"Not that the story need be long, but it
will take a long while to make it short."
— Henry David Thoreau

Tales from Firozsha Baag

Rohinton Mistry was born in Bombay in 1952. He emigrated
to Canada in 1975 and began working at a bank. He started
writing stories in 1983. While at the University of Toronto, he
won two Hart House literary prizes (for "One Sunday" and
"Auspicious Occasion") and in 1985 he won a *Canadian Fiction* Contributors' Prize. That same year, he left the bank to
devote himself full time to his writing.

TALES FROM
FIROZSHA BAAG

Rohinton Mistry

Penguin Books

Penguin Books Canada Limited, 2801 John Street,
Markham, Ontario, Canada, L3R 1B4
Penguin Books Ltd., Harmondsworth, Middlesex, England
Penguin Books, 40 West 23rd Street, New York, New York 10010 U.S.A.
Penguin Books Australia Ltd., Ringwood, Victoria, Australia
Penguin Books (N.Z.) Ltd., Private Bag, Takapuna, Auckland 9, New Zealand

First published by Penguin Books Canada Limited, 1987

Manufactured in Canada

Canadian Cataloguing in Publication Data
Mistry, Rohinton, 1952-
Tales from Firozsha Baag

(Penguin short fiction)
ISBN 0-14-009777-5

I. Title.   II. Series.

PS8576.I78T34 1987   C813'.54   C86-094731-9
PR9199.3.M57T34 1987

Contents

Acknowledgements

The following stories were previously published in slightly different versions. "Auspicious Occasion" in *The Fiddlehead*, No. 141, Autumn 1984 and *The New Press Anthology #2: Best Stories*, General Publishing, 1985. "One Sunday" in *The Antigonish Review*, Number 61, Spring 1985. "The Ghost of Firozsha Baag" in *Quarry*, Volume 35, Number 2, Spring 1986. "Condolence Visit" in *Canadian Fiction Magazine*, Number 50/51. "The Collectors" in Malahat Review, Number 72, 1985. "Of White Hairs and Cricket" in *Waves*, Volume 14, Number 3, Winter 1986. "Lend Me Your Light" in *The Toronto South Asian Review*, Volume 2, Number 3, Winter 1984. "Exercisers" in *Canadian Fiction Magazine*, Number 54. "Condolence Visit," "The Collectors" and "Lend Me Your Light" in *Coming Attractions #4*, Oberon Press.

The author gratefully acknowledges the assistance of the Explorations Program of the Canada Council and that of the Ontario Arts Council, which made it possible to write some of these stories.

Auspicious Occasion

Auspicious Occasion

With a bellow Rustomji emerged from the WC. He clutched his undone pyjama drawstring, an extreme rage distorting his yet un-
shaven features. He could barely keep the yellow-stained pyjamas
from falling.

"Mehroo! *Arré* Mehroo! Where are you?" he screamed. "I am
telling you, this is more than I can take! Today, of all days, on *Behram
roje*. Mehroo! Are you listening?"

Mehroo came, her slippers flopping in time — ploof ploof —
one two. She was considerably younger than her husband, having
been married off to a thirty-six-year-old man when she was a mere
girl of sixteen, before completing her final high-school year.
Rustomji, a successful Bombay lawyer, had been considered a fine
catch by Mehroo's parents — no one had anticipated that he would
be wearing dentures by the time he was fifty. Who, while trapped in
the fervour of matchmaking at the height of the wedding season,
could imagine a toothless gummy mouth, morning after morning,
greeting a woman in her absolute prime? No one. Certainly not
Mehroo. She came from an orthodox Parsi family which observed
all important days on the Parsi calendar, had the appropriate
prayers and ceremonies performed at the fire-temple, and even set

aside a room with an iron-frame bed and an iron stool for the women during their unclean time of the month.

Mehroo had welcomed her destiny and had carried to her new home all the orthodoxy of her parents'. Except for the separate "unclean" room which Rustomji would not hear of, she was permitted everything. In fact, Rustomji secretly enjoyed most of the age-old traditions while pretending indifference. He loved going to the fire-temple dressed up in his sparkling white *dugli*, starched white trousers, the carefully brushed *pheytoe* on his head — he had a fine head of hair, not yet gone the way of his teeth.

To Rustomji's present yelling Mehroo responded good-humouredly. She tried to remain calm on this morning which was to culminate in prayers at the fire-temple; nothing would mar the perfection of *Behram roje* if she could help it. This day on the Parsi calendar was particularly dear to her: on *Behram roje* her mother had given birth to her at the Awabai Petit Parsi Lying-In Hospital; it was also the day her *navjote* had been performed at the age of seven, when she was confirmed a Zoroastrian by the family priest, *Dustoor* Dhunjisha; and finally, Rustomji had married her on *Behram roje* fourteen years ago, with feasting and celebration continuing into the wee hours of the morning — it was said that not one beggar had gone hungry, such were the quantities of food dumped in the garbage cans of Cama Garden that day.

Indeed, *Behram roje* meant a lot to Mehroo. Which is why with a lilt in her voice she sang out: "Com—ing! Com—ing!"

Rustomji growled back, "You are deaf or what? Must I scream till my lungs burst?"

"Coming, coming! Two hands, so much to do, the *gunga* is late and the house is unswept — "

"*Arré* forget your *gunga-bunga*!" howled Rustomji. "That stinking lavatory upstairs is leaking again! God only knows what they do to make it leak. There I was, squatting — barely started — when someone pulled the flush. Then on my head I felt — pchuk — all wet! On my head!"

"On your head? Chhee chhee chhee! How horrible! How inauspicious! How…" and words failed her as she cringed and recoiled from the befouling event. Gingerly she peeked into the WC, fearing a deluge of ordure and filth. What she did see, however, was a steady leak — drip drip drip drip — rhythmical and regular, straight into the toilet bowl, so that using it was out of the question. Rustomji, still clutching his pyjama drawstring, a wild unravelled look about him, fumed behind her as she concluded her inspection.

"Why not call a good plumber ourselves this time instead of complaining to the Baag trustees?" Mehroo ventured. "They will once again do shoddy work."

"I will not spend one paisa of my hard-earned earnings! Those scoundrels sitting with piles of trust money hidden under their arses should pay for it!" stormed Rustomji, making sweeping gestures with the hand that was free of the pyjama string. "I will crap at their office, I will go to crap at their houses, I will crap on their doorsteps if necessary!"

"Hush, Rustomji, don't say such things on *Behram roje*," Mehroo chided. "If you still have to go, I will see if Hirabai next door does not mind."

"With her stupid husband there? A thousand times I've told you I will not step inside in Nariman's presence. Anyway, it is gone now. Vanished," said Rustomji with finality. "Now my whole day will be spoilt. And who knows," he added darkly with perverse satisfaction, "this may even lead to constipation."

"Nariman must have left for the library. I will ask Hirabai, you might have to go later. I am going there now to telephone the office, and when I come back I will make you a nice hot cup of tea. Drink that quickly, *gudh-gudh*, the urge will return," soothed Mehroo, and left. Rustomji decided to boil water for his bath. He felt unclean all over.

The copper vessel was already filled with water. But someone had forgotten to cover it, and plaster from the ceiling had dripped into it. It floated on the surface, little motes of white. Like the little motes that danced before Rustomji's eyes when he was very tired, after a long day in the hot, dusty courthouse, or when he was very angry, after shouting at the boys of Firozsha Baag for making a nuisance with their cricket in the compound.

Plaster had been dripping for some years now in his A Block flat, as it had been in most of the flats in Firozsha Baag. There had been a respite when Dr Mody, gadfly to the trustees (bless his soul), had pressed for improvement with the Baag management. But that period ended, and the trustees adopted a new policy to stop all maintenance work not essential to keep the buildings from being condemned.

Following a period of resistance, most of the tenants had taken to looking after their own flats, getting them replastered and painted. But to this day Rustomji stubbornly held out, calling his neighbours fools for making things easy for the trustees instead of suffering the discomfort of peeling walls till the scoundrels capitulated.

When the neighbours, under the leadership of Nariman Hansotia, had decided to pool some money and hire a contractor to paint the exterior of A Block, Rustomji, on principle, refused to hand over his share. The building had acquired an appalling patina of yellow and grey griminess. But even the likeable and retired Nariman, who drove every day except Sunday in his 1932 Mercedes-Benz to the Cawasji Framji Memorial Library to read the daily papers from around the world, could not persuade Rustomji to participate.

Totally frustrated, Nariman had returned to Hirabai: "That curmudgeon won't listen to reason, he has sawdust in his head. But if I don't make him the laughing-stock, my name isn't Nariman." Out of this exchange had grown an appended name: Rustomji-the-curmudgeon, and it had spread through Firozsha Baag, enjoying long life and considerable success.

And Nariman Hansotia had then convinced the neighbours to go ahead with the work, advising the contractor to leave untouched the exterior of Rustomji's flat. It would make Rustomji ashamed of himself, he thought, when the painting was finished and the sparkling façade of the building sported one begrimed square. But Rustomji was delighted. He triumphantly told everyone he met, "Mr Hansotia bought a new suit, and it has a patch on one knee!"

Rustomji chuckled now as he remembered the incident. He filled the copper vessel with fresh water and hoisted it onto the gas stove. The burner hesitated before it caught. He suspected the gas cylinder was about to run out; over a week ago he had telephoned the blasted gas company to deliver a new one. He wondered if there was going to be another shortage, like last year, when they had had to burn coals in a *sigri* — the weekly quota of kerosene had been barely enough to make the morning tea.

Tea, thank God for tea, he thought, anticipating with pleasure the second cup Mehroo had promised. He would drink it in copious draughts, piping hot, one continuous flow from cup to saucer to mouth. It just might induce his offended bowels to move and salvage something of this ill-omened morning. Of course, there was the WC of Hirabai Hansotia's that he would have to contend with — his bowels were recalcitrant in strange surroundings. It was a matter of waiting and seeing which would prevail: Mehroo's laxative tea or Hirabai's sphincter-tightening lavatory.

He picked up the *Times of India* and settled in his easy chair, waiting for the bath water to boil. Something would have to be done about the peeling paint and plaster; in some places the erosion was so bad, red brick lay exposed. The story went that these flats had been erected in an incredibly short time and with very little money. Cheap materials had been used, and sand carted from nearby Chaupatty beach had been mixed in abundance with substandard cement. Now during the monsoon season beads of moisture trickled down the walls, like sweat down a coolie's back, which considerably hastened the crumbling of paint and plaster.

From time to time, Mehroo pointed out the worsening problem, and Rustomji took refuge in railing at the trustees. But today he did not need to worry. She would never mention it on a day like *Behram roje*. There was not any time for argument. Her morning had started early: she had got the children ready for school and packed their lunch; cooked *dhandar-paatyo* and *sali-boti* for dinner; starched and ironed his white shirt, trousers, and *dugli*, all washed the night before, and her white blouse, petticoat and sari; and now those infernal people upstairs had made the WC leak. If Gajra, their *gunga*, did not arrive soon, Mehroo would also have to sweep and mop before she could decorate the entrance with coloured chalk designs, hang up the *tohrun* (waiting since the flowerwalla's six A.M. delivery) and spread the fragrance of *loban* through the flat — it was considered unlucky to omit or change the prescribed sequence of these things.

But celebrating in this manner was Mehroo's own choice. As far as Rustomji was concerned, these customs were dead and meaningless. Besides, he had repeatedly explained to her what he called the psychology of *gungas*: "If a particular day is important, never let the *gunga* know, pretend everything is normal. And never, never ask her to come earlier than usual, for she will deliberately come late." But Mehroo did not learn; she trusted, confided, and continued to suffer.

Gajra was the latest in a long line of *gungas* to toil at their house. Before her it had been Tanoo.

For two years, Tanoo came every morning to their flat to sweep and mop, do the dishes, and wash their clothes. A woman in her early seventies, tall and skinny, she was bow-legged and half blind, with an astonishing quantity of wrinkles on her face and limbs. Where her skin was not wrinkled, it was scaly and rough. She had large ears that stuck out under wisps of stringy, coconut-oiled grey hair, and wore spectacles (one lens of which was missing) balanced precariously on a thin pointed nose.

The trouble with Tanoo was that she was always breaking a dish or a cup or a saucer. Mehroo was prepared to overlook the inferior sweeping and mopping; the breakage, however, was a tangible loss which Rustomji said would one day ruin them if a stop was not put to it.

Tanoo was periodically threatened with pay cuts and other grimmer forms of retribution. But despite her good intentions and avowals and resolutions, there was never any improvement. Her dim eyes were further handicapped by hands which shook and fumbled because of old age and the long unhappiness of a life out of which her husband had fled after bringing into it two sons she single-handedly had to raise, and who were now drunkards, lazy good-for-nothings, and the sorrow of her old age.

"Poor, poor Tanoo," Mehroo would say, helpless to do anything. "Very sad," Rustomji would agree, but would not do more.

So plates and saucers continued to slip out of Tanoo's old, weary hands, continued to crash and shatter, causing Rustomji fiscal grief and Mehroo sorrow — sorrow because she knew that Tanoo would have to go. Rustomji too would have liked to feel sorrow and compassion. But he was afraid. He had decided long ago that this was no country for sorrow or compassion or pity — these were worthless and, at best, inappropriate.

There was a time during his college days, as a volunteer with the Social Service League, when he had thought differently (foolishly, he now felt). Sometimes, he still remembered those SSL camps fondly, the long train rides full of singing and merriment to remote villages lacking the most basic of necessities, where they dug roads and wells, built schoolhouses, and taught the villagers. Hard work, all of it, and yet so much fun, what a wonderful gang they had been, like Dara the Daredevil, the way he jumped in and out of moving trains, he called himself the Tom Mix of the locomotive; and Bajun the Banana Champion — at one camp he had eaten twenty-one of them, not small *ailchee* ones either, regular long green ones; every one had been a real character.

But Rustomji was not one to allow nostalgia to taint the colour of things as he saw them now. He was glad he had put it all behind him.

The way it ended for Tanoo, however, eased the blow a little for Mehroo. Tanoo arranged to leave Bombay and return to the village she had left so long ago, to end her days with her sister's family there. Mehroo was happy for her. Rustomji heaved a sigh of relief. He had no objections when Mehroo gave her generous gifts at the time of parting. He even suggested getting her a new pair of spectacles. But Tanoo declined the offer, saying she would not have much use for them in the village, with no china plates and saucers to wash.

And so, Tanoo departed and Gajra arrived: young and luscious, and notorious for tardiness.

Coconut hair oil was the only thing Gajra had in common with Tanoo. She was, despite her plumpness, quite pretty; she was, Rustomji secretly thought, voluptuous. And he did not tire of going into the kitchen while Gajra was washing dishes, crouched on her haunches within the parapet of the *mori*. When still a young boy, Rustomji had heard that most *gungas* had no use for underwear — neither brassiere or knickers. He had confirmed this several times through observation as a lad in his father's house. Gajra provided further proof, proof which popped out from beneath her short blouse during the exertion of sweeping or washing. With a deft movement she would tuck back the ample bosom into her *choli*, unabashed, but not before Rustomji had gazed his fill. Like two prime Ratnagiri mangoes they were, he felt, juicy and golden smooth.

"Her cups runneth over," he would then gleefully think, remembering time and time again the little joke from his beloved school days at St Xavier's. Though not given to proselytizing, the school had a custom of acquainting all its students, Catholic or otherwise, with the Lord's Prayer and the more popular Psalms.

Rustomji's one fervent wish was that some day Gajra's breasts should slip out far enough from under her *choli* to reveal her nipples. "*Dada Ormuzd*, just once let me see them, only once," he would yearn in his depths, trying to picture the nipples: now dark brown and the size of a gram but with the hidden power to swell; now uncontrollably aroused and black, large and pointed.

While waiting for his wish to come true, Rustomji enjoyed watching Gajra modify her sari each morning before she started work: she hauled it up between her thighs and tucked it in around the waist so it would not get wet in the *mori*. When altered like this, the layers produced a very large, very masculine lump over the crotch. But her movements while she, steatopygic, completed her daily transformation — bending her knees, thighs apart, patting her behind to smooth down the fabric — were extremely erotic for Rustomji.

Mehroo was usually present when this went on, so he would have to pretend to read the *Times of India*, looking surreptitiously from behind or over or under and taking his chances. Sometimes, he remembered a little Marathi rhyme he had picked up as a boy. It formed part of a song which was sung at every boisterous, rollicking party his father used to give for his Parsi colleagues from Central Bank. At that time, little Rustom had not understood the meaning, but it went:

> *Sakubai la zaoli*
> *Dadra chi khalti…*

After many years and many parties, as Rustom grew up, he was allowed to sit with the guests instead of being sent out to play in the compound. The day came when he was allowed his first sip of Scotch and soda from his father's glass. Mother had protested that he was too young, but father had said, "What is there in one sip, you think he will become a drunkard?" Rustom had enjoyed that first sip and had wanted more, to the delight of the guests. "Takes after his father, really likes his peg!" they had guffawed.

It was also around this time that Rustom started to understand the meaning of the rhyme and the song: it was about the encounter of a Parsi gentleman with a *gunga* he caught napping under a dark stairwell — he seduces her quite easily, then goes his merry way. Later, Rustom had sung it to his friends in St Xavier's, the song which he remembered today, on *Behram roje*, in his easy chair with the *Times of India*. He hoped Gajra would arrive before Mehroo finished using Hirabai's telephone. He could then ogle brazenly, unhindered.

But even as Rustomji thought his impure thoughts and relished them all, Mehroo returned; the office had promised to send the plumber right away. "I told him '*Bawa*, you are a Parsi too, you know how very important *Behram roje* is' and he said he understands, he will have the WC repaired today."

"The bloody swine understands? Hah! Now he knows it, he will purposely delay, to make you miserable. Go, be frank with the whole world; go, be unhappy." And Mehroo went, to make his tea.

The doorbell rang. Rustomji knew it must be Gajra. But even as he hurried to answer it, he sensed he was walking towards another zone of frustration, that his concupiscence would be thwarted as rudely as his bowels.

His instinct proved accurate. Mehroo rushed out from the kitchen as fast as her flopping slippers would allow, scolding and shooing Gajra away to do only the sweeping — the rest could wait till tomorrow — and leave. Sulking, Rustomji returned to the *Times of India*.

Mehroo then hurriedly made chalk designs at the entrance, not half as elaborate or colourful as planned. Time was running out; she had to get to the fire-temple by eleven. Dreading the inauspiciousness of a delay, she hung a *tohrun* over each doorway (the flowers, languishing since six A.M., luckily retained a spark of life) and went to dress.

When she was ready to leave, Rustomji was still coaxing his bowels with tea. Disgruntled over Gajra's abrupt departure, he nursed his loss silently, blaming Mehroo. "You go ahead," he said, "I will meet you at the fire-temple."

Mehroo took the H route bus. She looked radiant in her white sari, worn the Parsi way, across the right shoulder and over the forehead. The H route bus meandered through narrow streets of squalor once it left the Firozsha Baag neighbourhood. It went via Bhindi Bazaar, through Lohar Chawl and Crawford Market, crawling painfully amidst the traffic of cars and people, handcarts and trucks.

Usually, during a bus ride to the fire-temple, Mehroo attentively watched the scenes unfolding as the bus made its creeping way, wondering at the resilient ingenuity with which life was made liveable inside dingy little holes and inhospitable, frightful structures. Now, however, Mehroo sat oblivious to the bustle and meanness of lives on these narrow streets. None of it pierced the serenity with which she anticipated the perfect peace and calm she would soon be a part of inside the fire-temple.

She looked with pleasure at the white sari draping her person, and adjusted the border over her forehead. When she returned home, the sari would be full of the fragrance of sandalwood, absorbed from the smoke of the sacred fire. She would hang it up beside her bed instead of washing it, to savour the fragrance as long as it lasted. She remembered how, as a child, she would wait for her mother to return from the fire-temple so she could bury her face in her lap and breathe in the sandalwood smell. Her father's *dugli* gave off the same perfume, but her mother's white sari was better, it felt so soft. Then there was the ritual of *chasni*: all the brothers and sisters wearing their prayer caps would eagerly sit around the dining-table to partake of the fruit and sweets blessed during the day's prayer ceremonies.

Mehroo was a little saddened when she thought of her own children, who did not give a second thought to these things; she had to coax them to finish the *chasni* or it would sit for days, unnoticed and untouched.

Even as a child, Mehroo had adored going to the fire-temple. She loved its smells, its tranquillity, its priests in white performing their elegant, mystical rituals. Best of all she loved the inner sanctuary, the sanctum sanctorum, dark and mysterious, with marble floor and marble walls, which only the officiating priest could enter, to tend to the sacred fire burning in the huge, shining silver *afargaan* on its marble pedestal. She felt she could sit for hours outside the sanctuary, watching the flames in their dance of life, seeing the sparks fly up the enormous dark dome resembling the sky. It was her own private key to the universe, somehow making less frightening the notions of eternity and infinity.

In high school she would visit the fire-temple before exam week. Her offering of a sandalwood stick would be deposited in the silver tray at the door of the inner sanctuary, and she would reverently smear her forehead and throat with the grey ash left in the tray for this purpose. *Dustoor* Dhunjisha, in his flowing white robe, would always be there to greet her with a hug, always addressing her as his dear daughter. The smell of his robe would remind her of mother's sari fragrant with sandalwood. Serene and fortified, she would go to write her exam.

Dustoor Dhunjisha was now almost seventy-five, and was not always around when Mehroo went to the fire-temple. Some days, when he did not feel well, he stayed in his room and let a younger priest look after the business of prayer and worship. But today she hoped he would be present; she wanted to see that gentle face from her childhood, the long white beard, the reassuring paunch.

After marrying Rustomji and moving into Firozsha Baag, Mehroo had continued to go to *Dustoor* Dhunjisha for all ceremonies. In this, she risked the ire of the *dustoorji* who lived in their own block on the second floor. The latter believed that he had first claim to the business of Firozsha Baag tenants, that they should all patronize his nearby *agyaari* as long as he could accommodate them. But Mehroo persisted in her loyalty to Dhunjisha. She paid no attention to the high dudgeon the A Block priest directed at her, or to Rustomji's charges.

Under the priestly garb of Dhunjisha, protested Rustomji, lurked a salacious old man taking advantage of his venerable image: "Loves to touch and feel women, the old goat — the younger and fleshier, the more fun he has hugging and squeezing them." Mehroo did not believe it for a moment. She was always pleading with him not to say nasty things about such a holy figure.

But this was not all. Rustomji swore that Dhunjisha and his ilk had been known to exchange lewd remarks between lines of prayer, to slip them in amidst scripture recitals, especially on days of ceremony when sleek nubile women in their colourful finery attended in large numbers. The oft-repeated *Ashem Vahoo* was his favourite example:

> *Ashem Vahoo,*
> See the tits on that chickie-boo…

This version was a popular joke among the less religious, and Mehroo dismissed it as more of Rustomji's irreverence. He assured her they did it very skilfully and thus went undetected. Besides, the white kerchief all *dustoors* were required to wear over the nose and mouth, like masked bandits, to keep their breath from polluting the sacred fire, made it difficult to hear their muttering in the first place. Rustomji claimed it took a trained ear to sift through their mumbles and separate the prayers from the obscenities.

The H route bus stopped at Marine Lines. Mehroo alighted and walked down Princess Street, wondering about the heavy traffic. Cars and buses were backed up all the way on the flyover from Princess Street to Marine Drive.

She neared the fire-temple and saw parked outside its locked gates two police cars and a police van. Her step quickened. The last time the gates had been closed, as far as she knew, was during the Hindu-Muslim riots following partition; she was afraid to think what calamity had now come to pass. Parsis and non-Parsis were craning and peering through the bars of the gates; the same human curiosity had touched them all. A policeman was trying to persuade them to disperse.

Mehroo lingered on the periphery of the crowd, irresolute, then plunged into it. She saw *Dustoor* Kotwal leave the temple building and walk purposefully towards the gate. Jostling her way through the milling people, she attempted to get his attention. He was, like *Dustoor* Dhunjisha, a resident temple priest, and knew her well.

Dustoor Kotwal had an announcement for the Parsis: "All prayers and ceremonies scheduled for today have been cancelled, except the prayers for the dead." He was gone before Mehroo could reach the gate.

She now began to pick up alarming words in the crowd: "…murdered last night…stabbed in the back…police and CID…." Her spirits faltered. All this on *Behram roje* which she had done everything to make perfect? Why were things being so cruelly wrenched out of her control? She made up her mind to stay till she could speak to someone who knew what had happened.

Rustomji finished his cup of tea as Mehroo left. He decided to wait awhile before his bath, to give his obdurate bowels one more chance.

But after another ten minutes of the *Times of India* and not a murmur from his depths, he gave up. Getting things ready for the bath, he arched his back till his bottom stuck out, then raised one foot slightly and tensed. Nothing happened. Not even a little fart. He inspected his *dugli* and trousers: the starch was just right — not too limp, not too stiff. He rubbed his stomach and hoped he would not have to go later at the fire-temple; the WC there was horrid, with urine usually spattered outside the toilet bowl or excrement not flushed away. To look at it, it was not Parsis who used the WC, he felt, but uneducated, filthy, ignorant barbarians.

Rustomji performed his ablutions, trying to forget the disgusting leak from above while he had squatted below. Fortunately, with every mugful of hot water he scooped from the bucket and poured down his back, splashed on his face, and felt trickle down his crotch and thighs, that foul leak was reduced to a memory growing dimmer by the moment; the cleansing water which flowed down the drain swept away what remained of that memory to a distant remove; and once he had dried himself, it was blotted out completely. Rustomji was whole again.

Now all that lingered was the fresh refreshing scent, as the advertisement proclaimed, of lifegiving Lifebuoy Soap. Lifebuoy Soap and Johnnie Walker Scotch were the only two items which endured in the sumptuary laws passed down to Rustomji through three generations, and he relished them both. The one change wrought by the passing years was that Johnnie Walker Scotch, freely available under the British, could now be obtained only on the black market, and was responsible for Rustomji's continuing grief over the British departure.

Emerging from the bathroom, he was pleased to discover his bowels no longer bothered him. The desultoriness plaguing his morning hours had fled, and a new alacrity took charge of his actions. The bows on the *dugli* gave him some trouble as he dressed, usually it was Mehroo who tied these. But in his present mood he was more than a match for them. With a last brush to his brillian-tined hair he perched the *pheytoe* on it, gave a final tug of encouragement to the bows and surveyed himself in the mirror. Pleased with what he saw, he was ready for the fire-temple.

The H route bus stop was his destination as he stepped out buoyantly. The compound was deserted, the boys were all at school. In the evening, their noisy games would fill it with rowdiness and nuisance that he would have to combat if he was to enjoy peace and quiet. Confident of his control over them, he decided to pass the H route bus stop and walk further, to the A-1 Express, past Tar Gully and its menacing mouth. His starchy whiteness aroused in him feelings of resplendence and invincibility, and he had no objection to the viewing of his progress by the street.

There was a long queue at the A-1 bus stop. Rustomji disregarded the entire twisting, curving length and stationed himself at the head. He stared benignly into space, deaf to the protests of the queue's serpentine windings, and pondered the options of upper deck and lower deck. He decided on the lower — it might prove difficult to negotiate the steep flight of steps to the upper with as much poise as befitted his attire.

The bus arrived and the conductor was yelling out, even before it came to a standstill, "Upper deck upper deck! Everybody upper deck!" Rustomji, of course, had already settled the question. Ignor-ing the conductor, he grasped the overhead railing and stood jauntily on the lower deck. The usually belligerent conductor said nothing.

The bus approached Marine Lines, and Rustomji moved towards the door to prepare for his descent. He managed quite well despite the rough and bumpy passage of the bus. Without bruising his mien or his attire, he reached the door and waited.

But unbeknownst to Rustomji, on the upper deck sat fate in the form of a mouth chewing tobacco and betel nut, a mouth with a surfeit of juice and aching jaws crying for relief. And when the bus halted at Marine Lines, fate leaned out the window to release a generous quantity of sticky, viscous, dark red stuff.

Dugli gleaming in the midday sun, Rustomji emerged and stepped to the pavement. The squirt of tobacco juice caught him between the shoulder blades: blood red on sparkling white.

Rustomji felt it and whirled around. Looking up, he saw a face with crimson lips trickling juice, mouth chewing contentedly, and in an instant knew what had happened. He roared in agony, helpless, screaming as painfully as though it was a knife in the back, while the bus slowly pulled away.

"*Saala gandoo!* Filthy son of a whore! Shameless animal — spitting *paan* from the bus! Smash your face I will, you pimp…"

A small crowd gathered around Rustomji. Some were curious, a few sympathetic; but most were enjoying themselves.

"What happened? Who hurt the…"

"Tch tch, someone spat *paan* on his *dugli*…"

"Heh heh heh! *Bawaji* got *paan pichkari* right on his white *dugli*…"

"*Bawaji bawaji, dugli* looks very nice now, red and white, just like in technicolor…"

The taunting and teasing added to the outrage of tobacco juice made Rustomji do something dangerously foolish. He diverted his anger from the harmlessly receding bus to the crowd, overlooking the fact that unlike the bus, it was close enough to answer his vituperation with fury of its own.

"*Arré* you sisterfucking *ghatis*, what are you laughing for? Have you no shame? *Saala chootia* spat *paan* on my *dugli* and you think that is fun?"

A ripple of tension went through the crowd. It displaced the former lighthearted teasing they were indulging in at the spectacle of the *paan*-drenched *bawaji*.

"*Arré* who does he think he is, abusing us, giving such bad-bad *ghali*?" Someone pushed Rustomji from behind.

"*Bawaji*, we'll break all your bones. *Maaro saala bawajiko!*" Beat up the bloody *bawaji*.

"*Arré* your arse we'll tear to shreds!" People were jostling him from every side. The *pheytoe* was plucked from his head, and they tugged at the bows of the *dugli*.

All anger forgotten, Rustomji feared for his person. He knew he was in serious trouble. Not one friendly face in this group which was now looking for fun of a different sort. In panic he tried to undo the hostility: "*Arré* please *yaar*, why harass an old man? *Jaané dé, yaar.*" Let me go, friends.

Then his desperate search for a way out was rewarded — a sudden inspiration which just might work. He reached his fingers into his mouth, dislodged the dentures, and spat them out onto his palm. Two filaments of saliva, sparkling in the midday sun, momentarily connected the dentures to his gums. They finally broke and dribbled down his chin. With much effort and spittle, he sputtered: "Look, such an old man, no teeth even," and held out his hand for viewing.

The collapsed mouth and flapping lips appeased everyone. A general tittering spread through the assembly. Rustomji the clown was triumphant. He has restored to himself the harmlessness of the original entertaining spectacle, *pheytoe* back on head, teeth back in mouth.

Then, under the amused gaze of the crowd, Rustomji undid the bows of the *dugli* and removed it. Going to the fire-temple was out of the question. Tears of shame and rage welled in his eyes, and through the mist he saw the blood-red blotch. With the *dugli* off he still felt a little damp on the back — the juice had penetrated his shirt and *sudra* as well. For the second time that day he had been soiled in a most repulsive way.

Someone handed him a newspaper to wrap the *dugli* in; another picked up the packet of sandalwood he had dropped. At that moment, when Rustomji looked most helpless, a bus arrived and the crowd departed.

He was left alone, holding the newspapered *dugli* and the sandalwood in brown paper. The angle of his *pheytoe* had shifted, and he no longer looked or felt unassailable. Feebly, he hailed a taxi. It was a small Morris, and he had to stoop low to get in, to keep the *pheytoe* from being knocked off his head.

The horror of what Mehroo had found out at the fire-temple abated on the way home. Her thoughts turned to Rustomji; surely he should have finished his bath and arrived at the fire-temple, she had waited there for over two hours, first outside the gates, then inside. Maybe Rustomji has already found out, she hoped, maybe he knows the prayers were cancelled.

She turned the latchkey and entered the flat. Rustomji lay sprawled on the easy chair. Thrown on the teapoy beside him was his *dugli*, the blood-red *paan* stain prominent.

He was surprised to see her back so soon, looking so distressed. Mehroo always came from the fire-temple with something resembling beatitude shining on her face. Today she looked as though she had seen *sataan* himself inside the fire-temple, thought Rustomji.

She moved closer to the teapoy, and the light caught the *dugli*. She shrieked in terror: "*Dustoor* Dhunjisha's *dugli*! But...but...how did you — ?"

"What rubbish are you talking again? Some swine spat *paan* on my *dugli*." He decided not to mention his narrow escape. "Why would I have that fat rascal Dhunjisha's *dugli*?"

Mehroo sat down weakly. "God forgive you your words, you do not know *Dustoor* Dhunjisha was murdered!"

"What! In the fire-temple? But who would — ?"

"I will tell you everything if you wait for one minute. First I need a drink of water, I feel so tired."

Rustomji's stolidity was pierced through. He hurried to the kitchen for a glass of water. Mehroo then told how Dhunjisha had been stabbed by a *chasniwalla* employed at the fire-temple. The *chasniwalla* had confessed. He was trying to steal some silver trays from the fire-temple when Dhunjisha had unwittingly wandered into the room; the *chasniwalla* panicked and killed him. Then, to be rid of the corpse, he threw it in the sacred fire-temple well.

"They found the body this morning," continued Mehroo. "I was let inside later on, and the police were examining the body, nothing had been removed, he was still wearing his *dugli*, it looked exactly like..." She motioned towards Rustomji's on the teapoy, shuddered, and fell silent.

She began to busy herself. She carried her glass back to the kitchen along with Rustomji's teacup from earlier that morning, and lit the stove to get lunch ready. She came back, examined the blot of *paan* on his *dugli* and wondered aloud about the best way to remove the stain, then was silent again.

Rustomji heaved a sigh. "What is happening in the world I don't know. Parsi killing Parsi...*chasniwalla* and *dustoor*..."

He, too, fell silent, slowly shaking his head. He gazed pensively at the walls and ceiling, where bits of paint and plaster were waiting to peel, waiting to fall into their pots and pans, their vessels of water, their lives. Tomorrow, Gajra would come and sweep away the flakes of white from the floor; she would clean out the pots and pans, and fill fresh water into the vessels. The *Times of India* would arrive, he would read it as he sipped his tea, and see Nariman Hansotia drive past in his 1932 Mercedes-Benz to the Cawasji Framji Memorial Library to read the daily papers from around the world. Mehroo would wipe away with water the coloured chalk designs at the front entrance and take down the *tohrun* from over the doorways — the flowers would be dry shrunken scraps by morning.

Mehroo looked at Rustomji musing on the easy chair, and felt inside herself the melancholy of his troubled, distant gaze. This rare glimpse of the softness underneath his tough exterior touched her. She slipped away quietly to the bedroom, to change her sari.

The unravelled yards of crumpled fabric, unredeemed by sandalwood fragrance, were deposited on the bed. There was no point in folding and hanging up the sari beside the bed, it could go straight for washing. She regarded it with something close to despair and noticed, on the wall beside the bed, marks left by trickling water from last year's rains.

This year's monsoons were due soon; they would wash clean the narrow streets she had passed through that morning on her way to the fire-temple. And in the flat the rain would send new beads of moisture, to replace last year's marks with new imprints.

The aroma of *dhandar-paatyo*, wafting from the kitchen, gently penetrated her meditation. It reminded her that *Behram roje* was not over yet. But she returned to the kitchen and put off the stove — it would still be a while to lunch, she knew. Instead, she prepared two cups of tea. Between ten A.M. and four P.M. she never drank tea, it was one of her strictest rules. Today, for Rustomji's sake, she would make an exception.

She went back to him, asked if he was ready for lunch and, receiving the anticipated refusal, smiled to herself with a tender satisfaction — how well she knew her Rustomji. She felt very close to him at this moment.

He shook his head slowly from side to side, gazing pensively into the distance. "Stomach is still heavy. Must be constipated."

"And the WC?"

"Still leaking."

She re-emerged with the two cups she had left ready in the kitchen: "Another cup of tea then?"

Rustomji nodded gratefully.

One Sunday

One Sunday

Najamai was getting ready to lock up her flat in Firozsha Baag and take the train to spend the day with her sister's family in Bandra.

She bustled her bulk around, turning the keys in the padlocks of her seventeen cupboards, then tugged at each to ensure the levers had tumbled properly. Soon, she was breathless with excitement and exertion.

Her breathlessness reminded her of the operation she had had three years ago to remove fat tissue from the abdomen and breasts. The specialist had told her, "You will not notice any great difference in the mirror. But you will appreciate the results when you are over sixty. It will keep you from sagging."

Here she was at fifty-five, and would soon know the truth of his words if merciful God kept her alive for five more years. Najamai did not question the ways of merciful God, even though her Soli was taken away the very year after first Dolly and then Vera went abroad for higher studies.

Today would be the first Sunday that the flat would be empty for the whole day. "In a way it is good," she reflected, "that Tehmina next door and the Boyces downstairs use my fridge as much as they do. Anyone who has evil intentions about my empty flat will think twice when he sees the coming-going of neighbours."

Temporarily reconciled towards the neighbours whom she otherwise regarded as nuisances, Najamai set off. She nodded at the boys playing in the compound. Outside, it did not feel as hot, for there was a gentle breeze. She felt at peace with the world. It was a twenty-minute walk, and there would be plenty of time to catch the ten-fifteen express. She would arrive at her sister's well before lunch-time.

At eleven-thirty Tehmina cautiously opened her door and peered out. She made certain that the hallway was free of the risk of any confrontation with a Boyce on the way to Najamai's fridge. "It is shameful the way those people misuse the poor lady's goodness," thought Tehmina. "All Najamai said when she bought the fridge was to please feel free to use it. It was only out of courtesy. Now those Boyces behave as if they have a share in the ownership of the fridge."

She shuffled out in slippers and duster-coat, clutching one empty glass and the keys to Najamai's flat. She reeked of cloves, lodged in her mouth for two reasons: it kept away her attacks of nausea and alleviated her chronic toothaches.

Cursing the poor visibility in the hallway, Tehmina, circumspect, moved on. Even on the sunniest of days, the hallway persisted in a state of half-light. She fumbled with the locks, wishing her cataracts would hurry and ripen for removal.

Inside at last, she swung open the fridge door to luxuriate in the delicious rush of cold air. A curious-looking package wrapped in plastic caught her eye; she squeezed it, sniffed at it, decided against undoing it. The freezer section was almost bare; the Boyces' weekly packets of beef had not yet arrived.

Tehmina placed two ice-cubes in the empty glass she had brought along — the midday drink of chilled lemonade was as dear to her as the evening Scotch and soda — and proceeded to lock up the place. But she was startled in her battle with Najamai's locks and bolts by footsteps behind her.

"Francis!"

Francis did odd jobs. Not just for Tehmina and Najamai in

C Block, but for anyone in Firozsha Baag who required his services. This was his sole means of livelihood ever since he had been laid off or dismissed, it was never certain which, from the furniture store across the road where he used to be a delivery boy. The awning of that store still provided the only roof he had ever known. Strangely, the store owner did not mind, and it was a convenient location — all that Tehmina or Najamai or any of the other neighbours had to do was lean out of their verandas and wave or clap hands and he would come.

Grinning away as usual, Francis approached Tehmina.

"Stop staring, you idiot," started Tehmina, "and check if this door is properly locked."

"Yes, *bai*. But when will Najamai return? She said she would give me some work today."

"Never. Could not be for today. She won't be back till very late. You must have made a mistake." With a loud suck she moved the cloves to the other cheek and continued, "So many times I've told you to open your ears and listen properly when people tell you things. But no. You never listen."

Francis grinned again and shrugged his shoulders. In order to humour Tehmina he replied, "Sorry *bai*, it is my mistake." He stood only about five feet two but possessed strength which was out of all proportion to his light build. Once, in Tehmina's kitchen during a cleaning spree he had picked up the stone slab used for grinding spices. It weighed at least fifty pounds, and it was the way in which he lifted it, between thumb and fingertips, that amazed Tehmina. Later, she had reported the incident to Najamai. The two women had marvelled at his strength, giggling at Tehmina's speculation that he must be built like a bull.

As humbly as possible Francis now asked, "Do you have any work for me today?"

"No. And I do not like it, you skulking here in the hallway. When there is work we will call you. Now go away."

Francis left. Tehmina could be offensive, but he needed the few paise the neighbours graciously let him earn and the leftovers Najamai allowed him whenever there were any. So he returned to the shade of the furniture store awning.

While Tehmina was chilling her lemonade with Najamai's ice, downstairs, Silloo Boyce cleaned and portioned the beef into seven equal packets. She disliked being obligated to Najamai for the fridge, though it was a great convenience. "Besides," she argued with herself, "we do enough to pay her back, every night she borrows the newspaper. And every morning I receive her milk and bread so she does not have to wake up early. Madam will not even come down, my sons must carry it upstairs." Thus she mused and reasoned each Sunday, as she readied the meat in plastic bags which her son Kersi later stacked in Najamai's freezer.

Right now, Kersi was busy repairing his cricket bat. The cord around the handle had come unwound and had gathered in a black cluster at its base, leaving more than half the length of the handle naked. It looked like a clump of pubic hair, Kersi thought, as he untangled the cord and began gluing it back around the handle.

The bat was a size four, much too small for him, and he did not play a lot of cricket any more. But for some reason he continued to care for it. The willow still possessed spring enough to send a ball to the boundary line, in glaring contrast to his brother Percy's bat. The latter was in sad shape. The blade was dry and cracked in places; the handle, its rubber grip and cord having come off long ago, had split; and the joint where the blade met the handle was undone. But Percy did not care. He never had really cared for cricket, except during that one year when the Australian team was visiting, when he had spent whole days glued to the radio, listening to the commentary. Now it was aeroplanes all the time, model kits over which he spent hours, and Biggles books in which he buried himself.

But Kersi had wanted to play serious cricket ever since primary school. In the fifth standard he was finally chosen for the class team. On the eve of the match, however, the captain contracted mumps, and the vice-captain took over, promptly relegating Kersi to the extras and moving up his own crony. That was the end of serious cricket for Kersi. For a short while, his father used to take him and his Firozsha Baag friends to play at the Marine Drive *maidaan* on Sunday mornings. And nowadays, they played a little in the compound. But it was not the same. Besides, they were interrupted all the time by people like that mean old Rustomji in A Block. Of all the neighbours who yelled and scolded, Rustomji-the-curmudgeon did the loudest and the most. He always threatened to confiscate their bat and ball if they didn't stop immediately.

Kersi now used his bat mainly for killing rats. Rat poison and a variety of traps were also employed with unflagging vigilance. But most of the rat population, with some rodent sixth sense, circum-navigated the traps. Kersi's bat remained indispensable.

His mother was quite proud of his skill, and once she had bragged about it to Najamai upstairs: "So young, and yet so brave, the way he runs after the ugly things. And he never misses." This was a mistake, because Kersi was promptly summoned the next time Najamai spied a rat in her flat. It had fled into the daughters' room and Kersi rushed in after it. Vera had just finished her bath and was not dressed. She screamed, first when she saw the rat, and again, when Kersi entered after it. He found it hard to keep his eyes on the rat — it escaped easily. Soon after, Vera had gone abroad for higher studies, following her sister Dolly's example.

The first time that Kersi successfully used his bat against a rat, it had been quite messy. Perhaps it was the thrill of the chase, or his rage against the invader, or just an ignorance about the fragility of that creature of fur and bone. The bat had come down with such vehemence that the rat was badly squashed. A dark red stain had oozed across the floor, almost making him sick. He discovered how sticky that red smear was only when he tried to wipe it off with an old newspaper.

The beef was now ready for the freezer. With seven packets of meat, and Najamai's latchkeys in his pocket, Kersi plodded upstairs.

When Najamai's daughters had gone abroad, they took with them the youthful sensuality that once filled the flat, and which could drive Kersi giddy with excitement on a day like this, with no one home, and all before him the prospect of exploring Vera and Dolly's bedroom, examining their undies that invariably lay scat-tered around, running his hands through lacy frilly things, rubbing himself with these and, on one occasion, barely rescuing them from a sticky end. Now, exploration would yield nothing but Najamai's huge underclothes. Kersi could not think of them as bras and panties — their vastness forfeited the right to these dainty names.

Feeling sadness, loss, betrayal, he descended the stairs lifelessly. Each wooden step, with the passage of years and the weight of tenants, was worn to concavity, and he felt just as worn. Not so long ago, he was able to counter spells of low spirits and gloominess by turning to his Enid Blyton books. A few minutes was all it took before he was sharing the adventures of the Famous Five or the Secret Seven, an idyllic existence in a small English village, where he would play with dogs, ride horses in the meadows, climb hills, hike through the countryside, or, if the season was right, build a snowman and have a snowball fight.

But lately, this had refused to work, and he got rid of the books. Percy had made fun of him for clinging to such silly and childish fantasy, inviting him to share, instead, the experience of aerial warfare with Biggles and his men in the RAF.

Everything in Firozsha Baag was so dull since Pesi *paadmaroo* had been sent away to boarding school. And all because of that sissy Jehangir, the Bulsara Bookworm.

Francis was back in the hallway, and was disappointed when Kersi did not notice him. Kersi usually stopped to chat; he got on well with all the servants in the building, especially Francis. Kersi's father had taught him to play cricket but Francis had instructed him in kite-flying. With a kite and string bought with fifty paise earned for carrying Najamai's quota of rice and sugar from the rationing depot, and with the air of a mentor, he had taught Kersi everything he knew about kites.

But the time they spent together was anathema to Kersi's parents. They looked distastefully on the growing friendship, and all the neighbours agreed it was not proper for a Parsi boy to consort in this way with a man who was really no better than a homeless beggar, who would starve were it not for their thoughtfulness in providing him with odd jobs. No good would come of it, they said.

Much to their chagrin, however, when the kite-flying season of high winds had passed, Kersi and Francis started spinning tops and shooting marbles. These, too, were activities considered inappropriate for a Parsi boy.

At six-thirty, Tehmina went to Najamai's flat for ice. This was the hour of the most precious of all ice-cubes — she'd just poured herself two fingers of Scotch.

A red glow from the Ambica Saris neon display outside Firozsha Baag floated eerily over the compound wall. Though the street lamps had now come on, they hardly illuminated the hallway, and tonight's full moon was no help either. Tehmina cursed the locks eluding her efforts. But as she continued the unequal struggle by twilight, her armpits soaked with sweat, she admitted that life before the fridge had been even tougher.

In those days she had to venture beyond the compound of Firozsha Baag and buy ice from the Irani Restaurant in Tar Gully. It was not the money she minded but the tedium of it all. Besides, the residents of Tar Gully amused themselves by spitting from their tenement windows on all comers who were better-heeled than they. In impoverished Tar Gully she was certainly considered better-heeled, and many well-aimed globs had found their mark. On such evenings Tehmina, in tears, would return to her flat and rush to take a bath, cursing those satanic animals and fiends of Tar Gully. Meanwhile, the ice she had purchased would sit melting to a sliver.

As the door finally unlocked, Tehmina spied a figure at the far end of the darkened hallway. Heart racing a little, she wondered who it might be, and called out as authoritatively as she could, "*Kaun hai*? What do you want?"

The answer came: "*Bai*, it's only Francis."

The familiar voice gave her courage. She prepared to scold him. "Did I not tell you this morning not to loiter here? Did I not say we would call if there was work? Did I not tell you that Najamai would be very late? Tell me then, you rascal, what are you doing here?"

Francis was hungry. He had not eaten for two whole days, and had been hoping to earn something for dinner tonight. Unable to tolerate Tehmina much longer, he replied sullenly, "I came to see if Najamai had arrived," and turned to go.

But Tehmina suddenly changed her mind. "Wait here while I get my ice," she said, realizing that she could use his help to lock the door.

Inside, she decided it was best not to push Francis too far. One never knew when this type of person would turn vicious. If he wanted to, he could knock her down right now, ransack Najamai's flat and disappear completely. She shuddered at these thoughts, then composed herself.

From downstairs came the strains of "The Blue Danube." Tehmina swayed absently. Strauss! The music reminded her of a time when the world was a simpler, better place to live in, when trips to Tar Gully did not involve the risk of spit globs. She reached into the freezer, and "The Blue Danube" concluded. Grudgingly, Tehmina allowed that there was one thing about the Boyces: they had good taste in music. Those senseless and monotonous Hindi film-songs never blared from their flat as they did sometimes from the other blocks of Firozsha Baag.

In control of herself now, she briskly stepped out. "Come on, Francis," she said peremptorily, "help me lock this door. I will tell Najamai that you will be back tomorrow for her work." She held out the ring of keys and Francis, not yet appeased by her half-hearted attempt at pacification, slowly and resentfully reached for them.

Tehmina was thankful at asking him to wait. "If it takes him so long, I could never do it in this darkness," she thought, as he handed back the keys.

Silloo downstairs heard the door slam when Tehmina returned to her own flat. It was time to start dinner. She rose and went to the kitchen.

Najamai stepped off the train and gathered together her belong-ings: umbrella, purse, shopping-bag of leftovers, and cardigan. Sun-day night had descended in full upon the station, and the plat-forms and waiting-rooms were deserted. She debated whether to take the taxi waiting in the night or to walk. The station clock showed nine-thirty. Even if it took her forty minutes to walk instead of the usual twenty, it would still be early enough to stop at the Boyces' before they went to bed. Besides, the walk would be healthy and help digest her sister's *pupeta-noo-gose* and *dhandar-paatyo*. With any luck, tonight would be a night unencumbered by the pressure of gas upon her gut.

The moon was full, the night was cool, and Najamai enjoyed her little walk. She neared Firozsha Baag and glanced quickly at the menacing mouth of Tar Gully. In there, streetlights were few, and sections of it had no lights at all. Najamai wondered if she would be able to spot any of the pimps and prostitutes who were said to visit here after dark even though Tar Gully was not a red-light district. But it looked deserted.

She was glad when the walk was over. Breathing a little rapidly, she rang the Boyce doorbell.

"Hullo, hullo — just wanted to pick up today's paper. Only if you've finished with it."

"Oh yes," said Silloo, "I made everyone read it early."

"This is very sweet of you," said Najamai, raising her arm so Silloo could tuck the paper under it. Then, as Silloo reached for the flashlight, she protested: "No no, the stairs won't be dark, there's a full moon."

Lighting Najamai's way up the stairs at night was one of the many things Silloo did for her neighbour. She knew that if Najamai ever stumbled in the dark and fell down the stairs, her broken bones would be a problem for the Boyces. It was simpler to shine the flashlight and see her safely to the landing.

"Good-night," said Najamai and started up. Silloo waited. Like a spotlight in some grotesque cabaret, the torch picked up the arduous swaying of Najamai's buttocks. She reached the top of the stairs, breathless, thanked Silloo and disappeared.

Silloo restored the flashlight to its niche by the door. The sounds of Najamai's preparation for bed and sleep now started to drip downstairs, as relentlessly as a leaky tap. A cupboard slammed…the easy chair in the bedroom, next to the window by day, was dragged to the bedside…footsteps led to the extremities of the flat…after a suitable interval, the flush…then the sound of water again, not torrential this time but steady, gentle, from a faucet…footsteps again…

The flow of familiar sounds was torn out of sequence by Najamai's frantic cries.

"Help! Help! Oh quickly! Thief!"

Kersi and his mother were the first to reach the door. They were outside in time to see Francis disappear in the direction of Tar Gully. Najamai, puffing, stood at the top of the stairs. "He was hiding behind the kitchen door," she gasped. "The front door — Tehmina as usual — "

Silloo was overcome by furious indignation. "I don't know why, with her bad eyes, that woman must fumble and mess with your keys. What did he steal?"

"I must check my cupboards," Najamai panted. "That rascal of a loafer will have run far already."

Tehmina now shuffled out, still clad in the duster-coat, anxiously sucking cloves and looking very guilty. She had heard everything from behind her door but asked anyway, "What happened? Who was screaming?"

The senseless fluster irritated Kersi. He went indoors. Confused by what had happened, he sat on his bed and cracked the fingers of both hands. Each finger twice, expertly, once at the knuckle, then at the joint closest to the nail. He could also crack his toes — each toe just once, though — but he did not feel like it right now. Don't crack your fingers, they used to tell him, your hands will become fat and ugly. For a while then he had cracked his knuckles more fervently than ever, hoping they would swell into fists the size of a face. Such fists would be useful to scare someone off in a fight. But the hands had remained quite normal.

Kersi picked up his bat. The cord had set firmly around the handle and the glue was dry; the rubber grip could go back on. There was a trick to fitting it right; if not done correctly, the grip would not cover the entire handle, but hang over the tip, like uncircumcised foreskin. He rolled down the cylindrical rubber tube onto itself, down to a rubber ring. Then he slipped the ring over the handle and unrolled it. A condom was probably put on the same way, he thought; someone had showed him those things at school, only this looked like one with the tip lopped off. Just as in that joke about a book called *The Unwanted Child* by F. L. Burst.

He posed before the mirror and flourished the bat. Satisfied with his repair work, he sat down again. He felt angry and betrayed at the thought of Francis vanishing into Tar Gully. His anger, coupled with the emptiness of this Sunday which, like a promise unfulfilled, had primed him many hours ago, now made him succumb to the flush of heroics starting to sweep through him.

He glanced at himself in the mirror again and went outside with the bat.

A small crowd of C Block neighbours and their servants had gathered around Najamai, Silloo, and Tehmina. "I'm going to find him," Kersi announced grimly to this group.

"What rubbish are you talking?" his mother exclaimed. "In Tar Gully, alone at night?"

"Oh what a brave boy!" cried Najamai. "But maybe we should call the police."

Tehmina, by this time, was muttering *non sequiturs* about ice-cubes and Scotch and soda. Kersi repeated: "I'm going to find him."

This time Silloo said, "Your brother must go with you. Alone you'll be no match for that rascal. Percy! Bring the other bat and go with Kersi."

Obediently, Percy joined his brother and they set off in the direction of Tar Gully. Their mother shouted instructions after them: "Be careful for God's sake! Stay together and don't go too far if you cannot find him."

In Tar Gully the two drew a few curious glances as they strode along with cricket bats. But the hour was late and there were not many people around. Those who were, waited only for the final *Matka* draw to decide their financial destinies. Some of these men now hooted at Kersi and Percy. "Parsi *bawaji!* Cricket at night? Parsi *bawaji!* What will you hit, boundary or sixer?"

"Just ignore the bloody *ghatis*," said Percy softly. It was good advice; the two walked on as if it were a well-rehearsed plan, Percy dragging his bat behind him. Kersi carried his over the right shoulder to keep the puddles created by the overflowing gutters of Tar Gully from wetting it.

"It's funny," he thought, "just this morning I did not see any gutter spilling over when I went to the *bunya* for salt." Now they were all in full spate. The gutters of Tar Gully were notorious for their erratic habits and their stench, although the latter was never noticed by the denizens.

The *bunya*'s shop was closed for regular business but a small window was still open. The *bunya*, in his nocturnal role of bookie, was accepting last-minute *Matka* bets. Midnight was the deadline, when the winning numbers would be drawn from the earthen vessel that gave the game its name.

There was still no sign of Francis. Kersi and Percy approached the first of the tenements, with the familiar cow tethered out in front — it was the only one in this neighbourhood. Each morning, accompanied by the owner's comely daughter and a basket of cut green grass, it made the round of these streets. People would reverently feed the cow, buying grass at twenty-five paise a mouthful. When the basket was empty the cow would be led back to Tar Gully.

Kersi remembered one early morning when the daughter was milking the cow and a young man was standing behind her seated figure. He was bending over the girl, squeezing her breasts with both hands, while she did her best to work the cow's swollen udder. Neither of them had noticed Kersi as he'd hurried past. Now, as Kersi recalled the scene, he thought of Najamai's daughters, the rat in the bedroom, Vera's near-nude body, his dispossessed fantasy, and once again felt cheated, betrayed.

It was Percy who first spotted Francis and pointed him out to Kersi. It was also Percy who yelled "*Chor! Chor!* Stop him!" and galvanized the waiting *Matka* patrons into action.

Francis never had a chance. Three men in the distance heard the uproar and tripped him as he ran past. Without delay they started to punch him. One tried out a clumsy version of a dropkick but it did not work so well, and he diligently resumed with his fists. Then the others arrived and joined in the pounding.

The ritualistic cry of *"Chor! Chor!"* had rendered Francis into fair game in Tar Gully. But Kersi was horrified. This was not the way he had wanted it to end when he'd emerged with his bat. He watched in terror as Francis was slapped and kicked, had his arms twisted and his hair pulled, and was abused and spat upon. He looked away when their eyes met.

Then Percy shouted: "Stop! No more beating! We must take the thief back to the *bai* from whom he stole. She will decide!"

The notion of delivering the criminal to the scene of his crime and to his victim, like something out of a Hindi movie, appealed to this crowd. Kersi managed to shake off his numbness. Following Percy's example, he grabbed Francis by the arm and collar, signifying that this was their captive, no longer to be bashed around.

In this manner they led Francis back to Firozsha Baag — past the tethered cow, past the *bunya*'s shop, past the overflowing gutters of Tar Gully. Every once in a while someone would punch Francis in the small of his back or on his head. But Percy would remind the crowd of the *bai* who had been robbed, whereupon the procession would resume in an orderly way.

A crowd was waiting outside C Block. More neighbours had gathered, including the solitary Muslim tenant in Firozsha Baag, from the ground floor of B Block, and his Muslim servant. Both had a long-standing grudge against Francis over some incident with a prostitute, and were pleased at his predicament.

Francis was brought before Najamai. He was in tears and his knees kept buckling. "Why, Francis?" asked Najamai. "Why?"

Suddenly, a neighbour stepped out of the crowd and slapped him hard across the face: "You *budmaash*! You have no shame? Eating her food, earning money from her, then stealing from her, you rascal?"

At the slap, the gathering started to move in for a fresh round of thrashing. But Najamai screamed and the crowd froze. Francis threw himself at her feet, weeping. "*Bai*," he begged, "you hit me, you kick me, do whatever you want to me. But please don't let them, please!"

While he knelt before her, the Muslim servant saw his chance and moved swiftly. He swung his leg and kicked Francis powerfully in the ribs before the others could pull him away. Francis yelped like a dog and keeled over.

Najamai was formally expressing her gratitude to Silloo. "How brave your two sons are. If they had not gone after that rogue I would never have seen my eighty rupees again. Say thanks to Percy and Kersi, God bless them, such fine boys." Both of them pointedly ignored Tehmina who, by this time, had been established as the minor villain in the piece, for putting temptation in Francis's path.

Meanwhile, the crowd had dispersed. Tehmina was chatting with the Muslim neighbour. Having few friends in this building, he was endeavouring to ingratiate himself with her while she was still

vulnerable, and before she recovered from C Block's excom-
munication. By the light of the full moon he sympathized with her
version of the episode.

"Najamai knows my eyes are useless till these cataracts are
removed. Yet she wants me to keep her keys, look after her flat."
The cloves ventured to her lips, agitated, but she expertly sucked
them back to the safety of her cheeks. "How was I to know what
Francis would do? If only I could have seen his eyes. It is always so
dark in that hallway." And the Muslim neighbour shook his head
slowly, making clucking sounds with his tongue to show he
understood perfectly.

Back in her flat, Najamai chuckled as she pictured the two boys
returning with Francis. "How silly they looked. Going after poor
Francis with their big bats! As if he would ever have hurt them.
Wonder what the police will do to him now." She went into the kitchen, sniffing. A smell of ammonia was in the air and a pool of
yellowish liquid stood where Francis had been hiding behind the
kitchen door. She bent down, puzzled, and sniffed again, then
realized he must have lost control of his bladder when she
screamed.

She mopped and cleaned up, planning to tell Silloo tomorrow of
her discovery. She would also have to ask her to find someone to
bring the rations next week. Maybe it was time to overcome her
aversion to full-time servants and hire one who would live here,
and cook and clean, and look after the flat. Someone who would
also provide company for her, sometimes it felt so lonely being
alone in the flat.

Najamai finished in the kitchen. She went to the bedroom,
lowered her weight into the easy chair and picked up the Boyces'
Sunday paper.

Kersi was in the bathroom. He felt like throwing up, but returned
to the bedroom after retching without success. He sat on the bed
and picked up his bat. He ripped off the rubber grip and slowly,
meditatively, started to tear the freshly glued cord from around the
handle, bit by bit, circle by circle.

Soon, the cord lay on the floor in a black tangled heap, and the handle looked bald, exposed, defenceless. Never before had Kersi seen his cricket bat in this flayed and naked state. He stood up, grasped the handle with both hands, rested the blade at an angle to the floor, then smashed his foot down upon it. There was a loud crack as the handle snapped.

The Ghost of Firozsha Baag

The Ghost of Firozsha Baag

I always believed in ghosts. When I was little I saw them in my father's small field in Goa. That was very long ago, before I came to Bombay to work as ayah.

Father also saw them, mostly by the well, drawing water. He would come in and tell us, the *bhoot* is thirsty again. But it never scared us. Most people in our village had seen ghosts. Everyone believed in them.

Not like in Firozsha Baag. First time I saw a ghost here and people found out, how much fun they made of me. Calling me crazy, saying it is time for old ayah to go back to Goa, back to her *muluk*, she is seeing things.

Two years ago on Christmas Eve I first saw the *bhoot*. No, it was really Christmas Day. At ten o'clock on Christmas Eve I went to Cooperage Stadium for midnight mass. Every year all of us Catholic ayahs from Firozsha Baag go for mass. But this time I came home alone, the others went somewhere with their boyfriends. Must have been two o'clock in the morning. Lift in B Block was out of order, so I started up slowly. Thinking how easy to climb three floors when I was younger, even with a full bazaar-bag.

After reaching first floor I stopped to rest. My breath was coming fast-fast. Fast-fast, like it does nowadays when I grind curry *masala* on the stone. Jaakaylee, my *bai* calls out, Jaakaylee, is *masala* ready? Thinks a sixty-three-year-old ayah can make *masala* as quick as she used to when she was fifteen. Yes, fifteen. The day after my fourteenth birthday I came by bus from Goa to Bombay. All day and night I rode the bus. I still remember when my father took me to bus station in Panjim. Now it is called Panaji. Joseph Uncle, who was mechanic in Mazagaon, met me at Bombay Central Station. So crowded it was, people running all around, shouting, screaming, and coolies with big-big trunks on their heads. Never will I forget that first day in Bombay. I just stood in one place, not knowing what to do, till Joseph Uncle saw me. Now it has been forty-nine years in this house as ayah, believe or don't believe. Forty-nine years in Firozsha Baag's B Block and they still don't say my name right. Is it so difficult to say Jacqueline? But they always say Jaakaylee. Or worse, Jaakayl.

All the fault is of old *bai* who died ten years ago. She was in charge till her son brought a wife, the new *bai* of the house. Old *bai* took English words and made them Parsi words. Easy chair was *igeechur*, French beans was *ferach beech*, and Jacqueline became Jaakaylee. Later I found out that all old Parsis did this, it was like they made their own private language.

So then new *bai* called me Jaakaylee also, and children do the same. I don't care about it now. If someone asks my name I say Jaakaylee. And I talk Parsi-Gujarati all the time instead of Konkani, even with other ayahs. Sometimes also little bits of English.

But I was saying. My breath was fast-fast when I reached first floor and stopped for rest. And then I noticed someone, looked like in a white gown. Like a man, but I could not see the face, just body shape. *Kaun hai?* I asked in Hindi. Believe or don't believe, he vanished. Completely! I shook my head and started for second floor. Carefully, holding the railing, because the steps are so old, all slanting and crooked.

Then same thing happened. At the top of second floor he was waiting. And when I said, *kya hai?* believe or don't believe, he vanished again! Now I knew it must be a *bhoot*. I knew he would be on third floor also, and I was right. But I was not scared or anything.

I reached the third floor entrance and found my bedding which

I had put outside before leaving. After midnight mass I always sleep outside, by the stairs, because *bai* and *seth* must not be woken up at two A.M., and they never give me a key. No ayah gets key to a flat. It is something I have learned, like I learned forty-nine years ago that life as ayah means living close to floor. All work I do, I do on floors, like grinding *masala*, cutting vegetables, cleaning rice. Food also is eaten sitting on floor, after serving them at dining-table. And my bedding is rolled out at night in kitchen-passage, on floor. No cot for me. Nowadays, my weight is much more than it used to be, and is getting very difficult to get up from floor. But I am managing.

So Christmas morning at two o'clock I opened my bedding and spread out my *saterunjee* by the stairs. Then stopped. The *bhoot* had vanished, and I was not scared or anything. But my father used to say some ghosts play mischief. The ghost of our field never did, he only took water from our well, but if this ghost of the stairs played mischief he might roll me downstairs, who was to say. So I thought about it and rang the doorbell.

After many, many rings *bai* opened, looking very mean. Mostly she looks okay, and when she dresses in nice sari for a wedding or something, and puts on all bangles and necklace, she looks really pretty, I must say. But now she looked so mean. Like she was going to bite somebody. Same kind of look she has every morning when she has just woken up, but this was much worse and meaner because it was so early in the morning. She was very angry, said I was going crazy, there was no ghost or anything, I was just telling lies not to sleep outside.

Then *seth* also woke up. He started laughing, saying he did not want any ghost to roll me downstairs because who would make *chai* in the morning. He was not angry, his mood was good. They went back to their room, and I knew why he was feeling happy when crrr-crr crrr-crr sound of their bed started coming in the dark.

When he was little I sang Konkani songs for him. *Mogacha Mary* and *Hanv Saiba*. Big man now, he's forgotten them and so have I. Forgetting my name, my language, my songs. But complaining I'm not, don't make mistake. I'm telling you, to have a job I was very lucky because in Goa there was nothing to do. From Panjim to Bombay on the bus I cried, leaving behind my brothers and sisters and parents, and all my village friends. But I knew leaving was best thing. My father had eleven children and very small field. Coming to Bombay was only thing to do. Even schooling I got first year, at night. Then *bai* said I must stop because who would serve dinner when *seth* came home from work, and who would carry away dirty dishes? But that was not the real reason. She thought I stole her eggs. There were six eggs yesterday evening, she would say, only five this morning, what happened to one? She used to think I took it with me to school to give to someone.

I was saying, it was very lucky for me to become ayah in Parsi house, and never will I forget that. Especially because I'm Goan Catholic and very dark skin colour. Parsis prefer Manglorean Catholics, they have light skin colour. For themselves also Parsis like light skin, and when Parsi baby is born that is the first and most important thing. If it is fair they say, O how nice light skin just like parents. But if it is dark skin they say, *arré* what is this *ayah no chhokro*, ayah's child.

All this doing was more in olden days, mostly among very rich *bais* and *seths*. They thought they were like British only, ruling India side by side. But don't make mistake, not just rich Parsis. Even all Marathi people in low class Tar Gully made fun of me when I went to buy grocery from *bunya*. Blackie, blackie, they would call out. Nowadays it does not happen because very dark skin colour is common in Bombay, so many people from south are coming here, Tamils and Keralites, with their funny *illay illay poe poe* language. Now people more used to different colours.

But still not to ghosts. Everybody in B Block found out about the *bhoot* of the stairs. They made so much fun of me all the time, children and grown-up people also.

And believe or don't believe, that *was* a ghost of mischief. Because just before Easter he came back. Not on the stairs this time but right in my bed. I'm telling you, he was sitting on my chest and bouncing up and down, and I couldn't push him off, so weak I was feeling (I'm a proper Catholic, I was fasting), couldn't even scream or anything (not because I was scared — he was choking me). Then someone woke up to go to WC and put on a light in the passage where I sleep. Only then did the rascal *bhoot* jump off and vanish.

This time I did not tell anyone. Already they were making so much fun of me. Children in Firozsha Baag would shout, ayah *bhoot!* ayah *bhoot!* every time they saw me. And a new Hindi film had come out, *Bhoot Bungla*, about a haunted house, so they would say, like the man on the radio, in a loud voice: SEE TODAY, at APSARA CINEMA, R. K. Anand's NEW fillum *Bhoooot Bungla*, starring JAAKAYLEE of BLOCK B! Just like that! O they made a lot of fun of me, but I did not care, I knew what I had seen.

Jaakaylee, bai calls out, is it ready yet? She wants to check curry masala. Too thick, she always says, grind it again, make it smoother. And she is right, I leave it thick purposely. Before, when I did it fine, she used to send me back anyway. O it pains in my old shoulders, grinding this masala, but they will never buy the automatic machine. Very rich people, my bai-seth. He is a chartered accountant. He has a nice motorcar, just like A Block priest, and like the one Dr Mody used to drive, which has not moved from the compound since the day he died. Bai says they should buy it from Mrs Mody, she wants it to go shopping. But a masala machine they will not buy. Jaakaylee must keep on doing it till her arms fall out from shoulders.

How much teasing everyone was doing to me about the *bhoot*. It became a great game among boys, pretending to be ghosts. One who started it all was Dr Mody's son, from third floor of C Block. One day they call Pesi *paadmaroo* because he makes dirty wind all the time. Good thing he is in boarding-school now. That family came to Firozsha Baag only few years ago, he was doctor for animals, a really nice man. But what a terrible boy. Must have been so shameful for Dr Mody. Such a kind man, what a shock everybody got when he died. But I'm telling you, that boy did a bad thing one night.

Vera and Dolly, the two fashionable sisters from C Block's first floor, went to nightshow at Eros Cinema, and Pesi knew. After nightshow was over, tock-tock they came in their high-heel shoes. It was when mini-skirts had just come out, and that is what they were wearing. Very *esskey-messkey*, so short I don't know how their *mai-baap* allowed it. They said their daughters were going to foreign for studies, so maybe this kind of dressing was practice for over there. Anyway, they started up, the stairs were very dark. Then Pesi, wearing a white bedsheet and waiting under the staircase, jumped out shouting *bowe ré*. Vera and Dolly screamed so loudly, I'm telling you, and they started running.

Then Pesi did a really shameful thing. God knows where he got the idea from. Inside his sheet he had a torch, and he took it out and shined up into the girls' mini-skirts. Yes! He ran after them with his big torch shining in their skirts. And when Vera and Dolly reached the top they tripped and fell. That shameless boy just stood there with his light shining between their legs, seeing undies and everything, I'm telling you.

He ran away when all neighbours started opening their doors to see what is the matter, because everyone heard them screaming. All the men had good time with Vera and Dolly, pretending to be like concerned grown-up people, saying, it is all right, dears, don't worry, dears, just some bad boy, not a real ghost. And all the time petting-squeezing them as if to comfort them! Sheeh, these men!

Next day Pesi was telling his friends about it, how he shone the torch up their skirts and how they fell, and everything he saw. That boy, sheeh, terrible.

Afterwards, parents in Firozsha Baag made a very strict rule that no one plays the fool about ghosts because it can cause serious accident if sometime some old person is made scared and falls downstairs and breaks a bone or something or has heart attack. So there was no more ghost games and no more making fun of me. But I'm telling you, the *bhoot* kept coming every Friday night.

Curry is boiling nicely, smells very tasty. Bai *tells me don't forget about curry, don't burn the dinner. How many times have I burned the dinner in forty-nine years, I should ask her. Believe or don't believe, not one time.*

Yes, the *bhoot* came but he did not bounce any more upon my chest. Sometimes he just sat next to the bedding, other times he lay down beside me with his head on my chest, and if I tried to push him away he would hold me tighter. Or would try to put his hand up my gown or down from the neck. But I sleep with buttons up to my collar, so it was difficult for the rascal. O what a ghost of mischief he was! Reminded me of Cajetan back in Panjim always trying to do same thing with girls at the cinema or beach. His parents' house was not far from Church of St Cajetan for whom he was named, but this boy was no saint, I'm telling you.

Calunqute and Anjuna beaches in those days were very quiet and beautiful. It was before foreigners all started coming, and no hippie-bippie business with *charas* and *ganja*, and no big-big hotels or nothing. Cajetan said to me once, let us go and see the fishermen. And we went, and started to wade a little, up to ankles, and Cajetan said let us go more. He rolled up his pants over the knees and I pulled up my skirt, and we went in deeper. Then a big wave made everything wet. We ran out and sat on the beach for my skirt to dry.

Us two were only ones there, fishermen were still out in boats. Sitting on the sand he made all funny eyes at me, like Hindi film hero, and put his hand on my thigh. I told him to stop or I would tell my father who would give him solid pasting and throw him in the well where the *bhoot* would take care of him. But he didn't stop. Not till the fishermen came. Sheeh, what a boy that was.

Back to kitchen. To make good curry needs lots of stirring while boiling.

I'm telling you, that Cajetan! Once, it was feast of St Francis Xavier, and the body was to be in a glass case at Church of Bom Jesus. Once every ten years is this very big event for Catholics. They were not going to do it any more because, believe or don't believe, many years back some poor crazy woman took a bite from toe of St Francis Xavier. But then they changed their minds. Poor St Francis, it is not his luck to have a whole body — one day, Pope asked for a bone from the right arm, for people in Rome to see, and never sent it back; that is where it is till today.

But I was saying about Cajetan. All boys and girls from my village were going to Bom Jesus by bus. In church it was so crowded, and a long long line to walk by St Francis Xavier's glass case. Cajetan was standing behind my friend Lily, he had finished his fun with me, now it was Lily's turn. And I'm telling you, he kept bumping her and letting his hand touch her body like it was by accident in the crowd. Sheeh, even in church that boy could not behave.

And the ghost reminded me of Cajetan, whom I have not seen since I came to Bombay — what did I say, forty-nine years ago. Once a week the ghost came, and always on Friday. On Fridays I eat fish, so I started thinking, maybe he likes smell of fish. Then I just ate vegetarian, and yet he came. For almost a whole year the ghost slept with me, every Friday night, and Christmas was not far away.

And still no one knew about it, how he came to my bed, lay down with me, tried to touch me. There was one thing I was feeling so terrible about — even to Father D'Silva at Byculla Church I had not told anything for the whole year. Every time in confession I would keep completely quiet about it. But now Christmas was coming and I was feeling very bad, so first Sunday in December I told Father D'Silva everything and then I was feeling much better. Father D'Silva said I was blameless because it was not my wish to have the *bhoot* sleeping with me. But he gave three Hail Marys, and said eating fish again was okay if I wanted.

So on Friday of that week I had fish curry-rice and went to bed. And believe or don't believe, the *bhoot* did not come. After midnight, first I thought maybe he is late, maybe he has somewhere else to go. Then the clock in *bai*'s room went three times and I was really worried. Was he going to come in early morning while I was making tea? That would be terrible.

But he did not come. Why, I wondered. If he came to the bedding of a fat and ugly ayah all this time, now what was the matter? I could not understand. But then I said to myself, what are you thinking Jaakaylee, where is your head, do you really want the ghost to come sleep with you and touch you so shamefully?

After drinking my tea that morning I knew what had happened. The ghost did not come because of my confession. He was ashamed now. Because Father D'Silva knew about what he had been doing to me in the darkness every Friday night.

Next Friday night also there was no ghost. Now I was completely sure my confession had got rid of him and his shameless habits. But in a few days it would be Christmas Eve and time for midnight mass. I thought, maybe if he is ashamed to come into my bed, he could wait for me on the stairs like last year.

Time to cook rice now, time for seth *to come home. Best quality Basmati rice we use, always, makes such a lovely fragrance while cooking, so tasty.*

For midnight mass I left my bedding outside, and when I returned it was two A.M. But for worrying there was no reason. No ghost on any floor this time. I opened the bedding by the stairs, thinking about Cajetan, how scared he was when I said I would tell my father about his touching me. Did not ask me to go anywhere after that, no beaches, no cinema. Now same thing with the ghost. How scared men are of fathers.

And next morning *bai* opened the door, saying, good thing ghost took a holiday this year, if you had woken us again I would have killed you. I laughed a little and said Merry Christmas, *bai*, and she said same to me.

When *seth* woke up he also made a little joke. If they only knew that in one week they would say I had been right. Yes, on New Year's Day they would start believing, when there was really no ghost. Never has been since the day I told Father D'Silva in confession. But I was not going to tell them they were mistaken, after such fun they made of me. Let them feel sorry now for saying Jaakaylee was crazy.

Bai and *seth* were going to New Year's Eve dance, somewhere in Bandra, for first time since children were born. She used to say they were too small to leave alone with ayah, but that year he kept saying please, now children were bigger. So she agreed. She kept telling me what to do and gave telephone number to call in case of emergency. Such fuss she made, I'm telling you, when they left for Bandra I was so nervous.

I said special prayer that nothing goes wrong, that children would eat dinner properly, not spill anything, go to bed without crying or trouble. If *bai* found out she would say, what did I tell you, children cannot be left with ayah. And then she would give poor *seth* hell for it. He gets a lot anyway.

Everything went right and children went to sleep. I opened my bedding, but I was going to wait till they came home. Spreading out the *saterunjee*, I saw a tear in the white bedsheet used for covering — maybe from all pulling and pushing with the ghost — and was going to repair it next morning. I put off the light and lay down just to rest.

Then cockroach sounds started. I lay quietly in the dark, first to decide where it was. If you put a light on they stop singing and then you don't know where to look. So I listened carefully. It was coming from the gas stove table. I put on the light now and took my *chappal*. There were two of them, sitting next to cylinder. I lifted my *chappal*, very slowly and quietly, then phut! phut! Must say I am expert at cockroach-killing. The poison which *seth* puts out is really not doing much good, my *chappal* is much better.

I picked up the two dead ones and threw them outside, in Baag's backyard. Two cockroaches would make nice little snack for some rat in the yard, I thought. Then I lay down again after switching off light.

Clock in *bai-seth*'s room went twelve times. They would all be giving kiss now and saying Happy New Year. When I was little in Panjim, my parents, before all the money went, always gave a party on New Year's Eve. I lay on my bedding, thinking of those days. It is so strange that so much of your life you can remember if you think quietly in the darkness.

Must not forget rice on stove. With rice, especially Basmati, one minute more or one minute less, one spoon extra water or less water, and it will spoil, it will not be light and every grain separate.

So there I was in the darkness remembering my father and mother, Panjim and Cajetan, nice beaches and boats. Suddenly it was very sad, so I got up and put a light on. In *bai-seth*'s room their clock said two o'clock. I wished they would come home soon. I checked children's room, they were sleeping.

Back to my passage I went, and started mending the torn sheet. Sewing, thinking about my mother, how hard she used to work, how she would repair clothes for my brothers and sisters. Not only sewing to mend but also to alter. When my big brother's pants would not fit, she would open out the waist and undo trouser cuffs to make longer legs. Then when he grew so big that even with alter-ations it did not fit, she sewed same pants again, making a smaller waist, shorter legs, so little brother could wear. How much work my mother did, sometimes even helping my father outside in the small field, especially if he was visiting a *taverna* the night before.

But sewing and remembering brought me more sadness. I put away the needle and thread and went outside by the stairs. There is a little balcony there. It was so nice and dark and quiet, I just stood there. Then it became a little chilly. I wondered if the ghost was coming again. My father used to say that whenever a ghost is around it feels chilly, it is a sign. He said he always did in the field when the *bhoot* came to the well.

There was no ghost or anything so I must be chilly, I thought, because it is so early morning. I went in and brought my white bed-sheet. Shivering a little, I put it over my head, covering up my ears. There was a full moon, and it looked so good. In Panjim sometimes we used to go to the beach at night when there was a full moon, and father would tell us about when he was little, and the old days when Portuguese ruled Goa, and about grandfather who had been to Portugal in a big ship.

Then I saw *bai-seth*'s car come in the compound. I leaned over the balcony, thinking to wave if they looked up, let them know I had not gone to sleep. Then I thought, no, it is better if I go in quietly before they see me, or *bai* might get angry and say, what are you doing outside in middle of night, leaving children alone inside. But she looked up suddenly. I thought, O my Jesus, she has already seen me.

And then she screamed. I'm telling you, she screamed so loudly I almost fell down faint. It was not angry screaming, it was frightened screaming, *bhoot! bhoot!* and I understood. I quickly went inside and lay down on my bedding.

It took some time for them to come up because she sat inside the car and locked all doors. Would not come out until he climbed upstairs, put on every staircase light to make sure the ghost was gone, and then went back for her.

She came in the house at last and straight to my passage, shaking me, saying wake up, Jaakaylee, wake up! I pretended to be sleeping deeply, then turned around and said, Happy New Year, *bai*, everything is okay, children are okay.

She said, yes yes, but the *bhoot* is on the stairs! I saw him, the one you saw last year at Christmas, he is back, I saw him with my own eyes!

I wanted so much to laugh, but I just said, don't be afraid, *bai*, he will not do any harm, he is not a ghost of mischief, he must have just lost his way.

Then she said, Jaakaylee, you were telling the truth and I was angry with you. I will tell everyone in B Block you were right, there really is a *bhoot*.

I said *bai*, let it be now, everyone has forgotten about it, and no one will believe anyway. But she said, when *I* tell them, they will believe.

And after that many people in Firozsha Baag started to believe in the ghost. One was *dustoorji* in A Block. He came one day and taught *bai* a prayer, *saykasté saykasté sataan*, to say it every time she was on the stairs. He told her, because you have seen a *bhoot* on the balcony by the stairs, it is better to have a special Parsi prayer ceremony there so he does not come again and cause any trouble. He said, many years ago, near Marine Lines where Hindus have their funerals and burn bodies, a *bhoot* walked at midnight in the middle of the road, scaring motorists and causing many accidents. Hindu priests said prayers to make him stop. But no use. *Bhoot* kept walking at midnight, motorists kept having accidents. So Hindu priests called me to do a *jashan*, they knew Parsi priest has most powerful prayers of all. And after I did a *jashan* right in the middle of the road, everything was all right.

Bai listened to all this talk of *dustoorji* from A Block, then said she would check with *seth* and let him know if they wanted a balcony *jashan*. Now *seth* says yes to everything, so he told her, sure sure, let *dustoorji* do it. It will be fun to see the exkoriseesum, he said, some big English word like that.

Dustoorji was pleased, and he checked his Parsi calendar for a good day. On that morning I had to wash whole balcony floor specially, then *dustoorji* came, spread a white sheet, and put all prayer items on it, a silver thing in which he made fire with sandalwood and *loban*, a big silver dish, a *lotta* full of water, flowers, and some fruit.

When it was time to start saying prayers *dustoorji* told me to go inside. Later, *bai* told me that was because Parsi prayers are so powerful, only a Parsi can listen to them. Everyone else can be badly damaged inside their soul if they listen.

So *jashan* was done and *dustoorji* went home with all his prayer things. But when people in Firozsha Baag who did not believe in the ghost heard about prayer ceremony, they began talking and mocking.

Some said Jaakaylee's *bai* has gone crazy, first the ayah was seeing things, and now she has made her *bai* go mad. *Bai* will not talk to those people in the Baag. She is really angry, says she does not want friends who think she is crazy. She hopes *jashan* was not very powerful, so the ghost can come again. She wants everyone to see him and know the truth like her.

Busy eating, bai-seth are. Curry is hot, they are blowing whoosh-whoosh on their tongues but still eating, they love it hot. Secret of good curry is not only what spices to put, but also what goes in first, what goes in second, and third, and so on. And never cook curry with lid on pot, always leave it open, stir it often, stir it to urge the flavour to come out.

So *bai* is hoping the ghost will come again. She keeps asking me about ghosts, what they do, why they come. She thinks because I saw the ghost first in Firozsha Baag, it must be my speciality or something. Especially since I am from village — she says village people know more about such things than city people. So I tell her about the *bhoot* we used to see in the small field, and what my father said when he saw the *bhoot* near the well. *Bai* enjoys it, even asks me to sit with her at table, bring my separate mug, and pours a cup for me, listening to my ghost-talk. She does not treat me like servant all the time.

One night she came to my passage when I was saying my rosary and sat down with me on the bedding. I could not believe it, I stopped my rosary. She said, Jaakaylee, what is it Catholics say when they touch their head and stomach and both sides of chest? So I told her, Father, Son, and Holy Ghost. Right right! she said, I remember it now, when I went to St Anne's High School there were many Catholic girls and they used to say it always before and after class prayer, yes, Holy Ghost. Jaakaylee, you don't think this is that Holy Ghost you pray to, do you? And I said, no *bai*, that Holy Ghost has a different meaning, it is not like the *bhoot* you and I saw.

Yesterday she said, Jaakaylee, will you help me with something? All morning she was looking restless, so I said, yes *bai*. She left the table and came back with her big scissors and the flat cane *soopra* I use for winnowing rice and wheat. She said, my granny showed me a little magic once, she told me to keep it for important things only. The *bhoot* is, so I am going to use it. If you help me. It needs two Parsis, but I'll do it with you.

I just sat quietly, a little worried, wondering what she was up to now. First, she covered her head with a white *mathoobanoo*, and gave me one for mine, she said to put it over my head like a scarf. Then, the two points of scissors she poked through one side of *soopra*, really tight, so it could hang from the scissors. On two chairs we sat face to face. She made me balance one ring of scissors on my finger, and she balanced the other ring on hers. And we sat like that, with *soopra* hanging from scissors between us, our heads covered with white cloth. Believe or don't believe, it looked funny and scary at the same time. When *soopra* became still and stopped swinging around she said, now close your eyes and don't think of anything, just keep your hand steady. So I closed my eyes, wondering if *seth* knew what was going on.

Then she started to speak, in a voice I had never heard before. It seemed to come from very far away, very soft, all scary. My hair was standing, I felt chilly, as if a *bhoot* was about to come. This is what she said: if the ghost is going to appear again, then *soopra* must turn.

Nothing happened. But I'm telling you, I was so afraid I just kept my eyes shut tight, like she told me to do. I wanted to see nothing which I was not supposed to see. All this was something completely new for me. Even in my village, where everyone knew so much about ghosts, magic with *soopra* and scissors was unknown.

Then *bai* spoke once more, in that same scary voice: if the ghost is going to appear again, upstairs or downstairs, on balcony or inside the house, this year or next year, in daylight or in darkness, for good purpose or for bad purpose, then *soopra* must surely turn.

Believe or don't believe, this time it started to turn, I could feel the ring of the scissors moving on my finger. I screamed and pulled away my hand, there was a loud crash, and *bai* also screamed.

Slowly, I opened my eyes. Everything was on the floor, scissors were broken, and I said to *bai*, I'm very sorry I was so frightened, *bai*, and for breaking your big scissors, you can take it from my pay.

She said, you scared me with your scream, Jaakaylee, but it is all right now, nothing to be scared about, I'm here with you. All the worry was gone from her face. She took off her *mathoobanoo* and patted my shoulder, picked up the broken scissors and *soopra*, and took it back to kitchen.

Bai was looking very pleased. She came back and said to me, don't worry about broken scissors, come, bring your mug, I'm making tea for both of us, forget about *soopra* and ghost for now. So I removed my *mathoobanoo* and went with her.

Jaakaylee, O Jaakaylee, she is calling from dining-room. They must want more curry. Good thing I took some out for my dinner, they will finish the whole pot. Whenever I make Goan curry, nothing is left over. At the end seth always takes a piece of bread and rubs it round and round in the pot, wiping every little bit. They always joke, Jaakaylee, no need today for washing pot, all cleaned out. Yes, it is one thing I really enjoy, cooking my Goan curry, stirring and stirring, taking the aroma as it boils and cooks, stirring it again and again, watching it bubbling and steaming, stirring and stirring till it is ready to eat.

Condolence Visit

Condolence Visit

Yesterday had been the tenth day, *dusmoo*, after the funeral of
Minocher Mirza. *Dusmoo* prayers were prayed at the fire-temple,
and the widow Mirza awaited with apprehension the visitors who
would troop into the house over the next few weeks. They would
come to offer their condolence, share her grief, poke and pry into
her life and Minocher's with a thousand questions. And to gratify
them with answers she would have to relive the anguish of the most
trying days of her life.

The more tactful ones would wait for the first month, *maasiso*, to
elapse before besieging her with sympathy and comfort. But not
the early birds; they would come flocking from today. It was open
season, and Minocher Mirza had been well-known in the Parsi
community of Bombay.

After a long and troubled illness, Minocher had suddenly eased
into a condition resembling a state of convalescence. Minocher
and Daulat had both understood that it was only a spurious convalescence, there would be no real recovery. All the same, they were
thankful his days and nights passed in relative comfort. He was
able to wait for death freed from the agony which had racked his
body for the past several months.

And as it so often happens in such cases, along with relief from physical torment, the doubts and fears which had tortured his mind released their hold as well. He was at peace with his being which was soon to be snuffed out.

Daulat, too, felt at peace because her one fervent prayer was being answered. Minocher would be allowed to die with dignity, without being reduced to something less than human; she would not have to witness any more of his suffering.

Thus Minocher had passed away in his sleep after six days spent in an inexplicable state of grace and tranquillity. Daulat had cried for the briefest period; she felt it would be sinful to show anything but gladness when he had been so fortunate in his final days.

Now, however, the inescapable condolence visits would make her regurgitate months of endless pain, nights spent sleeplessly, while she listened for his breath, his sighs, his groans, his vocalization of the agony within. For bearers of condolences and sympathies she would have to answer questions about the illness, about doctors and hospitals, about nurses and medicines, about X-rays and blood reports. She would be requested (tenderly but tenaciously, as though it was their rightful entitlement) to recreate the hell her beloved Minocher had suffered, instead of being allowed to hold on to the memory of those final blessed six days. The worst of it would be the repetition of details for different visitors at different hours on different days, until that intensely emotional time she had been through with Minocher would be reduced to a dry and dull lesson learned from a textbook which she would parrot like a schoolgirl.

Last year, Daulat's nephew Sarosh, the Canadian immigrant who now answered to the name of Sid, had arrived from Toronto for a visit, after ten years. Why he had never gone back he would not say, nor did he come to see her any more. After all that she and Minocher had done for him. But he did bring her a portable cassette tape recorder from Canada, remembering her fondness for music, so she could tape her favourite songs from All India Radio's two Western music programs: "Merry Go Round" and "Saturday Date." Daulat, however, had refused it, saying "Poor Minocher sick in bed, and I listen to music? Never." She would not change her mind despite Sarosh-Sid's recounting of the problems he had had getting it through Bombay customs.

Now she wished she had accepted the gift. It could be handy, she thought with bitterness, to tape the details, to squeeze all of her and Minocher's suffering inside the plastic case, and proffer it to the visitors who came propelled by custom and convention. When they held out their right hands in the condolence-handshake position (fingertips of left hand tragically supporting right elbow, as though the right arm, overcome with grief, could not make it on its own) she could thrust towards them the cassette and recorder: "You have come to ask about my life, my suffering, my sorrow? Here, take and listen. Listen on the machine, everything is on tape. How my Minocher fell sick, where it started to pain, how much it hurt, what doctor said, what specialist said, what happened in hospital. This R button? Is for Rewind. Some part you like, you can hear it again, hear it ten times if you want: how nurse gave wrong medicine but my Minocher, sharp even in sickness, noticed different colour of pills and told her to check; how wardboy always handled the bedpan savagely, shoving it underneath as if doing sick people a big favour; how Minocher was afraid when time came for sponge bath, they were so careless and rough — felt like number three sandpaper on his bedsores, my brave Minocher would joke. What? The FF button? Means Fast Forward. If some part bores you, just press FF and tape will turn to something else: like how in hospital Minocher's bedsores were so terrible it would bring tears to my eyes to look, all filled with pus and a bad smell on him always, even after sponge bath, so I begged of doctor to let me take him home; how at home I changed dressings four times a day using sulfa ointment, and in two weeks bedsores were almost gone; how, as time went by and he got worse, his friends stopped coming when he needed them most, friends like you, now listening to this tape. Huh? This letter P? Stands for Pause. Press it if you want to shut off machine, if you cannot bear to hear more of your friend Minocher's suffering…"

Daulat stopped herself. Ah, the bitter thoughts of a tired old woman. But of what use? It was better not to think of these visits which were as inevitable as Minocher's death. The only way out was to lock up the flat and leave Firozsha Baag, live elsewhere for the next few weeks. Perhaps at a boarding-house in Udwada, town of the most sacrosanct of all fire-temples. But though her choice of location would be irreproachable, the timing of her trip would generate the most virulent gossip and criticism the community was capable of, to weather which she possessed neither the strength nor the audacity. The visits would have to be suffered, just as Minocher had suffered his sickness, with forbearance.

The doorbell startled Daulat. This early in the morning could not bring a condolence visitor. The clock was about to strike nine as she went to the door.

Her neighbour Najamai glided in, as fluidly as the smell of slightly rancid fat that always trailed her. The pounds shed by her bulk in recent years constantly amazed Daulat. Today the smell was supplemented by *dhansaak masala*, she realized, as the odours found and penetrated her nostrils. It was usually possible to tell what Najamai had been cooking; she carried a bit of her kitchen with her wherever she went.

Although about the same age as Daulat, widowhood had descended much earlier upon Najamai, turning her into an authority on the subject of Religious Rituals And The Widowed Woman. This had never bothered Daulat before. But the death of Minocher offered Najamai unlimited scope, and she had made the best of it, besetting and bombarding Daulat with advice on topics ranging from items she should pack in her valise for the four-day Towers Of Silence vigil, to the recommended diet during the first ten days of mourning. Her counselling service had to close, however, with completion of the death rituals. Then Daulat was again able to regard her in the old way, with a mixture of tolerance and mild dislike.

"Forgive me for ringing your bell so early in the morning but I wanted to let you know, if you need chairs or glasses, just ask me."

"Thanks, but no one will — "

"No no, you see, yesterday was *dusmoo*, I am counting carefully. How quickly ten days have gone by! People will start visiting from today, believe me. Poor Minocher, so popular, he had so many friends, they will all visit — "

"Yes, they will, and I must get ready," said Daulat, interrupting what threatened to turn into an early morning prologue to a condolence visit. She found it hard to judge her too harshly, Najamai had had her share of sorrow and rough times. Her Soli had passed away the very year after the daughters, Vera and Dolly, had gone abroad for higher studies. The sudden burden of loneliness must have been horrible to bear. For a while, her large new refrigerator had helped to keep up a flow of neighbourly companionship, drawn forth by the offer of ice and other favours. But after the Francis incident, that, too, ceased. Tehmina refused to have anything to do with the fridge or with Najamai (her conscience heavy and her cataracts still unripe), and Silloo Boyce downstairs had also drastically reduced its use (though her conscience was clear, her sons Kersi and Percy had saved the day).

So Najamai, quite alone and spending her time wherever she was tolerated, now spied Minocher's pugree. "Oh, that's so nice, so shiny and black! And in such good condition!" she rhapsodized.

It truly was an elegant piece of headgear, and many years ago Minocher had purchased a glass display case for it. Daulat had brought it out into the living-room this morning.

Najamai continued: "You know, pugrees are so hard to find these days, this one would bring a lot of money. But you must never sell it. Never. It is your Minocher's, so always keep it." With these ex-hortatory words she prepared to leave. Her eyes wandered around the flat for a last minute scrutiny, the sort that evoked mild dislike for her in Daulat.

"You must be very busy today, so I'll — " Najamai turned towards Minocher's bedroom and halted in mid-sentence, in consterna-tion: "*O baap ré!* The lamp is still burning! Beside Minocher's bed — that's wrong, very wrong!"

"Oh, I forgot all about it," lied Daulat, feigning dismay. "I was so busy. Thanks for reminding, I'll put it out."

But she had no such intention. When Minocher had breathed his last, the *dustoorji* from A Block had been summoned and had given her careful instructions on what was expected of her. The first and most important thing, the *dustoorji* had said, was to light a small oil lamp at the head of Minocher's bed; this lamp, he said, must burn for four days and nights while prayers were performed at the Towers Of Silence. But the little oil lamp became a source of comfort in a house grown quiet and empty for the lack of one silent feeble man, one shadow. Daulat kept the lamp lit past the prescribed four days, replenishing it constantly with coconut oil.

"Didn't *dustoorji* tell you?" asked Najamai. "For the first four days the soul comes to visit here. The lamp is there to welcome the soul. But after four days prayers are all complete, you know, and the soul must now quickly-quickly go to the Next World. With the lamp still burning the soul will be attracted to two different places: here, and the Next World. So you must put it out, you are confusing the soul," Najamai earnestly concluded.

Nothing can confuse my Minocher, thought Daulat, he will go where he has to go. Aloud she said, "Yes, I'll put it out right away."

"Good, good," said Najamai, "and oh, I almost forgot to tell you, I have lots of cold-drink bottles in the fridge, Limca and Goldspot, nice and chilled, if you need them. Few years back, when visitors were coming after Dr Mody's *dusmoo*, I had no fridge, and poor Mrs Mody had to keep running to Irani restaurant. But you are lucky, just come to me."

What does she think, I'm giving a party the day after *dusmoo*? thought Daulat. In the bedroom she poured more oil in the glass, determined to keep the lamp lit as long as she felt the need. Only, the bedroom door must remain closed, so the tug-of-war between two worlds, with Minocher's soul in the middle, would not provide sport for visitors.

She sat in the armchair next to what had been Minocher's bed and watched the steady, unflickering flame of the oil lamp. Like Minocher, she thought, reliable and always there; how lucky I was to have such a husband. No bad habits, did not drink, did not go to the racecourse, did not give me any trouble. Ah, but he made up for it when he fell sick. How much worry he caused me then, while he still had the strength to argue and fight back. Would not eat his food, would not take his medicine, would not let me help with anything.

In the lamp glass coconut oil, because it was of the unrefined type, rested golden-hued on water, a natant disc. With a pure sootless flame the wick floated, a little raft upon the gold. And Daulat, looking for answers to difficult questions, stared at the flame. Slowly, across the months, borne upon the flame-raft came the incident of the Ostermilk tin. It came without the anger and frustration she had known then, it came in a new light. And she could not help smiling as she remembered.

It had been the day of the monthly inspection for bedbugs. Due to the critical nature of this task, Daulat tackled it with a zeal unreserved for anything else. She worked side by side with the servant. Minocher had been comfortable in the armchair, and the mattress was turned over. The servant removed the slats, one by one, while Daulat, armed with a torch, examined every crack and corner, every potential redoubt. Then she was ready to spray the mixture of Flit and Tik-20, and pulled at the handle of the pump.

But before plunging in the piston she glimpsed, between the bedpost and the wall, a large tin of Ostermilk on the floor. The servant dived under to retrieve it. The tin was shut tight, she had to pry the lid open with a spoon. And as it came off, there rose a stench powerful enough to rip to shreds the hardy nostrils of a latrine-basket collector. She quickly replaced the lid, fanning the air vigorously with her hand. Minocher seemed to be dozing off, olfactory nerves unaffected. Was he trying to subdue a smile? Daulat could not be sure. But the tin without its lid was placed outside the back door, in hopes that the smell would clear in a while.

The bedbug inspection was resumed and the Flitting finished without further interruption. Minocher's bed was soon ready, and he fell asleep in it.

The smell of the Ostermilk tin had now lost its former potency. Daulat squinted at the contents: a greyish mass of liquids and solids, no recognizable shapes or forms amongst them. With a stick she explored the gloppy, sloppy mess. Gradually, familiar objects began to emerge, greatly transmogrified but retaining enough of their original states to agitate her. She was now able to discern a square of fried egg, exhume a piece of toast, fish out an orange pip. So! This is what he did with his food! How *could* he get better if he did not eat. Indignation drove her back to his bedroom. She refused to be responsible for him if he was going to behave in this way. Sickness or no sickness, I will have to tell him straight.

But Minocher was fast asleep, snoring gently. Like a child, she thought, and her anger had melted away. She did not have the heart to waken him; he had spent all night tossing and turning. Let him sleep. But from now on I will have to watch him carefully at mealtimes.

Beside the oil lamp Daulat returned to the present. Talking to visitors about such things would not be difficult. But they would be made uncomfortable, not knowing whether to laugh or keep the condolence-visit-grimness upon their faces. The Ostermilk tin would have to remain their secret, hers and Minocher's. As would the oxtail soup, whose turn it now was to sail silently out of the past, on the golden disc, on the flame-raft of Minocher's lamp.

At the butcher's, Daulat and Minocher had always argued about oxtail which neither had ever eaten. Minocher wanted to try it, but she would say with a shudder, "See how they hang like snakes. How can you even think of eating that? It will bring bad luck, I won't cook it."

He called her superstitious. Oxtail, however, remained a dream deferred for Minocher. After his illness commenced, Daulat shopped alone, and at the meat market she would remember Minocher's penchant for trying new things. She picked her way cautiously over the wet, slippery floors, weaving through the narrow aisles between the meat stalls, avoiding the importunating hands that thrust shoulders and legs and chops before her. But she forced herself to stop before the pendent objects of her dread and fix them with a long, hard gaze, as though to stare them down and overcome her aversion.

She was often tempted to buy oxtail and surprise Minocher — something different might revive his now almost-dead appetite. But the thought of evil and misfortune associated with all things serpentine dissuaded her each time. Finally, when Minocher had entered the period of his pseudo-convalescence, he awakened after a peaceful night and said, "Do me a favour?" Daulat nodded, and he smiled wickedly: "Make oxtail soup." And that day, they dined on what had made her cringe for years, the first hearty meal for both since the illness had commandeered the course of their lives.

Daulat rose from the armchair. It was time now to carry out the plan she had made yesterday, walking past the Old-Age Home For Parsi Men, on her way back from the fire-temple. If Minocher could, he would want her to. Many were the times he had gone through his wardrobe selecting things he did not need or wear any longer, wrapped them in brown paper and string, and carried them to the Home for distribution.

Beginning with the ordinary items of everyday wear, she started sorting them: *sudras*, underwear, two spare *kustis*, sleeping suits, light cotton shirts for wearing around the house. She decided to make parcels right away — why wait for the prescribed year or six months and deny the need of the old men at the Home if she could (and Minocher certainly could) give today?

When the first heap of clothing took its place upon brown paper spread out on his bed, something wrenched inside her. The way it had wrenched when he had been pronounced dead by the doctor. Then it passed, as it had passed before. She concentrated on the clothes; one of each in every parcel: *sudra*, underpants, sleeping suit, shirt would make it easier to distribute.

Bent over the bed, she worked unaware of her shadow on the wall, cast by the soft light of the oil lamp. Though the curtainless window was open, the room was half-dark because the sun was on the other side of the flat. But half-dark was light enough in this room into which had been concentrated her entire universe for the duration of her and Minocher's ordeal. Every little detail in this room she knew intimately: the slivered edge of the first compartment of the chest of drawers where a *sudra* could snag, she knew to avoid; the little trick, to ease out the shirt drawer which always stuck, she was familiar with; the special way to jiggle the key in the lock of the Godrej cupboard she had mastered a long time ago.

The Godrej steel cupboard Daulat tackled next. This was the difficult one, containing the "going-out" clothes: suits, ties, silk shirts, fashionable bush shirts, including some foreign ones sent by their Canadian nephew, Sarosh-Sid, and the envy of Minocher's friends. This cupboard would be the hard one to empty out, with each garment holding memories of parties and New Year's Eve dances, weddings and *navjotes*. Strung out on the hangers and spread out on the shelves were the chronicles of their life together, beginning with the Parsi formal dress Minocher had worn on the day of their wedding: silk *dugli*, white silk shirt, and the magnificent pugree. And to commence her life with him all she had had to do was move from her parents' flat in A Block to Minocher's in C Block. Yes, they were the only childhood sweethearts in Firozsha Baag who had got married, all the others had gone their separate ways.

The pugree was in its glass case in the living-room where Daulat had left it earlier. She went to it now and opened the case. It gleamed the way it had forty years ago. How grand he had looked then, with the pugree splendidly seated on his head! There was only one other occasion when he had worn it since, on the wedding of Sarosh-Sid, who had been to them the son they never had. Sarosh's papers had arrived from the Canadian High Commission in New Delhi, and three months after the wedding he had emigrated with his brand new wife. They divorced a year later because she did not like it in Canada. For the wedding, Minocher had wanted Sarosh to wear the pugree, but he had insisted (like the modern young man that he was) on an English styled double-breasted suit. So Minocher had worn it instead. Pugree-making had become a lost art due to modern young men like Sarosh, but Minocher had known how to take care of his. Hence its mint condition.

Daulat took the pugree and case back into the bedroom as she went looking for the advertisement she had clipped out of the *Jam-E-Jamshed*. It had appeared six days ago, on the morning after she had returned from the Towers Of Silence: "Wanted — a pugree in good condition. Phone no. ————— ." Yesterday, Daulat had dialled the number; the advertiser was still looking. He was coming today to inspect Minocher's pugree.

The doorbell rang. It was Najamai. Again. In her wake followed Ramchandra, lugging four chairs of the stackable type. The idea of a full-time servant who would live under her roof had always been disagreeable to Najamai, but she had finally heeded the advice of the many who said that a full-time servant was safer than an odd-job man, he became like one of the family, responsible and loyal. Thus Najamai had taken the plunge; now the two were inseparable.

They walked in, her rancid-fat-*dhansaak-masala* smell embroidered by the attar of Ramchandra's hair oil. The combination made Daulat wince.

"Forgive me for disturbing you again, I was just now leaving with Ramu, many-many things to do today, and I thought, what if poor Daulat needs chairs? So I brought them now only, before we left. That way you will…"

Daulat stopped listening. Good thing the bedroom door was shut, or Najamai would have started another oil lamp exegesis.

Would this garrulous busybody never leave her alone? There were extra chairs in the dining-room she could bring out.

With Sarosh's cassette recorder, she could have made a tape for Najamai too. It would be a simple one to make, with many pauses during which Najamai did all the talking: Neighbour Najamai Take One — "Hullo, come in" — (long pause) — "hmm, right" — (short pause) — "yes yes, that's okay" — (long pause) — "right, right." It would be easy, compared to the tape for condolence visitors.

"...you are listening, no? So chairs you can keep as long as you like, don't worry, Ramchandra can bring them back after a month, two months, after friends and relatives stop visiting. Come on Ramu, come on, we're getting late."

Daulat shut the door and withdrew into her flat. Into the silence of the flat. Where moments of life past and forgotten, moments lost, misplaced, hidden away, were all waiting to be recovered. They were like the stubs of cinema tickets she came across in Minocher's trouser pockets or jackets, wrung through the laundry, crumpled and worn thin but still decipherable. Or like the old program for a concert at Scot's Kirk by the Max Mueller Society of Bombay, found in a purse fallen, like Scot's Kirk, into desuetude. On the evening of the concert Minocher, with a touch of sarcasm, had quipped: Indian audience listens to German musicians inside a church built by skirted men — truly Bombay is cosmopolitan. The encore had been *Für Elise*. The music passed through her mind now, in the silent flat, by the light of the oil lamp: the beginning in A minor, full of sadness and nostalgia and an unbearable yearning for times gone by; then the modulation into C major, with its offer of hope and strength and understanding. This music, felt Daulat, was like a person remembering — if you could hear the sound of the working of remembrance, the mechanism of memory, *Für Elise* was what it would sound like.

Suddenly, remembering was extremely important, a deep-seated need surfacing, manifesting itself in Daulat's flat. All her life those closest to her had reminisced about events from their lives; she, the audience, had listened, sometimes rapt, sometimes impatient. Grandmother would sit her down and tell stories from years gone by; the favourite one was about her marriage and the elaborate matchmaking that preceded it. Mother would talk about her Girl

Guide days, with a faraway look in her eyes; she still had her dark blue Girl Guide satchel, faded and frayed.

When grandmother had died no music was allowed in the house for three months. Even the neighbours, in all three blocks, had silenced their radios and gramophones for ten days. No one was permitted to play in the compound for a month. In those old days, the compound was not flagstoned, and clouds of dust were raised by the boys of Firozsha Baag as they tore about playing their games. The greatest nuisance was, of course, to the ground floor: furniture dusted and cleaned in the morning was recoated by nightfall. The thirty-day interdiction against games was a temporary reprieve for those tenants. That month, membership in the Cawasji Framji Memorial Library rose, and grandmother's death converted several boys in the Baag to reading. During that time, Daulat's mother introduced her to kitchen and cooking — there was now room for one more in that part of the flat.

Daulat had become strangers with her radio shortly after Minocher's illness started. But the childhood proscription against music racked her with guilt whenever a strand of melody strayed into her room from the outside world. Minocher's favourite song was "At the Balalaika." He had taken her to see *Balalaika* starring Nelson Eddy at a morning show. It was playing at the Eros Cinema, it was his fourth time, and he was surprised that she had never seen the film before. How did the song…she hummed it, out of tune: At the Balalaika, one summer night a table laid for two, was just a private heaven made for two…

The wick of the oil lamp crackled. It did this when the oil was low. She fetched the bottle and filled the glass, shaking out the last drop, then placed the bottle on the windowsill: a reminder to replenish the oil.

Outside, the peripatetic vendors started to arrive, which meant it was past three o'clock. Between one and three was nap time, and the watchman at the gate of Firozsha Baag kept out all hawkers, according to the instructions of the management. The potato-and-onion man got louder as he approached now, "Onions rupee a kilo, potatoes two rupees," faded after he went past, to the creaky obligato of his thirsty-for-lubrication cart as it jounced through the compound. He was followed by the fishwalli, the

eggman, the biscuitwalla; and the ragman who sang with a sono-
rous vibrato:

> Of old saris and old clothes I am collector,
> Of new plates and bowls in exchange I am giver...

From time to time, B.E.S.T. buses thundered past and all sounds were
drowned out. Finally came the one Daulat was waiting for. She
waved the empty bottle at the oilwalla, purchased a quarter litre,
and arranged with him to knock at her door every alternate day. She
was not yet sure when she would be ready to let the lamp go out.

The clock showed half past four when she went in with the bottle. Minocher's things lay in neat brown paper packages, ready for
the Old-Age Home. She shut the doors of the cupboards now
almost empty; the clothes it took a man a lifetime to wear and enjoy, she thought, could be parcelled away in hours.

The man would soon arrive to see Minocher's pugree. She
wondered what it was that had made him go to the trouble of
advertising. Perhaps she should never have telephoned. Unless he
had a good reason, she was not going to part with it. Definitely not
if he was just some sort of collector.

The doorbell. Must be him, she thought, and looked through the
peephole.

But standing outside were second cousin Moti and her two
grandsons. Moti had not been at the funeral. Daulat did not open
the door immediately. She could hear her admonishing the two little boys: "Now you better behave properly or I will not take you
anywhere ever again. And if she serves Goldspot or Vimto or
something, be polite, leave some in the glass. Drink it all and you'll
get a pasting when you get home."

Daulat had heard enough. She opened the door and Moti, laden
with eau de cologne, fell on her neck with properly woeful utterances
and tragic tones. "O Daulat, Daulat! What an unfortunate thing to
happen to you! O very wrong thing has come to pass! Poor Minocher
gone! Forgive me for not coming to the funeral, but my Gustadji's
gout was so painful that day. Completely impossible. I said to Gustadji, least I can do now is visit you soon as possible after *dusmoo*."

Daulat nodded, trying to look grateful for the sympathy Moti was so desperate to offer to fulfil her duties. It was almost time to reach for her imaginary cassette player.

"Before you start thinking what a stupid woman I am to bring two little boys to a condolence visit, I must tell you that there was no one at home they could stay with. And we never leave them alone. It is so dangerous. You heard about that vegetablewalla in Bandra? Broke into a flat, strangled a child, stole everything. Cleaned it out completely. *Parvar Daegar!* Save us from such wicked madmen!"

Daulat led the way into the living-room, and Moti sat on the sofa. The boys occupied Najamai's loaned chairs. The bedroom door was open just a crack, revealing the oil lamp with its steady un-wavering flame. Daulat shut it quickly lest Moti should notice and comment about the unorthodoxy of her source of comfort.

"Did he suffer much before the end? I heard from Ruby — you know Ruby, sister of Eruch Uncle's son-in-law Shapur, she was at the funeral — that poor Minocher was in great pain the last few days."

Daulat reached in her mind for the start switch of the cassette player. But Moti was not yet ready: "Couldn't the doctors do something? From what we hear these days, they can cure almost anything."

"Well," said Daulat, "our doctor was very helpful, but it was a hopeless case, he told me, we were just prolonging the agony."

"You know, I was reading in the *Indian Express* last week that doctors in China were able to make" — here, Moti lowered her voice in case the grandsons were listening, shielded her mouth with one hand, and pointed to her lap with the other — "a man's Part. His girlfriend ran off with another man and he was very upset. So he chopped off" — in a whisper — "his own Part, in frustration, and flushed it down the toilet. Later, in hospital, he regretted doing it, and God knows how, but the doctors made for him" — in a whisper again — "a New Part, out of his own skin and all. They say it works and everything. Isn't that amazing?"

"Yes, very interesting," said Daulat, relieved that Moti had, at least temporarily, forsaken the prescribed condolence visit questioning.

The doorbell again. Must be the young man for the pugree this time.

But in stepped ever-solicitous Najamai. "Sorry, sorry. Very sorry, didn't know you had company. Just wanted to see if you were okay, and let you know I was back. In case you need anything." Then leaning closer conspiratorially, rancid-fat-*dhansaak-masala* odours overwhelming Daulat, she whispered, "Good thing, no, I brought the extra chairs."

Daulat calculated quickly. If Najamai stayed, as indeed she was eager to, Moti would drift even further from the purpose of her visit. So she invited her in. "Please come and sit, meet my second cousin Moti. And these are her grandsons. Moti was just now telling me a very interesting case about doctors in China who made" — copying Moti's whisper — "a New Part for a man."

"A new part? But that's nothing new. They do it here also now, putting artificial arms-legs and little things inside hearts to make blood pump properly."

"No no," said Moti. "Not a new part. This was" — in a whisper, dramatically pointing again to her lap for Najamai's benefit — "a New Part! And he can do everything with it. It works. Chinese doctors made it."

"Oh!" said Najamai, now understanding. "A New Part!"

Daulat left the two women to ponder the miracle, and went to the kitchen. There was a bottle of Goldspot in the icebox for the children. The kettle was ready and she poured three cups of tea. The doorbell rang for the third time while she arranged the tray. She was about to abandon it and go to the door but Najamai called out, "It's all right, I'll open it, don't worry, finish what you are doing."

Najamai said: "Yes?" to the young man standing outside.

"Are you Mrs Mirza?"

"No no, but come in. Daulat! There's a young man asking for you."

Daulat settled the tray on the teapoy before the sofa and went to the door. "You're here to see the pugree. Please come in and sit." He took one of Najamai's loaned chairs.

Najamai and Moti exchanged glances. Come for the pugree? What was going on?

The young man noticed the exchange and felt obliged to say something. "Mrs Mirza is selling Mr Mirza's pugree to me. You see, my fiancée and I, we decided to do everything, all the ceremonies, the proper traditional way at our wedding. In correct Parsi dress and all."

Daulat heard him explain in the next room and felt relieved. It was going to be all right, parting with the pugree would not be difficult. The young man's reasons would have made Minocher exceedingly happy.

But Najamai and Moti were aghast. Minocher's pugree being sold and the man barely digested by vultures at the Towers Of Silence! Najamai decided she had to take charge. She took a deep breath and tilted her chin pugnaciously. "Look here, *bawa*, it's very nice to hear you want to do it the proper Parsi way. So many young men are doing it in suits and ties these days. Why, one wedding I went to, the boy was wearing a shiny black suit with lacey, frilly-frilly shirt and bow tie. Exactly like Dhobitalao Goan wedding of a Catholic it was looking! So believe me when I say that we are very happy about yours."

She paused, took another deep breath, and prepared for a fortissimo finale. "But this poor woman who is giving you the pugree, her beloved husband's funeral was only ten days ago. Yesterday was *dusmoo*, and her tears are barely dry! And today you are taking away his pugree. It is not correct! You must come back later!" Then Najamai went after Daulat, and Moti followed.

The young man could see them go into a huddle from where he sat, and could hear them as well. Moti was saying, "Your neighbour is right, this is not proper. Wait for a few days."

And Najamai was emboldened to the point of presenting one of her theories. "You see, with help of prayers, the soul usually crosses over after four days. But sometimes the soul is very attached to this world and takes longer to make the crossing. And as long as the soul is here, everything such as clothes, cup-saucer, brush-comb, all must be kept same way they were, exactly same. Or the soul becomes very unhappy."

The young man was feeling extremely uncomfortable. He, of course, had not known that Daulat had been widowed as recently as ten days ago. Once again he felt obliged to say something. He cleared his throat: "Excuse me." But it was washed away in the downpour of Najamai's words.

He tried again, louder this time: "Excuse me, please!"

Najamai and Moti turned around sharply and delivered a challenging "Yes?"

"Excuse me, but maybe I should come back later for the pugree, the wedding is three months away."

"Yes! Yes!" said Moti and Najamai in unison. The latter continued: "I don't want you thinking I'm stirring my ladle in your pot, but that would be much better. Come back next month, after *maasiso*. You can try it on today if you like, see if it fits. In that there is no harm. Just don't take it away from the place where the soul expects it to be."

"I don't want to give any trouble," said the young man. "It's all right, I can try it later, the wedding is three months away. I'm sure it will fit."

Daulat, with the pugree in her hands, approached the young man. "If you think it is bad luck to wear a recently dead man's pugree and you are changing your mind, that's okay with me." The young man vigorously shook his head from side to side, protesting, as Daulat continued: "But let me tell you, my Minocher would be happy to give it to you if he were here. He would rejoice to see someone get married in his pugree. So if you want it, take it today."

The young man looked at Moti and Najamai's flabbergasted countenances, then at Daulat waiting calmly for his decision. The tableau of four persisted: two women slack-jawed with disbelief; another holding a handsome black pugree; and in the middle an embarrassed young man pulled two ways, like Minocher's soul, in a tug-of-war between two worlds.

The young man broke the spell. He reached out for the pugree and gently took it from Daulat's hands.

"Come," she smiled, and walked towards the bedroom, to the dressing-table.

"Excuse me," he said to Najamai and Moti, who were glaring resentfully, and followed. He placed the pugree on his head and looked in the mirror.

"See, it fits perfectly," said Daulat.

"Yes," he answered, "it does fit perfectly." He took it off, caressed it for a moment, then asked hesitantly, "How much…?"

Daulat held up her hand; she had prepared for this moment. Though she had dismissed very quickly the thought of selling it, she had considered asking for its return after the wedding. Now, however, she shook her head and took the pugree from the young man. Carefully, she placed it in the glass case and handed it back to him.

"It is yours, wear it in good health. And take good care of it for my Minocher."

"I will, oh thank you," said the young man. "Thank you very much." He waited for a moment, then softly, shyly added, "And God bless you."

Daulat smiled. "If you have a son, maybe he will wear it, too, on his wedding." The young man nodded, smiling back.

She saw him to the door and returned to the living-room. Moti and Najamai were sipping half-heartedly at their tea, looking somewhat injured. The children had finished their cold drink. They were swishing the shrunken ice-cubes around in the forbidden final quarter inch of liquid, left in their glasses as they'd been warned to, to attest to their good breeding. An irretrievably mixed up and confusing bit of testimony.

A beggar was crying outside, "Firstfloorwalla *bai*! Take pity on the poor! Secondfloorwalla *bai*! Help the hungry!"

Presently, Najamai rose. "Have to leave now, Ramchandra must be ready with dinner."

Moti took the opportunity to depart as well, offering the fidgetiness of the two little boys for an excuse.

Daulat was alone once more. Leaving the cups and glasses where they stood with their dregs of tea and Goldspot, she went into Minocher's room. It was dark except for the glow of the oil lamp. The oil was low again and she reached for the bottle, then changed her mind.

From under one of the cups in the living-room she retrieved a saucer and returned to his room. She stood before the lamp for a moment, looking deep into the flame, then slid the saucer over the glass. She covered it up completely, the way his face had been covered with a white sheet ten days ago.

In a few seconds the lamp was doused, snuffed out. The afterglow of the wick persisted; then it, too, was gone. The room was in full darkness.

Daulat sat in the armchair. The first round, at least, was definitely hers.

The Collectors

The Collectors

When Dr Burjor Mody was transferred from Mysore to assume the principalship of the Bombay Veterinary College, he moved into Firozsha Baag with his wife and son Pesi. They occupied the vacant flat on the third floor of C Block, next to the Bulsara family.

Dr Mody did not know it then, but he would be seeing a lot of Jehangir, the Bulsara boy; the boy who sat silent and brooding, every evening, watching the others at play, and called *chaarikhao* by them — quite unfairly, since he never tattled or told tales — (Dr Mody would call him, affectionately, the observer of C Block). And Dr Mody did not know this, either, at the time of moving, that Jehangir Bulsara's visits at ten A.M. every Sunday would become a source of profound joy for himself. Or that just when he would think he had found someone to share his hobby with, someone to mitigate the perpetual disappointment about his son Pesi, he would lose his precious Spanish dancing-lady stamp and renounce Jehangir's friendship, both in quick succession. And then two years later, he himself would — but *that* is never knowable.

Soon after moving in, Dr Burjor Mody became the pride of the Parsis in C Block. C Block, like the rest of Firozsha Baag, had a surfeit of low-paid bank clerks and bookkeepers, and the arrival of Dr Mody permitted them to feel a little better about themselves. More importantly, in A Block lived a prominent priest, and B Block boasted a chartered accountant. Now C Block had a voice in Baag matters as important as the others did.

While C Block went about its routine business, confirming and authenticating the sturdiness of the object of their pride, the doctor's big-boned son Pesi established himself as leader of the rowdier elements among the Baag's ten-to-sixteen population. For Pesi, too, it was routine business; he was following a course he had mapped out for himself ever since the family began moving from city to city on the whims and megrims of his father's employer, the government.

To account for Pesi's success was the fact of his brutish strength. But he was also the practitioner of a number of minor talents which appealed to the crowd where he would be leader. The one no doubt complemented the other, the talents serving to dissemble the brutish qualifier of strength, and the brutish strength encouraging the crowd to perceive the appeal of his talents.

Hawking, for instance, was one of them. Pesi could summon up prodigious quantities of phlegm at will, accompanied by sounds such as the boys had seldom heard except in accomplished adults: deep, throaty, rasping, resonating rolls which culminated in a pthoo, with the impressive trophy landing in the dust at their feet, its size leaving them all slightly envious. Pesi could also break wind that sounded like questions, exclamations, fragments of the chromatic scale, and clarion calls, while the others sniffed and discussed the merits of pungency versus tonality. This ability earned him the appellation of Pesi *paadmaroo*, and he wore the sobriquet with pride.

Perhaps his single most important talent was his ability to improvise. The peculiarities of a locale were the raw material for his inventions. In Firozsha Baag, behind the three buildings, or blocks, as they were called, were spacious yards shared by all three blocks. These yards planted in Pesi's fecund mind the seed from which grew a new game: stoning-the-cats.

Till the arrival of the Mody family the yards were home for stray and happy felines, well fed on scraps and leftovers disgorged regularly as clockwork, after mealtimes, by the three blocks. The ground floors were the only ones who refrained. They voiced their protests in a periodic cycle of reasoning, pleading, and screaming of obscenities, because the garbage collected outside their windows where the cats took up permanent residency, miaowing, feasting and caterwauling day and night. If the cascade of food was more than the cats could devour, the remainder fell to the fortune of the rats. Finally, flies and insects buzzed and hovered over the dregs, little pools of pulses and curries fermenting and frothing, till the *kuchrawalli* came next morning and swept it all away.

The backyards of Firozsha Baag constituted its squalid underbelly. And this would be the scenario for stoning-the-cats, Pesi decided. But there was one hitch: the backyards were off limits to the boys. The only way in was through the *kuchrawalli*'s little shack standing beyond A Block, where her huge ferocious dog, tied to the gate, kept the boys at bay. So Pesi decreed that the boys gather at the rear windows of their homes, preferably at a time of day when the adults were scarce, with the fathers away at work and the mothers not yet finished with their afternoon naps. Each boy brought a pile of small stones and took turns, chucking three stones each. The game could just as easily have been stoning-the-rats; but stoned rats quietly walked away to safety, whereas the yowls of cats provided primal satisfaction and verified direct hits: no yowl, no point.

The game added to Pesi's popularity — he called it a howling success. But the parents (except the ground floor) complained to Dr Mody about his son instigating their children to torment poor dumb and helpless creatures. For a veterinarian's son to harass animals was shameful, they said.

As might be supposed, Pesi was the despair of his parents. Over the years Dr Mody had become inured to the initial embarrassment in each new place they moved to. The routine was familiar: first, a spate of complaints from indignant parents claiming their sons *bugree nay dhoor thai gaya* — were corrupted to become useless as dust; next, the protestations giving way to sympathy when the neighbours saw that Pesi was the worm in the Modys' mango.

And so it was in Firozsha Baag. After the furor about stoning-the-cats had died down, the people of the Baag liked Dr Mody more than ever. He earned their respect for the initiative he took in Baag matters, dealing with the management for things like broken lifts, leaking water tanks, crumbling plaster, and faulty wiring. It was at his urging that the massive iron gate, set in the stone wall which ran all around the buildings, compound and backyards, was repaired, and a watchman installed to stop beggars and riff-raff. (And although Dr Mody would be dead by the time of the *Shiv Sena* riots, the tenants would remember him for the gate which would keep out the rampaging mobs.) When the Bombay Municipality tried to appropriate a section of Baag property for its road-widening scheme, Dr Mody was in the forefront of the battle, winning a compromise whereby the Baag only lost half the proposed area. But the Baag's esteem did nothing to lighten the despair for Pesi that hung around the doctor.

At the birth of his son, Dr Mody had deliberated long and hard about the naming. Peshotan, in the Persian epic, *Shah-Nameh*, was the brother of the great Asfandyar, and a noble general, lover of art and learning, and man of wise counsel. Dr Mody had decided his son would play the violin, acquire the best from the cultures of East and West, thrill to the words of Tagore and Shakespeare, appreciate Mozart and Indian ragas; and one day, at the proper moment, he would introduce him to his dearest activity, stamp-collecting.

But the years passed in their own way. Fate denied fruition to all of Dr Mody's plans; and when he talked about stamps, Pesi laughed and mocked his beloved hobby. This was the point at which, hurt and confused, he surrendered his son to whatever destiny was in store. A perpetual grief entered to occupy the void left behind after the aspirations for his son were evicted.

The weight of grief was heaviest around Dr Mody when he returned from work in the evenings. As the car turned into the compound he usually saw Pesi before Pesi saw him, in scenes which made him despair, scenes in which his son was abusing someone, fighting, or making lewd gestures.

But Dr Mody was careful not to make a public spectacle of his despair. While the car made its way sluggishly over the uneven flagstones of the compound, the boys would stand back and wave him through. With his droll comments and jovial countenance he was welcome to disrupt their play, unlike two other car-owners of Firozsha Baag: the priest in A Block and the chartered accountant in B who habitually berated, from inside their vehicles, the sons of bank clerks and bookkeepers for blocking the driveway with their games. Their well-worn curses had become so predictable and ineffective that sometimes the boys chanted gleefully, in unison with their nemeses: "Worse than *saala* animals!" or "*junglee* dogs-cats have more sense!" or "you *sataans* ever have any lesson-*paani* to do or not!"

There was one boy who always stayed apart from his peers — the Bulsara boy, from the family next door to the Modys. Jehangir sat on the stone steps every evening while the gentle land breezes, drying and cooling the sweaty skins of the boys at play, blew out to sea. He sat alone through the long dusk, a source of discomfiture to the others. They resented his melancholy, watching presence.

Dr Mody noticed Jehangir, too, on the stone steps of C Block, the delicate boy with the build much too slight for his age. Next to a hulk like Pesi he was diminutive, but things other than size underlined his frail looks: he had slender hands, and forearms with fine downy hair. And while facial fuzz was incipient in most boys of his age (and Pesi was positively hirsute), Jehangir's chin and upper lip were smooth as a young woman's. But it pleased Dr Mody to see him evening after evening. The quiet contemplation of the boy on the steps and the noise and activity of the others at play came together in the kind of balance that Dr Mody was always looking for and was quick to appreciate.

Jehangir, in his turn, observed the burly Dr Mody closely as he walked past him each evening. When he approached the steps after parking his car, Jehangir would say *"Sahibji"* in greeting, and smile wanly. He saw that despite Dr Mody's constant jocularity there was something painfully empty about his eyes. He noticed the peculiar way he scratched the greyish-red patches of psoriasis on his elbows, both elbows simultaneously, by folding his arms across his chest. Sometimes Jehangir would arise from the stone steps and the two would go up together to the third floor. Dr Mody asked him once, "You don't like playing with the other boys? You just sit and watch them?" The boy shook his head and blushed, and Dr Mody did not bring up the matter after that.

Gradually, a friendship of sorts grew between the two. Jehangir touched a chord inside the doctor which had lain silent for much too long. Now affection for the boy developed and started to linger around the region hitherto occupied by grief bearing Pesi's name.

II

One evening, while Jehangir sat on the stone steps waiting for Dr Mody's car to arrive, Pesi was organizing a game of *naargolio*. He divided the boys into two teams, then discovered he was one short. He beckoned to Jehangir, who said he did not want to play. Scowling, Pesi handed the ball to one of the others and walked over to him. He grabbed his collar with both hands, jerking him to his feet. *"Arré choosya!"* he yelled, "want a pasting?" and began dragging him by the collar to where the boys had piled up the seven flat stones for *naargolio*.

At that instant, Dr Mody's car turned into the compound, and he spied his son in one of those scenes which could provoke despair. But today the despair was swept aside by rage when he saw that Pesi's victim was the gentle and quiet Jehangir Bulsara. He left the car in the middle of the compound with the motor running. Anger glinted in his eyes. He kicked over the pile of seven flat stones as he walked blindly towards Pesi who, having seen his father, had released Jehangir. He had been caught by his father often enough to know that it was best to stand and wait. Jehangir, meanwhile, tried to keep back the tears.

Dr Mody stopped before his son and slapped him hard, once on each cheek, with the front and back of his right hand. He waited, as if debating whether that was enough, then put his arm around Jehangir and led him to the car.

He drove to his parking spot. By now, Jehangir had control of his tears, and they walked to the steps of C Block. The lift was out of order. They climbed the stairs to the third floor and knocked. He waited with Jehangir.

Jehangir's mother came to the door. "*Sahibji*, Dr Mody," she said, a short, middle-aged woman, very prim, whose hair was always in a bun. Never without a *mathoobanoo*, she could do wonderful things with that square of fine white cloth which was tied and knotted to sit like a cap on her head, snugly packeting the bun. In the evenings, after the household chores were done, she removed the *mathoobanoo* and wore it in a more conventional manner, like a scarf.

"Sahibji," she said, then noticed her son's tear-stained face. *"Arré,* Jehangoo, what happened, who made you cry?" Her hand flew automatically to the *mathoobanoo,* tugging and adjusting it as she did whenever she was concerned or agitated.

To save the boy embarrassment, Dr Mody intervened: "Go, wash your face while I talk to your mother." Jehangir went inside, and Dr Mody told her briefly about what had happened. "Why does he not play with the other boys?" he asked finally.

"Dr Mody, what to say. The boy never wants even to go out. *Khoedai salaamat raakhé,* wants to sit at home all the time and read story books. Even this little time in the evening he goes because I force him and tell him he will not grow tall without fresh air. Every week he brings new-new story books from school. First, school library would allow only one book per week. But he went to Father Gonzalves who is in charge of library and got special permission for two books. God knows why he gave it."

"But reading is good, Mrs Bulsara."

"I know, I know, but a mania like this, all the time?"

"Some boys are outdoor types, some are indoor types. You shouldn't worry about Jehangir, he is a very good boy. Look at my Pesi, now there is a case for worry," he said, meaning to reassure her.

"No, no. You mustn't say that. Be patient, *Khoedai* is great," said Mrs Bulsara, consoling him instead. Jehangir returned, his eyes slightly red but dry. While washing his face he had wet a lock of his hair which hung down over his forehood.

"Ah, here comes my indoor champion," smiled Dr Mody, and patted Jehangir's shoulder, brushing back the lock of hair. Jehangir did not understand, but grinned anyway; the doctor's joviality was infectious. Dr Mody turned again to the mother. "Send him to my house on Sunday at ten o'clock. We will have a little talk."

After Dr Mody left, Jehangir's mother told him how lucky he was that someone as important and learned as Burjor Uncle was taking an interest in him. Privately, she hoped he would encourage the boy towards a more all-rounded approach to life and to the things other boys did. And when Sunday came she sent Jehangir off to Dr Mody's promptly at ten.

Dr Mody was taking his bath, and Mrs Mody opened the door. She was a dour-faced woman, spare and lean — the opposite of her husband in appearance and disposition, yet retaining some quality from long ago which suggested that it had not always been so. Jehangir had never crossed her path save when she was exchanging civilities with his mother, while making purchases out by the stairs from the vegetablewalla or fruitwalla.

Not expecting Jehangir's visit, Mrs Mody stood blocking the doorway and said: "Yes?" Meaning, what nuisance now?

"Burjor Uncle asked me to come at ten o'clock."

"Asked you to come at ten o'clock? What for?"

"He just said to come at ten o'clock."

Grudgingly, Mrs Mody stepped aside. "Come in then. Sit down there." And she indicated the specific chair she wanted him to oc- cupy, muttering something about a *baap* who had time for strangers' children but not for his own son.

Jehangir sat in what must have been the most uncomfortable chair in the room. This was his first time inside the Modys' flat, and he looked around with curiosity. But his gaze was quickly restricted to the area of the floor directly in front of him when he realized that he was the object of Mrs Mody's watchfulness.

Minutes ticked by under her vigilant eye. Jehangir was grateful when Dr Mody emerged from the bedroom. Being Sunday, he had eschewed his usual khaki half-pants for loose and comfortable white pyjamas. His *sudra* hung out over it, and he strode vigorously, feet encased in a huge pair of *sapaat*. He smiled at Jehangir, who happily noted the crow's-feet appearing at the corners of his eyes. He was ushered into Dr Mody's room, and man and boy both seemed glad to escape the surveillance of the woman.

The chairs were more comfortable in Dr Mody's room. They sat at his desk and Dr Mody opened a drawer to take out a large book.

"This was the first stamp album I ever had," said Dr Mody. "It was given to me by my Nusserwanji Uncle when I was your age. All the pages were empty." He began turning them. They were covered with stamps, each a feast of colour and design. He talked as he turned the pages, and Jehangir watched and listened, glancing at the stamps flying past, at Dr Mody's face, then at the stamps again.

Dr Mody spoke not in his usual booming, jovial tones but softly, in a low voice charged with inspiration. The stamps whizzed by, and his speech was gently underscored by the rustle of the heavily laden pages that seemed to turn of their own volition in the quiet room. (Jehangir would remember this peculiar rustle when one day, older, he'd stand alone in this very room, silenced now forever, and turn the pages of Nusserwanji Uncle's album.) Jehangir watched and listened. It was as though a mask had descended over Dr Mody, a faraway look upon his face, and a shining in the eyes which heretofore Jehangir had only seen sad with despair or glinting with anger or just plain and empty, belying his constant drollery. Jehangir watched, and listened to the euphonious voice hinting at wondrous things and promises and dreams.

The album on the desk, able to produce such changes in Dr Mody, now worked its magic through him upon the boy. Jehangir, watching and listening, fascinated, tried to read the names of the countries at the top of the pages as they sped by: Antigua...Australia...Belgium...Bhutan...Bulgaria...and on through to Malta and Mauritius...Romania and Russia...Togo and Tonga...and a final blur through which he caught Yugoslavia and Zanzibar.

"Can I see it again?" he asked, and Dr Mody handed the album to him.

"So what do you think? Do you want to be a collector?"

Jehangir nodded eagerly and Dr Mody laughed. "When Nusserwanji Uncle showed me his collection I felt just like that. I'll tell your mother what to buy for you to get you started. Bring it here next Sunday, same time."

And next Sunday Jehangir was ready at nine. But he waited by his door with a Stamp Album For Beginners and a packet of 100 Assorted Stamps — All Countries. Going too early would mean sitting under the baleful eyes of Mrs Mody.

Ten o'clock struck and the clock's tenth bong was echoed by the Modys' doorchimes. Mrs Mody was expecting him this time and did not block the doorway. Wordlessly, she beckoned him in. Burjor Uncle was ready, too, and came out almost immediately to rescue him from her arena.

"Let's see what you've got there," he said when they were in his room. They removed the cellophane wrapper, and while they worked Dr Mody enjoyed himself as much as the boy. His deepest wish appeared to be coming true: he had at last found someone to share his hobby with. He could not have hoped for a finer neophyte than Jehangir. His young recruit was so quick to learn how to identify and sort stamps by countries, learn the different currencies, spot watermarks. Already he was skilfully folding and moistening the little hinges and mounting the stamps as neatly as the teacher.

When it was almost time to leave, Jehangir asked if he could examine again Nusserwanji Uncle's album, the one he had seen last Sunday. But Burjor Uncle led him instead to a cupboard in the corner of the room. "Since you enjoy looking at my stamps, let me show you what I have here." He unlocked its doors.

Each of the cupboard's four shelves was piled with biscuit tins and sweet tins: round, oval, rectangular, square. It puzzled Jehangir: all this bore the unmistakable stamp of the worthless hoardings of senility, and did not seem at all like Burjor Uncle. But Burjor Uncle reached out for a box at random and showed him inside. It was chock-full of stamps! Jehangir's mouth fell open. Then he gaped at the shelves, and Burjor Uncle laughed. "Yes, all these tins are full of stamps. And that big cardboard box at the bottom contains six new albums, all empty."

Jehangir quickly tried to assign a number in his mind to the stamps in the containers of Maghanlal Biscuitwalla and Lokmanji Mithaiwalla, to all of the stamps in the round tins and the oval tins, the square ones and the oblong ones. He failed.

Once again Dr Mody laughed at the boy's wonderment. "A lot of stamps. And they took me a lot of years to collect. Of course, I am lucky I have many contacts in foreign countries. Because of my job, I meet the experts from abroad who are invited by the Indian Government. When I tell them about my hobby they send me stamps from their countries. But no time to sort them, so I pack them in boxes. One day, after I retire, I will spend all my time with my stamps." He paused, and shut the cupboard doors. "So what you have to do now is start making lots of friends, tell them about your hobby. If they also collect, you can exchange duplicates with them. If they don't, you can still ask them for all the envelopes they may be throwing away with stamps on them. You do something for them, they will do something for you. Your collection will grow depending on how smart you are."

He hesitated, and opened the cupboard again. Then he changed his mind and shut it — it wasn't yet time for the Spanish dancing-lady stamp.

III

On the pavement outside St Xavier's Boys School, not far from the ornate iron gates, stood two variety stalls. They were the stalls of *Patla Babu* and *Jhaaria Babu*. Their real names were never known. Nor was known the exact source of the schoolboy inspiration that named them thus, many years ago, after their respective thinness and fatness.

Before the schoolboys arrived in the morning, the two would unpack their cases and set up the displays, beating the beggars to the choice positions. Occasionally, there were disputes if someone's space was violated. The beggars did not harbour great hopes for alms from schoolboys but they stood there, nonetheless, like mute lessons in realism and the harshness of life. Their patience was rewarded when they raided the dustbins after breaks and lunches.

At the end of the school day the pavement community packed up. The beggars shuffled off into the approaching dark, *Patla Babu* went home with his cases, and *Jhaaria Babu* slept near the school gate under a large tree to whose trunk he chained his boxes during the night.

The two sold a variety of nondescript objects and comestibles, uninteresting to any save the eyes and stomachs of schoolboys: *supari*, A-1 chewing gum (which, in a most ungumlike manner, would, after a while, dissolve in one's mouth), *jeeragoli*, marbles, tops, *aampapud* during the mango season, pens, Camel Ink, pencils, rulers, and stamps in little cellophane packets.

Patla Babu and *Jhaaria Babu* lost some of their goods regularly due to theft. This was inevitable when doing business outside a large school like St Xavier's, with a population as varied as its was. The loss was an operating expense stoically accepted, like the success or failure of the monsoons, and they never complained to the school authorities or held it against the boys. Besides, business was good despite the losses: insignificant items like a packet of *jeeragoli* worth ten paise, or a marble of the kind that sold three for five paise. More often than not, the stealing went on for the excitement of it, out of bravado or on a dare. It was called "flicking" and was done without any malice towards *Patla* and *Jhaaria*.

Foremost among the flickers was a boy in Jehangir's class called Eric D'Souza. A tall, lanky fellow who had been suspended a couple of times, he had had to repeat the year on two occasions, and held out the promise of more repetitions. Eric also had the reputation of doing things inside his half-pants under cover of his desk. In a class of fifty boys it was easy to go unobserved by the teacher, and only his immediate neighbours could see the ecstasy on his face and the vigorous back and forth movement of his hand. When he grinned at them they looked away, pretending not to have noticed anything.

Jehangir sat far from Eric and knew of his habits only by hearsay. He was oblivious to Eric's eye which had been on him for quite a while. In fact, Eric found Jehangir's delicate hands and fingers, his smooth legs and thighs very desirable. In class he gazed for hours, longingly, at the girlish face, curly hair, long eyelashes.

Jehangir and Eric finally got acquainted one day when the class filed out for games period. Eric had been made to kneel down by the door for coming late and disturbing the class, and Jehangir found himself next to him as he stood in line. From his kneeling position Eric observed the smooth thighs emerging from the half-pants (half-pants was the school uniform requirement), winked at him and, unhindered by his underwear, inserted a pencil up the pant leg. He tickled Jehangir's genitals seductively with the eraser end, expertly, then withdrew it. Jehangir feigned a giggle, too shocked to say anything. The line started to move for the playground.

Shortly after this incident, Eric approached Jehangir during breaktime. He had heard that Jehangir was desperate to acquire stamps.

"*Arré* man, I can get you stamps, whatever kind you want," he said.

Jehangir stopped. He had been slightly confused ever since the pass with the pencil; Eric frightened him a little with his curious

habits and forbidden knowledge. But it had not been easy to ac-
cumulate stamps. Sundays with Burjor Uncle continued to be as
fascinating as the first. He wished he had new stamps to show —
the stasis of his collection might be misinterpreted as lack of interest. He asked Eric: "Ya? You want to exchange?"

"No *yaar*, I don't collect. But I'll get them for you. As a favour,
man."

"Ya? What kind do you have?"

"I don't have, man. Come on with me to *Patla* and *Jhaaria*, just
show me which ones you want. I'll flick them for you."

Jehangir hesitated. Eric put his arm around him: "C'mon man,
what you scared for, I'll flick. You just show me and go away."
Jehangir pictured the stamps on display in cellophane wrappers:
how well they would add to his collection. He imagined album
pages bare no more but covered with exquisite stamps, each one
mounted carefully and correctly, with a hinge, as Burjor Uncle had
showed him to.

They went outside, Eric's arm still around him. Crowds of
schoolboys were gathered around the two stalls. A multitude of
groping, exploring hands handled the merchandise and browsed
absorbedly, a multitude that was a prerequisite for flicking to
begin. Jehangir showed Eric the individually wrapped stamps he
wanted and moved away. In a few minutes Eric joined him
triumphantly.

"Got them?"

"Ya ya. But come inside. He could be watching, man."

Jehangir was thrilled. Eric asked, "You want more or what?"

"Sure," said Jehangir.

"But not today. On Friday. If you do me a favour in visual period
on Thursday."

Jehangir's pulse speeded slightly — visual period, with its
darkened hall and projector, and the intimacy created by the
teacher's policing abilities temporarily suspended. He
remembered Eric's pencil. The cellophane-wrapped stamp packets
rustled and crackled in his hand. And there was the promise of
more. There had been nothing unpleasant about the pencil. In fact
it had felt quite, well, exciting. He agreed to Eric's proposal.

On Thursday, the class lined up to go to the Visual Hall. Eric stood behind Jehangir to ensure their seats would be together.

When the room was dark he put his hand on Jehangir's thigh and began caressing it. He took Jehangir's hand and placed it on his crotch. It lay there inert. Impatient, he whispered, "Do it, man, c'mon!" But Jehangir's lacklustre stroking was highly unsatisfactory. Eric arrested the hand, reached inside his pants and said, "OK, hold it tight and rub it like this." He encircled Jehangir's hand with his to show him how. When Jehangir had attained the right pressure and speed he released his own hand to lean back and sigh contentedly. Shortly, Jehangir felt a warm stickiness fill his palm and fingers, and the hardness he held in his hand grew flaccid.

Eric shook off the hand. Jehangir wiped his palm with his hanky. Eric borrowed the hanky to wipe himself. "Want me to do it for you?" he asked. But Jehangir declined. He was thinking of his hanky. The odour was interesting, not unpleasant at all, but he would have to find some way of cleaning it before his mother found it.

The following day, Eric presented him with more stamps. Next Thursday's assignation was also fixed.

And on Sunday Jehangir went to see Dr Mody at ten o'clock. The wife let him in, muttering something under her breath about being bothered by inconsiderate people on the one day that the family could be together.

Dr Mody's delight at the new stamps fulfilled Jehangir's every expectation: "Wonderful, wonderful! Where did you get them all? No, no, forget it, don't tell me. You will think I'm trying to learn your tricks. I already have enough stamps to keep me busy in my retirement. Ha! ha!"

After the new stamps had been examined and sorted Dr Mody said, "Today, as a reward for your enterprise, I'm going to show you a stamp you've never seen before." From the cupboard of biscuit and sweet tins he took a small satin-covered box of the type in which rings or bracelets are kept. He opened it and, without removing the stamp from inside, placed it on the desk.

The stamp said España Correos at the bottom and its denomination was noted in the top left corner: 3 PTAS. The face of the stamp featured a flamenco dancer in the most exquisite detail and colour. But it was something in the woman's countenance, a look, an ineffable sparkle he saw in her eyes, which so captivated Jehangir.

Wordlessly, he studied the stamp. Dr Mody waited restlessly as the seconds ticked by. He kept fidgeting till the little satin-covered box was shut and back in his hands, then said, "So you like the Spanish dancing-lady. Everyone who sees it likes it. Even my wife who is not interested in stamp-collecting thought it was beautiful. When I retire I can spend more time with the Spanish dancing-lady. And all my other stamps." He relaxed once the stamp was locked again in the cupboard.

Jehangir left, carrying that vision of the Spanish dancer in his head. He tried to imagine the stamp inhabiting the pages of his album, to greet him every time he opened it, with the wonderful sparkle in her eyes. He shut the door behind him and immediately, as though to obliterate his covetous fantasy, loud voices rose inside the flat.

He heard Mrs Mody's, shrill in argument, and the doctor's, beseeching her not to yell lest the neighbours would hear. Pesi's name was mentioned several times in the quarrel that ensued, and accusations of neglect, and something about the terrible affliction on a son of an unloving father. The voices followed Jehangir as he hurried past the inquiring eyes of his mother, till he reached the bedroom at the other end of the flat and shut the door.

When the school week started, Jehangir found himself looking forward to Thursday. His pulse was racing with excitement when visual period came. To save his hanky this time he kept some paper at hand.

Eric did not have to provide much guidance. Jehangir discovered he could control Eric's reactions with variations in speed, pressure, and grip. When it was over and Eric offered to do it to him, he did not refuse.

The weeks sped by and Jehangir's collection continued to grow, visual period by visual period. Eric's and his masturbatory partnership was whispered about in class, earning the pair the title of *moothya-maroo*. He accompanied Eric on the flicking forays, helping to swell the milling crowd and add to the browsing hands. Then he grew bolder, studied Eric's methods, and flicked a few stamps himself.

But this smooth course of stamp-collecting was about to end.

Patla Babu and *Jhaaria Babu* broke their long tradition of silence and complained to the school. Unlike marbles and *supari*, it was not a question of a few paise a day. When Eric and Jehangir struck, their haul could be totalled in rupees reaching double digits; the loss was serious enough to make the *Babus* worry about their survival.

The school assigned the case to the head prefect to investigate. He was an ambitious boy, always snooping around, and was also a member of the school debating team and the Road Safety Patrol. Shortly after the complaint was made he marched into Jehangir's class one afternoon just after lunch break, before the teacher returned, and made what sounded very much like one of his debating speeches: "Two boys in this class have been stealing stamps from *Patla Babu* and *Jhaaria Babu* for the past several weeks. You may ask: who are those boys? No need for names. They know who they are and I know who they are, and I am asking them to return the stamps to me tomorrow. There will be no punishment if this is done. The *Babus* just want their stamps back. But if the missing stamps are not returned, the names will be reported to the principal and to the police. It is up to the two boys."

Jehangir tried hard to appear normal. He was racked with trepidation, and looked to the unperturbed Eric for guidance. But Eric ignored him. The head prefect left amidst mock applause from the class.

After school, Eric turned surly. Gone was the tender, cajoling manner he reserved for Jehangir, and he said nastily: "You better bring back all those fucking stamps tomorrow." Jehangir, of course, agreed. There was no trouble with the prefect or the school after the stamps were returned.

But Jehangir's collection shrunk pitiably overnight. He slept badly the entire week, worried about explaining to Burjor Uncle the sudden disappearance of the bulk of his collection. His mother assumed the dark rings around his eyes were due to too much reading and not enough fresh air. The thought of stamps or of *Patla Babu* or *Jhaaria Babu* brought an emptiness to his stomach and a bitter taste to his mouth. A general sense of ill-being took possession of him.

He went to see Burjor Uncle on Sunday, leaving behind his

stamp album. Mrs Mody opened the door and turned away silently. She appeared to be in a black rage, which exacerbated Jehangir's own feelings of guilt and shame.

He explained to Burjor Uncle that he had not bothered to bring his album because he had acquired no new stamps since last Sunday, and also, he was not well and would not stay for long.

Dr Mody was concerned about the boy, so nervous and uneasy; he put it down to his feeling unwell. They looked at some stamps Dr Mody had received last week from his colleagues abroad. Then Jehangir said he'd better leave.

"But you *must* see the Spanish dancing-lady before you go. Maybe she will help you feel better. Ha! ha!" and Dr Mody rose to go to the cupboard for the stamp. Its viewing at the end of each Sunday's session had acquired the significance of an esoteric ritual.

From the next room Mrs Mody screeched: "Burjorji! Come here at once!" He made a wry face at Jehangir and hurried out.

In the next room, all the vehemence of Mrs Mody's black rage of that morning poured out upon Dr Mody: "It has reached the limit now! No time for your own son and Sunday after Sunday sitting with some stranger! What does he have that your own son does not? Are you a *baap* or what? No wonder Pesi has become this way! How can I blame the boy when his own *baap* takes no interest…"

"Shh! The boy is in the next room! What do you want, that all the neighbours hear your screaming?"

"I don't care! Let them hear! You think they don't know already? You think you are…"

Mrs Bulsara next door listened intently. Suddenly, she realized that Jehangir was in there. Listening from one's own house was one thing — hearing a quarrel from inside the quarrellers' house was another. It made feigning ignorance very difficult.

She rang the Modys' doorbell and waited, adjusting her *mathoobanoo*. Dr Mody came to the door.

"Burjorji, forgive me for disturbing your stamping and collecting work with Jehangir. But I must take him away. Guests have arrived unexpectedly. Jehangir must go to the Irani, we need cold drinks."

"That's okay, he can come next Sunday." Then added, "He *must*

come next Sunday," and noted with satisfaction the frustrated turning away of Mrs Mody who waited out of sight of the doorway.
"Jehangir! Your mother is calling."

Jehangir was relieved at being rescued from the turbulent waters
of the Mody household. They left without further conversation, his
mother tugging in embarrassment at the knots of her *mathoobanoo*.

As a result of this unfortunate outburst, a period of awkwardness
between the women was unavoidable. Mrs Mody, though far from
garrulous, had never let her domestic sorrows and disappointments interfere with the civilities of neighbourly relations, which
she respected and observed at all times. Now for the first time since
the arrival of the Modys in Firozsha Baag these civilities experienced a hiatus.

When the *muchhiwalla* arrived next morning, instead of striking
a joint deal with him as they usually did, Mrs Mody waited till Mrs
Bulsara had finished. She stationed an eye at her peephole as he
emphasized the freshness of his catch. "Look *bai*, it is *saféd paani*,"
he said, holding out the pomfret and squeezing it near the gills till
white fluid oozed out. After Mrs Bulsara had paid and gone, Mrs
Mody emerged, while the former took her turn at the peephole.
And so it went for a few days till the awkwardness had run its course
and things returned to normal.

But not so for Jehangir; on Sunday, he once again had to leave
behind his sadly depleted album. To add to his uneasiness, Mrs
Mody invited him in with a greeting of "Come *bawa* come," and
there was something malignant about her smile.

Dr Mody sat at his desk, shoulders sagging, his hands dangling
over the arms of the chair. The desk was bare — not a single stamp
anywhere in sight, and the cupboard in the corner locked. The
absence of his habitual, comfortable clutter made the room cold
and cheerless. He was in low spirits; instead of the crow's-feet at the
corners of his eyes were lines of distress and dejection.

"No album again?"

"No. Haven't got any new stamps yet," Jehangir smiled nervously.

Dr Mody scratched the psoriasis on his elbows. He watched
Jehangir carefully as he spoke. "Something very bad has happened
to the Spanish dancing-lady stamp. Look," and he displayed the
satin-covered box minus its treasure. "It is missing." Half-fearfully,

he looked at Jehangir, afraid he would see what he did not want to. But it was inevitable. His last sentence evoked the head prefect's thundering debating-style speech of a few days ago, and the ugliness of the entire episode revisited Jehangir's features — a final ignominious postscript to Dr Mody's loss and disillusion.

Dr Mody shut the box. The boy's reaction, his silence, the absence of his album, confirmed his worst suspicions. More humiliatingly, it seemed his wife was right. With great sadness he rose from his chair. "I have to leave now, something urgent at the College." They parted without a word about next Sunday.

Jehangir never went back. He thought for a few days about the missing stamp and wondered what could have happened to it. Burjor Uncle was too careful to have misplaced it; besides, he never removed it from its special box. And the box was still there. But he did not resent him for concluding he had stolen it. His guilt about *Patla Babu* and *Jhaaria Babu*, about Eric and the stamps was so intense, and the punishment deriving from it so inconsequential, almost non-existent, that he did not mind this undeserved blame. In fact, it served to equilibrate his scales of justice.

His mother questioned him the first few Sundays he stayed home. Feeble excuses about homework, and Burjor Uncle not having new stamps, and it being boring to look at the same stuff every Sunday did not satisfy her. She finally attributed his abnegation of stamps to sensitivity and a regard for the unfortunate state of the Modys' domestic affairs. It pleased her that her son was capable of such concern. She did not press him after that.

IV

Pesi was no longer to be seen in Firozsha Baag. His absence brought relief to most of the parents at first, and then curiosity. Gradually, it became known that he had been sent away to a boarding-school in Poona.

The boys of the Baag continued to play their games in the compound. For better or worse, the spark was lacking that lent unpredictability to those languid coastal evenings of Bombay; evenings which could so easily trap the unwary, adult or child, within a circle of lassitude and depression in which time hung heavy and suffocating.

Jehangir no longer sat on the stone steps of C Block in the evenings. He found it difficult to confront Dr Mody day after day. Besides, the boys he used to watch at play suspected some kind of connection between Pesi's being sent away to boarding-school, Jehangir's former friendship with Dr Mody, and the emerging of Dr Mody's constant sorrow and despair (which he had tried so hard to keep private all along, and had succeeded, but was now visible for all to see). And the boys resented Jehangir for whatever his part was in it — they bore him open antagonism.

Dr Mody was no more the jovial figure the boys had grown to love. When his car turned into the compound in the evenings, he still waved, but no crow's-feet appeared at his eyes, no smile, no jokes.

Two years passed since the Mody family's arrival in Firozsha Baag.

In school, Jehangir was as isolated as in the Baag. Most of his effeminateness had, of late, transformed into vigorous signs of impending manhood. Eric D'Souza had been expelled for attempting to sodomize a junior boy. Jehangir had not been involved in this affair, but most of his classmates related it to the furtive activities of their callow days and the stamp-flicking. *Patla Babu* and *Jhaaria Babu* had disappeared from the pavement outside St Xavier's. The Bombay police, in a misinterpretation of the nation's mandate: *garibi hatao* — eradicate poverty, conducted periodic round-ups of pavement dwellers, sweeping into their vans beggars and street-vendors, cripples and alcoholics, the homeless and the hungry, and dumped them somewhere outside the city limits; when the human detritus made its way back into the city, another clean-up was scheduled. *Patla* and *Jhaaria* were snared in one of these raids, and never found their way back. Eyewitnesses said their stalls were smashed up and *Patla Babu* received a *lathi* across his forehead for trying to salvage some of his inventory. They were not seen again.

Two years passed since Jehangir's visits to Dr Mody had ceased.

It was getting close to the time for another transfer for Dr Mody. When the inevitable orders were received, he went to Ahmedabad to make arrangements. Mrs Mody was to join her husband after a few days. Pesi was still in boarding-school, and would stay there.

So when news arrived from Ahmedabad of Dr Mody's death of heart failure, Mrs Mody was alone in the flat. She went next door with the telegram and broke down.

The Bulsaras helped with all the arrangements. The body was brought to Bombay by car for a proper Parsi funeral. Pesi came from Poona for the funeral, then went back to boarding-school.

The events were talked about for days afterwards, the stories spreading first in C Block, then through A and B. Commiseration for Mrs Mody was general. The ordeal of the body during the two-day car journey from Ahmedabad was particularly horrifying, and was discussed endlessly. Embalming was not allowed according to Parsi rituals, and the body in the trunk, although packed with ice, had started to smell horribly in the heat of the Deccan Plateau which the car had had to traverse. Some hinted that this torment suffered by Dr Mody's earthly remains was the Almighty's punishment for neglecting his duties as a father and making Mrs Mody so unhappy. Poor Dr Mody, they said, who never went a day without a bath and talcum powder in life, to undergo this in death. Someone even had, on good authority, a count of the number of eau de cologne bottles used by Mrs Mody and the three occupants of the car over the course of the journey — it was the only way they could draw breath, through cologne-watered handkerchiefs. And it was also said that ever after, these four could never tolerate eau de cologne — opening a bottle was like opening the car trunk with Dr Mody's decomposing corpse.

A year after the funeral, Mrs Mody was still living in Firozsha Baag. Time and grief had softened her looks, and she was no longer the harsh and dour-faced woman Jehangir had seen during his first Sunday visit. She had decided to make the flat her permanent home now, and the trustees of the Baag granted her request "in view of the unfortunate circumstances."

There were some protests about this, particularly from those whose sons or daughters had been postponing marriages and families till flats became available. But the majority, out of respect for Dr Mody's memory, agreed with the trustees' decision. Pesi continued to attend boarding-school.

One day, shortly after her application had been approved by the trustees, Mrs Mody visited Mrs Bulsara. They sat and talked of old times, when they had first moved in, and about how pleased Dr Mody had been to live in a Parsi colony like Firozsha Baag after years of travelling, and then the disagreements she had had with her husband over Pesi and Pesi's future; tears came to her eyes, and also to Mrs Bulsara's, who tugged at a corner of her *mathoobanoo* to reach it to her eyes and dry them. Mrs Mody confessed how she had hated Jehangir's Sunday visits although he was such a fine boy, because she was worried about the way poor Burjorji was neglecting Pesi: "But he could not help it. That was the way he was. Sometimes he would wish *Khoedai* had given him a daughter instead of a son. Pesi disappointed him in everything, in all his plans, and..." and here she burst into uncontrollable sobs.

Finally, after her tears subsided she asked, "Is Jehangir home?" He wasn't. "Would you ask him to come and see me this Sunday? At ten? Tell him I won't keep him long."

Jehangir was a bit apprehensive when his mother gave him the message. He couldn't imagine why Mrs Mody would want to see him.

On Sunday, as he prepared to go next door, he was reminded of the Sundays with Dr Mody, the kindly man who had befriended him, opened up a new world for him, and then repudiated him for something he had not done. He remembered the way he would scratch the greyish-red patches of psoriasis on his elbows. He could still picture the sorrow on his face as, with the utmost reluctance, he had made his decision to end the friendship. Jehangir had not blamed Dr Mody then, and he still did not; he knew how overwhelmingly the evidence had been against him, and how much that stamp had meant to Dr Mody.

Mrs Mody led him in by his arm: "Will you drink something?"

"No, thank you."

"Not feeling shy, are you? You always were shy." She asked him about his studies and what subjects he was taking in high school. She told him a little about Pesi, who was still in boarding-school and had twice repeated the same standard. She sighed. "I asked you to come today because there is something I wanted to give you. Something of Burjor Uncle's. I thought about it for many days. Pesi is not interested, and I don't know anything about it. Will you take his collection?"

"The album in his drawer?" asked Jehangir, a little surprised.

"Everything. The album, all the boxes, everything in the cupboard. I know you will use it well. Burjor would have done the same."

Jehangir was speechless. He had stopped collecting stamps, and they no longer held the fascination they once did. Nonetheless, he was familiar with the size of the collection, and the sheer magnitude of what he was now being offered had its effect. He remembered the awe with which he had looked inside the cupboard the first time its doors had been opened before him. So many sweet tins, cardboard boxes, biscuit tins…

"You will take it? As a favour to me, yes?" she asked a second time, and Jehangir nodded. "You have some time today? Whenever you like, just take it." He said he would ask his mother and come back.

There was a huge, old iron trunk which lay under Jehangir's bed. It was dented in several places and the lid would not shut properly. Undisturbed for years, it had rusted peacefully beneath the bed. His mother agreed that the rags it held could be thrown away and the stamps temporarily stored in it till Jehangir organized them into albums. He emptied the trunk, wiped it out, lined it with brown paper and went next door to bring back the stamps.

Several trips later, Dr Mody's cupboard stood empty. Jehangir looked around the room in which he had once spent so many happy hours. The desk was in exactly the same position, and the two chairs. He turned to go, almost forgetting, and went back to the desk. Yes, there it was in the drawer, Dr Mody's first album, given him by his Nusserwanji Uncle.

He started to turn the heavily laden pages. They rustled in a peculiar way — what was it about that sound? Then he remembered: that first Sunday, and he could almost hear Dr Mody again, the soft inspired tones speaking of promises and dreams, quite different from his usual booming, jovial voice, and that faraway look in his eyes which had once glinted with rage when Pesi had tried to bully him…

Mrs Mody came into the room. He shut the album, startled: "This is the last lot." He stopped to thank her but she interrupted: "No, no. What is the thank-you for? You are doing a favour to me by taking it, you are helping me to do what Burjor would like." She took his arm. "I wanted to tell you. From the collection one stamp is missing. With the picture of the dancing-lady."

"I know!" said Jehangir. "That's the one Burjor Uncle lost and thought that I…"

Mrs Mody squeezed his arm which she was still holding and he fell silent. She spoke softly, but without guilt: "He did not lose it. I destroyed it." Then her eyes went moist as she watched the disbelief on his face. She wanted to say more, to explain, but could not, and clung to his arm. Finally, her voice quavering pitiably, she managed to say, "Forgive an old lady," and patted his cheek. Jehangir left in silence, suddenly feeling very ashamed.

Over the next few days, he tried to impose some order on that greatly chaotic mass of stamps. He was hoping that sooner or later his interest in philately would be rekindled. But that did not happen; the task remained futile and dry and boring. The meaningless squares of paper refused to come to life as they used to for Dr Mody in his room every Sunday at ten o'clock. Jehangir shut the trunk and pushed it back under his bed where it had lain untroubled for so many years.

From time to time his mother reminded him about the stamps: "Do something Jehangoo, do something with them." He said he would when he felt like it and had the time; he wasn't interested for now.

Then, after several months, he pulled out the trunk again from under his bed. Mrs Bulsara watched eagerly from a distance, not daring to interrupt with any kind of advice or encouragement: her Jehangoo was at that difficult age, she knew, when boys automatically did the exact reverse of what their parents said.

But the night before, Jehangir's sleep had been disturbed by a faint and peculiar rustling sound seeming to come from inside the trunk. His reasons for dragging it out into daylight soon became apparent to Mrs Bulsara.

The lid was thrown back to reveal clusters of cockroaches. They tried to scuttle to safety, and he killed a few with his slipper. His mother ran up now, adding a few blows of her own *chappal*, as the creatures began quickly to disperse. Some ran under the bed into hard-to-reach corners; others sought out the trunk's deeper recesses.

A cursory examination showed that besides cockroaches, the

trunk was also infested with white ants. All the albums had been ravaged. Most of the stamps which had not been destroyed outright were damaged in one way or another. They bore haphazard perforations and brown stains of the type associated with insects and household pests.

Jehangir picked up an album at random and opened it. Almost immediately, the pages started to fall to pieces in his hands. He remembered what Dr Mody used to say: "This is my retirement hobby. I will spend my retirement with my stamps." He allowed the tattered remains of Burjor Uncle's beloved pastime to drop back slowly into the trunk.

He crouched beside the dented, rusted metal, curious that he felt no loss or pain. Why, he wondered. If anything, there was a slight sense of relief. He let his hands stray through the contents, through worthless paper scraps, through shreds of the work of so many Sunday mornings, stopping now and then to regard with detachment the bizarre patterns created by the mandibles of the insects who had feasted night after night under his bed, while he slept.

With an almost imperceptible shrug, he arose and closed the lid. It was doubtful if anything of value remained in the trunk.

Of White Hairs and Cricket

Of White Hairs and Cricket

The white hair was trapped in the tweezers. I pulled it taut to see if it was gripped tightly, then plucked it.

"Aaah!" grimaced Daddy. "Careful, only one at a time." He continued to read the *Times Of India*, spreading it on the table.

"It *is* only one," I said, holding out the tweezers, but my annoyance did not register. Engrossed in the classifieds, he barely looked my way. The naked bulb overhead glanced off the stainless steel tweezers, making a splotch of light dart across the Murphy Radio calendar. It danced over the cherubic features of the Murphy Baby, in step with the tweezers' progress on Daddy's scalp. He sighed, turned a page, and went on scrutinizing the columns.

Each Sunday, the elimination of white hairs took longer than the last time. I'm sure Daddy noticed it too, but joked bravely that laziness was slowing me down. Percy was always excused from this task. And if I pointed it out, the answer was: your brother's college studies are more important.

Daddy relied on my nimble fourteen-year-old fingers to uproot the signposts of mortality sprouting week after week. It was unappetizing work, combing through his hair greasy with day-old pomade, isolating the white ones, or the ones just beginning to turn — half black and half white, and somehow more repulsive. It was always difficult to decide whether to remove those or let them go till next Sunday, when the whiteness would have spread upward to their tips.

The Sunday edition of the *Times Of India* came with a tabloid of comics: Mandrake the Magician, The Phantom, and Maggie and Jiggs in "Bringing Up Father." The drab yellow tablecloth looked festive with the vivid colours of the comics, as though specially decorated for Sunday. The plastic cloth smelled stale and musty. It was impossible to clean perfectly because of the floral design embossed upon its surface. The swirly grooves were ideal for trapping all kinds of dirt.

Daddy reached up to scratch a spot on his scalp. His aaah surprised me. He had taught me to be tough, always. One morning when we had come home after cricket, he told Mummy and *Mamaiji*, "Today my son did a brave thing, as I would have done. A powerful shot was going to the boundary, like a cannonball, and he blocked it with his bare shin." Those were his exact words. The ball's shiny red fury, and the audible crack — at least, I think it was audible — had sent pain racing through me that nearly made my eyes overflow. Daddy had clapped and said, "Well-fielded, sir, well-fielded." So I waited to rub the agonized bone until attention was no longer upon me. I wish Percy had not lost interest in cricket, and had been there. My best friend, Viraf from A Block, was immensely impressed. But that was all a long time ago, many months ago, now Daddy did not take us for cricket on Sunday mornings.

I paused in my search. Daddy had found something in the classifieds and did not notice. By angling the tweezers I could aim the bulb's light upon various spots on the Murphy Radio calendar: the edges of the picture, worn and turned inward; the threadbare loop of braid sharing the colour of rust with the rusty nail it hung by; a corroded staple clutching twelve thin strips — the perforated residue of months ripped summarily over a decade ago when their days and weeks were played out. The baby's smile, posed with finger to chin, was all that had fully endured the years. Mummy and Daddy called it so innocent and joyous. That baby would now be the same age as me. The ragged perimeter of the patch of crumbled wall it tried to hide strayed outward from behind, forming a kind of dark and jagged halo around the baby. The picture grew less adequate, daily, as the wall kept losing plaster and the edges continued to curl and tatter.

Other calendars in the room performed similar enshroudings: the Cement Corporation skyscraper; the Lifebuoy Soap towel-wrapped woman with long black hair; the Parsi calendar, pictureless but showing the English and Parsi names for the months, and the *roje* in Gujarati beside each date, which Mummy and *Mamaiji* consulted when reciting their prayers. All these hung well past their designated time span in the world of months and years, covering up the broken promises of the Firozsha Baag building management.

"Yes, this is it," said Daddy, tapping the paper, "get me the scissors."

Mamaiji came out and settled in her chair on the veranda. Seated, there was no trace of the infirmity that caused her to walk doubled over. Doctors said it was due to a weak spine that could not erect against the now inordinate weight of her stomach. From photographs of Mummy's childhood, I knew *Mamaiji* had been a big handsome woman, with a majestic countenance. She opened her bag of spinning things, although she had been told to rest her eyes after the recent cataract operation. Then she spied me with the tweezers.

"Sunday dawns and he makes the child do that *duleendar* thing again. It will only bring bad luck." She spoke under her breath, arranging her spindle and wool; she was not looking for a direct confrontation. "Plucking out hair as if it was a slaughtered chicken. An ill-omened thing, I'm warning you, Sunday after Sunday. But no one listens. Is this anything to make a child do, he should be out playing, or learning how to do *bajaar*, how to bargain with butcher and *bunya*." She mumbled softly, to allow Daddy to pretend he hadn't heard a thing.

I resented her speaking against Daddy and calling me a child. She twirled the spindle, drawing fibres into thread from the scrap of wool in her left hand as the spindle descended. I watched, expecting — even wishing — the thread to break. Sometimes it did, and then it seemed to me that *Mamaiji* was overcome with disbelief, shocked and pained that it could have happened, and I would feel sorry and rush to pick it up for her. The spindle spun to the floor this time without mishap, hanging by a fine, brand new thread. She hauled it up, winding the thread around the extended thumb and little finger of her left hand by waggling the wrist in little clockwise and counter-clockwise half-turns, while the index and middle fingers clamped tight the source: the shred of wool resembling a lock of her own hair, snow white and slightly tangled.

Mamaiji spun enough thread to keep us all in *kustis*. Since Grandpa's death, she spent more and more time spinning, so that now we each had a spare *kusti* as well. The *kustis* were woven by a professional, who always praised the fine quality of the thread; and even at the fire-temple, where we untied and tied them during prayers, they earned the covetous glances of other Parsis.

I beheld the spindle and *Mamaiji*'s co-ordinated feats of dexterity with admiration. All spinning things entranced me. The descending spindle was like the bucket spinning down into the sacred Bhikha Behram Well to draw water for the ones like us who went there to pray on certain holy days after visiting the fire-temple. I imagined myself clinging to the base of the spindle, sinking into the dark well, confident that *Mamaiji* would pull me up with her waggling hand before I drowned, and praying that the thread would not break. I also liked to stare at records spinning on the old 78-rpm gramophone. There was one I was particularly fond of: its round label was the most ethereal blue I ever saw. The lettering was gold. I played this record over and over, just to watch its wonderfully soothing blue and gold rotation, and the concentric rings of the shiny black shellac, whose grooves created a spiral effect if the light was right. The gramophone cabinet's warm smell of wood and leather seemed to fly right out of this shellacked spiral, while I sat close, my cheek against it, to feel the hum and vibration of the turntable. It was so cosy and comforting. Like missing school because of a slight cold, staying in bed all day with a book, fussed over by Mummy, eating white rice and soup made specially for me.

Daddy finished cutting out and re-reading the classified advertisement. "Yes, this is a good one. Sounds very promising." He picked up the newspaper again, then remembered what *Mamaiji* had muttered, and said softly to me, "If it is so *duleendar* and will bring bad luck, how is it I found this? These old people — " and gave a sigh of mild exasperation. Then briskly: "Don't stop now, this week is very important." He continued, slapping the table merrily at each word: "Every-single-white-hair-out."

There was no real enmity between Daddy and *Mamaiji*, I think they even liked each other. He was just disinclined towards living with his mother-in-law. They often had disagreements over me, and it was always *Mamaiji* versus Mummy and Daddy. *Mamaiji* firmly believed that I was underfed. Housebound as she was, the only food accessible to her was the stuff sold by door-to-door vendors, which I adored but was strictly forbidden: *samosa*, *bhajia*, *sev-ganthia*; or the dinners she cooked for herself, separately, because she said that Mummy's cooking was insipidity itself: "Tasteless as spit, refuses to go down my throat."

So I, her favourite, enjoyed from time to time, on the sly, hot sear-ing curries and things she purchased at the door when Daddy was at work and Mummy in the kitchen. Percy shared, too, if he was around; actually, his iron-clad stomach was much better suited to those flaming snacks. But the clandestine repasts were invariably uncovered, and the price was paid in harsh and unpleasant words. *Mamaiji* was accused of trying to burn to a crisp my stomach and intestines with her fiery, ungodly curries, or of exposing me to dysentery and diphtheria: the cheap door-to-door foodstuff was allegedly cooked in filthy, rancid oil — even machine oil, unfit for human consumption, as was revealed recently by a government in-vestigation. *Mamaiji* retorted that if they did their duty as parents she would not have to resort to secrecy and *chori-chhoopi*; as it was, she had no choice, she could not stand by and see the child starve.

All this bothered me much more than I let anyone know. When the arguments started I would say that all the shouting was giving me a headache, and stalk out to the steps of the compound. My guilty conscience, squirming uncontrollably, could not witness the quarrels. For though I was an eager partner in the conspiracy with *Mamaiji*, and acquiesced to the necessity for secrecy, very often I spilled the beans — quite literally — with diarrhoea and vomiting, which *Mamaiji* upheld as undeniable proof that lack of proper regular nourishment had enfeebled my bowels. In the throes of these bouts of effluence, I promised Mummy and Daddy never again to eat what *Mamaiji* offered, and confessed all my past sins. In

Mamaiji's eyes I was a traitor, but sometimes it was also fun to listen to her scatalogical reproaches: "*Muà ugheeparoo!* Eating my food, then shitting and tattling all over the place. Next time I'll cork you up with a big *bootch* before feeding you."

Mummy came in from the kitchen with a plateful of toast fresh off the Criterion: unevenly browned, and charred in spots by the vagaries of its kerosene wick. She cleared the comics to one side and set the plate down.

"Listen to this," Daddy said to her, "just found it in the paper: 'A Growing Concern Seeks Dynamic Young Account Executive, Self-Motivated. Four-Figure Salary and Provident Fund.' I think it's perfect." He waited for Mummy's reaction. Then: "If I can get it, all our troubles will be over."

Mummy listened to such advertisements week after week: har-bingers of hope that ended in disappointment and frustration. But she always allowed the initial wave of optimism to lift her, riding it with Daddy and me, higher and higher, making plans and dream-ing, until it crashed and left us stranded, awaiting the next adver-tisement and the next wave. So her silence was surprising.

Daddy reached for a toast and dipped it in the tea, wrinkling his nose. "Smells of kerosene again. When I get this job, first thing will be a proper toaster. No more making burnt toast on top of the Criterion."

"I cannot smell kerosene," said Mummy.

"Smell this then," he said, thrusting the tea-soaked piece at her nose, "smell it and tell me," irritated by her ready contradiction. "It's these useless wicks. The original Criterion ones from England used to be so good. One trim and you had a fine flame for months." He bit queasily into the toast. "Well, when I get the job, a Bombay Gas Company stove and cylinder can replace it." He laughed. "Why not? The British left seventeen years ago, time for their stove to go as well."

He finished chewing and turned to me. "And one day, you must go, too, to America. No future here." His eyes fixed mine, urgently. "Somehow we'll get the money to send you. I'll find a way."

His face filled with love. I felt suddenly like hugging him, but we never did except on birthdays, and to get rid of the feeling I looked away and pretended to myself that he was saying it just to humour me, because he wanted me to finish pulling his white hairs. Fortunately, his jovial optimism returned.

"Maybe even a fridge is possible, then we will never have to go upstairs to that woman. No more obligations, no more favours. You won't have to kill any more rats for her." Daddy waited for us to join in. For his sake I hoped that Mummy would. I did not feel like mustering any enthusiasm.

But she said sharply, "All your *shaik-chullee* thoughts are flying again. Nothing happens when you plan too much. Leave it in the hands of God."

Daddy was taken aback. He said, summoning bitterness to retaliate, "You are thinking I will never get a better job? I'll show all of you." He threw his piece of toast onto the plate and sat back. But he recovered as quickly, and made it into a joke. He picked up the newspaper. "Well, I'll just have to surprise you one day when I throw out the kerosene stoves."

I liked the kerosene stoves and the formidable fifteen-gallon storage drum that replenished them. The Criterion had a little round glass window in one corner of its black base, and I would peer into the murky depths, watching the level rise as kerosene poured through the funnel; it was very dark and cool and mysterious in there, then the kerosene floated up and its surface shone under the light bulb. Looking inside was like lying on Chaupatty beach at night and gazing at the stars, in the hot season, while we stayed out after dinner till the breeze could rise and cool off the walls baking all day in the sun. When the stove was lit and the kitchen dark, the soft orange glow through its little mica door reminded me of the glow in the fire-temple *afargaan*, when there wasn't a blazing fire because hardly any sandalwood offerings had been left in the silver *thaali*; most people came only on the holy days. The Primus stove was fun, too, pumped up hot and roaring, the kerosene emerging under pressure and igniting into sharp blue flames. Daddy was the only one who lit it; every year, many women died in their kitchens because of explosions, and Daddy said that though many of them were not accidents, especially the dowry cases, it was still a dangerous stove if handled improperly.

Mummy went back to the kitchen. I did not mind the kerosene smell, and ate some toast, trying to imagine the kitchen without the stoves, with squat red gas cylinders sitting under the table instead. I had seen them in shop windows, and I thought they were ugly. We would get used to them, though, like everything else. At night, I stood on the veranda sometimes to look at the stars. But it was not the same as going to Chaupatty and lying on the sand, quietly, with only the sound of the waves in the dark. On Saturday nights, I would make sure that the stoves were filled, because Mummy made a very early breakfast for Daddy and me next morning. The milk and bread would be arriving in the pre-dawn darkness while the kettle was boiling and we got ready for cricket with the boys of Firozsha Baag.

We always left by seven o'clock. The rest of the building was just starting to wake up: Nariman Hansotia would be aligning, on the parapet of his ground floor veranda, his razor and shaving brush and mirror beside two steaming cups, one of boiling water and the other of tea, and we often wondered if he ever dipped the brush in the wrong cup; and the old spinster Tehmina, still waiting for her cataracts to ripen, would be saying her prayers facing the rising sun, with her duster-coat hoisted up and slung over the left shoulder, her yellowing petticoat revealed, to untie and tie her thick rope-like *kusti* around the waist; and the *kuchrawalli* would be sweeping the compound, making her rounds from door to door with broom and basket, collecting yesterday's garbage. If she happened to cross Tehmina's line of vision, all the boys were sure to have a fine time, because Tehmina, though blurry with cataracts, would recognize the *kuchrawalli* and let loose at her with a stream of curses fouler than any filth in the garbage basket, for committing the unspeakable crime of passing in front of her, thereby polluting her prayers and vitiating their efficacy.

Even Daddy laughed, but he hurried us along as we lingered there to follow the ensuing dialogue. We picked our way through sleeping streets. The pavement dwellers would stretch, and look for a place to relieve themselves. Then they would fold up their cardboard pieces and roll away their plastics before the street sweepers arrived and the traffic got heavy. Sometimes, they would start a small fire if they had something to cook for breakfast, or else try to beg from people who came to the Irani restaurant for their morning *chai* and bun. Occasionally, Mummy would wrap up leftovers from the night before for Daddy and me to distribute to them along the way.

It had been such a long time since we last played cricket. Flying kites had also become a thing of the past. One by one, the things I held dear were leaving my life, I thought gloomily. And Francis. What about poor Francis? Where was he now, I wondered. I wished he was still working in the Baag. That awful thrashing he got in Tar Gully was the fault of Najamai and Tehmina, those stupid old women. And Najamai saying he stole eighty rupees was nonsense, in my opinion; the absent-minded cow must have forgotten where she left the money.

I put down the tweezers and reached for the comics. Daddy looked up. "Don't stop now, it should be perfect this week. There will be an interview or something."

Avoiding his eye, I said stolidly, "I'm going to read the comics," and walked out to the compound steps. When I turned at the doorway Daddy was still looking at me. His face was like *Mamaiji*'s when the thread broke and slipped through his fingers and the spindle fell to the floor. But I kept walking, it was a matter of pride. You always did what you said you were going to do.

The comics did not take long. It used to be more fun when Daddy and I had a race to the door to grab the *Times*, and pretended to fight over who would read the comics first. I thought of the lines on Daddy's forehead, visible so clearly from my coign of vantage with the tweezers. His thinning hair barely gave off a dull lustre with its day-old pomade, and the Sunday morning stubble on his chin was flecked with grey and white.

Something — remorse, maybe just pity — stirred inside, but I quashed it without finding out. All my friends had fathers whose hair was greying. Surely they did not spend Sunday mornings doing what I did, or they would have said something. They were not like me, there was nothing that was too private and personal for them. They would talk about anything. Especially Pesi. He used to describe for us how his father passed gas, enhancing the narrative with authentic sound effects. Now he was in boarding-school. His father was dead.

From our C Block stone steps I could observe the entire length of the compound, up to A Block at the far end. Dr Sidhwa's black

Fiat turned in at the gate and trundled laboriously over the rough-hewn flagstones of Firozsha Baag. He waved as he went past. He looked so much like Pesi's father. He had the same crow's-feet at the corners of his eyes that Dr Mody used to have, and even their old cars seemed identical, except that Dr Mody healed animals and Dr Sidhwa, humans. Most of us had been treated by him at one time or another. His house and dispensary were within walking distance of Firozsha Baag, even a sick person's walking distance; he was a steadfast Parsi, seen often at fire-temples; and he always drove over for his house-calls. What more could we want in a doctor?

The car stopped at the far end of the compound. Dr Sidhwa heaved out, he was a portly man, and reached in for his bag. It must be an emergency in A Block, I decided, for someone to call him on Sunday. He slammed the door, then opened and slammed it again, harder now. The impact rocked the old car a little, but the door shut properly this time. Viraf emerged from the steps of A Block. I waved to him to let him know I was waiting.

Viraf was my best friend. Together we learned bicycling, on a rented contraption of bent spokes and patchwork tyres from Cecil Cycles of Tar Gully: Fifty Paise Per Hour. Daddy used to take us to practise at Chaupatty on the wide pavements by the beach. They were deserted in the early morning — pavement dwellers preferred the narrow side streets — except for pigeons gathering in anticipation of the pigeon-man, who arrived when the streets stirred to life. We took turns, and Daddy ran behind, holding the seat to keep us steady. Daddy also taught the two of us to play cricket. Mummy had been angry when he brought home the bat and ball, asking where the money had come from. His specialty on his own school team had been bowling, and he taught us the leg break and off break, and told us about the legendary Jasu Patel, born with a defective wrist which turned out to be perfect for spin bowling, and how Jasu had mastered the dreaded curl spin which was eventually feared by all the great international batsmen.

Cricket on Sunday mornings became a regular event for the boys in Firozsha Baag. Between us we almost had a complete kit; all that was missing was a pair of bails, and wicket-keeping gloves. Daddy took anyone who wanted to play to the Marine Drive *maidaan*, and organized us into teams, captaining one team himself. We went early, before the sun got too hot and the *maidaan* overcrowded. But then one Sunday, halfway through the game, Daddy said he was going to rest for a while. Sitting on the grass a little distance away, he seemed so much older than he did when he was batting, or bowling leg breaks. He watched us with a faraway expression on his face. Sadly, as if he had just realized something and wished he hadn't.

There was no cricket at the *maidaan* after that day. Since we were not allowed to go alone, our games were now confined to the Firozsha Baag compound. Its flagstoned surface would not accept the points of stumps, and we chalked three white lines on the compound's black stone wall. But the compound was too cramped for cricket. Besides, the uneven ground made the ball bounce and rear erratically. After a few shattered panes of glass and several complaints from neighbours, the games ceased.

I waved again to Viraf and gave our private signal, "OO ooo OO ooo," which was like a yodel. He waved back, then took the doctor's bag and accompanied him into A Block. His polite demeanor made me smile. That Viraf. Shrewd fellow, he knew the things to do to make grownups approve of him, and was always welcome at all the homes in Firozsha Baag. He would be back soon.

I waited for at least half an hour. I cracked all my fingers and knuckles, even the thumbs. Then I went to the other end of the compound. After sitting on the steps there for a few minutes, I got impatient and climbed upstairs to find out why Viraf was buttering up the doctor.

But Dr Sidhwa was on his way down, carrying his black bag. I said, "*Sahibji*, doctor," and he smiled at me as I raced up to the third floor. Viraf was standing at the balcony outside his flat. "What's all the *muskaa-paalis* for the doctor?"

He turned away without answering. He looked upset but I did not ask what the matter was. Words to show concern were always beyond me. I spoke again, in that easygoing debonair style which all of us tried to perfect, right arm akimbo and head tilted ever so slightly, "Come on *yaar*, what are your plans for today?"

He shrugged his shoulders, and I persisted, "Half the morning's over, man, don't be such a cry-baby."

"Fish off," he said, but his voice shook. His eyes were red, and he rubbed one as if there was something in it. I stood quietly for a while, looking out over the balcony. His third-floor balcony was my favourite spot, you could see the road beyond Firozsha Baag, and sometimes, on a sunny day, even a corner of Chaupatty beach with the sun gleaming on the waves. From my ground floor veranda the compound's black stone wall was all that was visible.

Hushed voices came from the flat, the door was open. I looked into the dining-room where some A Block neighbours had gathered around Viraf's mother. "How about Ludo or Snakes-and-Ladders?" I tried. If he shrugged again I planned to leave. What else could I do?

"Okay," he said, "but stay quiet. If *Mumma* sees us she'll send us out."

No one saw as we tiptoed inside, they were absorbed in whatever the discussion was about. "*Puppa* is very sick," whispered Viraf, as we passed the sickroom. I stopped and looked inside. It was dark. The smell of sickness and medicines made it stink like the waiting room of Dr Sidhwa's dispensary. Viraf's father was in bed, lying on his back, with a tube through his nose. There was a long needle stuck into his right arm, and it glinted cruelly in a thin shaft of sunlight that had suddenly slunk inside the darkened room. I shivered. The needle was connected by a tube to a large bottle which hung upside down from a dark metal stand towering over the bed.

Viraf's mother was talking softly to the neighbours in the dining-room. "…in his chest got worse when he came home last night. So many times I've told him, three floors to climb is not easy at your age with your big body, climb one, take rest for a few minutes, then climb again. But he won't listen, does not want people to think it is too much for him. Now this is the result, and what I will do I don't know. Poor little Viraf, being so brave when the doctor…"

Supine, his rotundity had spread into a flatness denying the huge bulk. I remembered calling Viraf a cry-baby, and my face flushed with shame. I swore I would apologize. Daddy was slim and wiry, although there were the beginnings of a small pot, as Mummy called it. He used to run and field with us at cricket. Viraf's father had sat on the grass the one time he took us. The breath came loud and rasping. His mouth was a bit open. It resembled a person snoring, but was uneven, and the sound suggested pain. I noticed the lines on his brow, like Daddy's, only Daddy's were less deep.

Over the rasp of his breath came the voice of Viraf's mother. "…to exchange with someone on the ground floor, but that also is no. Says I won't give up my third-floor paradise for all the smell and noise of a ground-floor flat. Which is true, up here even B.E.S.T. bus rattle and rumble does not come. But what use of paradise if you are not alive in good health to enjoy it? Now doctor says intensive care but Parsi General Hospital has no place. Better to stay here than other hospitals, only…"

My eyes fixed on the stone-grey face of Viraf's father, I backed out of the sickroom, unseen. The hallway was empty. Viraf was waiting for me in the back room with the boards for Ludo and Snakes-and-Ladders. But I sneaked through the veranda and down the stairs without a word.

The compound was flooded in sunshine as I returned to the other end. On the way I passed the three white stumps we had once chalked on the compound wall's black stone. The lines were very faint, and could barely be seen, lost amongst more recent scribbles and abandoned games of noughts and crosses.

Mummy was in the kitchen, I could hear the roaring of the Primus stove. *Mamaiji*, sinister in her dark glasses, sat by the veranda window, sunlight reflecting off the thick, black lenses with leather blinders at the sides; after her cataract operation the doctor had told her to wear these for a few months.

Daddy was still reading the *Times* at the dining-table. Through the gloom of the light bulb I saw the Murphy Baby's innocent and joyous smile. I wondered what he looked like now. When I was two years old, there was a Murphy Baby Contest, and according to Mummy and Daddy my photograph, which had been entered, should have won. They said that in those days my smile had been just as, if not more, innocent and joyous.

The tweezers were lying on the table. I picked them up. They glinted pitilessly, like that long needle in Viraf's father. I dropped them with a shudder, and they clattered against the table.

Daddy looked up questioningly. His hair was dishevelled as I had left it, and I waited, hoping he would ask me to continue. To offer to do it was beyond me, but I wanted desperately that he should ask me now. I glanced at his face discreetly, from the corner of my eye.

The lines on his forehead stood out all too clearly, and the stubble flecked with white, which by this hour should have disappeared down the drain with the shaving water. I swore to myself that never again would I begrudge him my help; I would get all the white hairs, one by one, if he would only ask me; I would concentrate on the tweezers as never before, I would do it as if all our lives were riding on the efficacy of the tweezers, yes, I would continue to do it Sunday after Sunday, no matter how long it took.

Daddy put down the newspaper and removed his glasses. He rubbed his eyes, then went to the bathroom. How tired he looked, and how his shoulders drooped; his gait lacked confidence, and I'd never noticed that before. He did not speak to me even though I was praying hard that he would. Something inside me grew very heavy, and I tried to swallow, to dissolve that heaviness in saliva, but swallowing wasn't easy either, the heaviness was blocking my throat.

I heard the sound of running water. Daddy was preparing to shave. I wanted to go and watch him, talk to him, laugh with him at the funny faces he made to get at all the tricky places with the razor, especially the cleft in his chin.

Instead, I threw myself on the bed. I felt like crying, and buried my face in the pillow. I wanted to cry for the way I had treated Viraf, and for his sick father with the long, cold needle in his arm and his rasping breath; for *Mamaiji* and her tired, darkened eyes spinning thread for our *kustis*, and for Mummy growing old in the dingy kitchen smelling of kerosene, where the Primus roared and her dreams were extinguished; I wanted to weep for myself, for not being able to hug Daddy when I wanted to, and for not ever saying thank you for cricket in the morning, and pigeons and bicycles and dreams; and for all the white hairs that I was powerless to stop.

The Paying Guests

The Paying Guests

Khorshedbai emerged from her room with a loosely newspapered package cradled in her arms. Then, as she had been doing every morning at eleven o'clock for the past four weeks, she began strewing its smelly contents over the veranda.

The veranda sat in the L of the flat's two rooms. She was careful to let nothing fall by the door to her room. That she was on the ground floor of B Block, exposed to curious eyes passing in the compound, had not discouraged her for four weeks and did not discourage her now. None of the neighbours would interfere. Why, she did not know for certain. Perhaps out of respect for her grey hair. She also had the vague notion that praying every day at the *agyaari* had something to do with it.

Her work was methodical and thorough. She commenced with the window and its parapet, tossing onion skin, coconut husk, egg shells trailing gluey white, potato peelings, one strip of a banana skin, cauliflower leaves, and orange rind, all along the inside ledge. An eggshell rolled off. She picked it up and cracked it — there, that would keep it from falling — and replaced it on the parapet, between the coconut husk and potato peelings.

Pleased with her arrangement, Khorshedbai stepped to the door leading to the other room. Locked from the inside, as usual. The cowards. She draped the balance of the banana skin over the door handle, hung an elongated shred of fatty gristle from the knob, and scattered the remaining assorted peels and skins over the doorstep. The several bangles on her bony wrists tinkled softly: a delicate accompaniment while she worked over the veranda. Gentle though the sound was, it always annoyed her, announcing her presence like a cowbell. She pushed the bangles higher. Tight, around the forearms. To get rid of them without offending Ardesar would be such a comfort. The gold wedding bangle, encircling her wrist for forty years now, was the only one she cared for.

Khorshedbai reversed three paces and regarded her handiwork with satisfaction. Especially the length of gristle, which was pendulating gently with the weight of the bone at its extremity. Only one thing remained now. Collected from the pavement as an afterthought while returning from the *agyaari*, she hurled it against the locked door.

Dog faeces spattered the lower panel with a smack. Bits of it clung, the rest fell on the step. Behind the locked door Kashmira puzzled over the soft thud. She was alone with little Adil. The sound was quite different from the rustle and tinkle of the past four weeks, but she stayed where she was, behind the safety of the locked door. She could wait to find out what it was till Boman came home from work. Four weeks of calm and restrained littering had still not alleviated her fear that Khorshedbai would one day explode into an uncontrollable, shrieking madwoman. Or she could collapse into a whimpering mass of helplessness. If it did happen, Kashmira hoped it would be the latter.

Outside, Khorshedbai was delighted with the results. Had it dried up completely, it would not have stuck. But this was perfect. She crumpled up the newspaper and turned to leave, then stopped. Another afterthought — she raised her eyes heavenward in thanks and shredded the pages of *The Indian Express* into tiny pieces. She scattered them, tossed them, hither and thither, little paper medallions gently falling, to decorate the floor and window ledge and door. Traces of prance and glee crept into her step; she became a little girl indulging in forbidden fun. Strewing to the left and to the right, and up to the ceiling to watch it all float downward. The sari slipped off her head (she *always* kept her head covered) and the left shoulder (she deftly restored the fabric), and her bangles, having escaped the forearms to the freedom of the wrists, sounded louder, the fragile tinkles now a solid row of jingle-jangles.

From behind the locked door it sounded as though Khorshedbai had finally entered that long-feared state of frenzy, and Kashmira was worried. Khorshedbai could usually be controlled by Ardesar with his gentle voice of reason. She had heard him before, speaking so calmly and tenderly to his wife; it always brought a lump to Kashmira's throat.

Ardesar had tried to dissuade Khorshedbai every day since she conceived of this scheme four weeks ago. That first morning, after tasting victory in the court case in which they had faced eviction, she woke up and said that Pestonji had given her a gift in the night. Whistling with his little red beak and fluttering his bright green wings in her dream, she said, he had revealed how to teach next door a lesson they would never forget. Ardesar had pleaded with her, but forty years of marriage should have taught him better. When Khorshed was resolved for fight and revenge nothing could stop her.

Now Ardesar could watch no more, after that nasty thing she hurled. Away, away from the door, away from this, this insane and filthy behaviour, he turned. Wringing his hands, he formed four words with his lips, over and over, in urgent supplication: *Dada Ormuzd*, forgive her. He paced the room in distress, stopping now and then to straighten and re-straighten the photoframes on the shelf. What was he to do? He could not question Pestonji's dream-dictums without hurting his beloved Khotty. No, he could never do that. Besides, who was to say what dreams were all about, even scientists still knew so very little about the universe and its mysterious forces. He pulled out a chair as if to sit, then continued to pace. He repeatedly touched the bald spot on his head, fingered its peripheral strands, and tried to push the glasses (which had not strayed) up on his nose.

Khorshedbai curbed her frolic. She came in as the last little pieces of *The Indian Express* floated to the floor behind her. Ardesar took her arm, murmuring: "O Khotty my life, what have you done, that thing you threw. We will have to answer one day to The One

Up There. This must stop before…"

She pulled away her arm and went to the empty parrot cage. With hands clasped before her chest and eyes closed she stood before it for a few moments, then turned to Ardesar. "They started it, why should we stop? Six months of court-and-lawyer nonsense. Eviction notices! Ha! He gives me eviction notices! With his ties and jackets, trying to be a *sahib*, and his good-mornings and good-evenings, thinks he is better than me." Her hardness disappeared for a moment as she appealed to him pleadingly: "I was never this way before, was I?"

"But Khotty my life, that, that thing you threw! And you know it is their flat, they have a right to…"

"A right to what? Put us on the street? Don't we have rights? At last to have a roof, eat a little *daar-roteli*, and finish our days in peace? No one will peck me to pieces, they better learn."

"But we leave soon as the other place is vacant. Tell them, they are good people."

"For you the whole world is good people." Her gesture to encompass humanity tinkled the bangles again. She pushed them towards the elbows. "The other place is not ready. Might never be. Nothing is certain in life. Only birth, marriage, and death, my poor mother used to say. At our age you want to go begging again for rooms in *dharmsaalas*?"

"But that dirty, that thing…"

"That thing, that thing, that thing! Trembling in your pyjamas every day instead of helping. And if He did not want me to throw it, then why was it on the pavement outside the *agyaari*? And why did He give me the idea? It is not easy to…"

Ardesar stopped listening. He did not mind Khorshedbai's scolding. The uncertainty of things was worrying her. That was all. Besides, he was far away from this room now as he fed the pigeons flocking the wide pavements along Chaupatty beach, cooing to them as they played and nibbled in his hand, while the sound of the tide coming in offered a continuo to the occasional whirr of their gentle wings.

Locked inside her room with little Adil, Kashmira heard the drone of Khorshedbai's determined voice and Ardesar's soft one for a long time. Sometimes she wished she could eavesdrop with greater clarity. After Boman came home she would unlock her door; they would clean up the mess as usual, then relax outside.

Kashmira needed at least one hour every evening on the veranda before going to bed. She said it felt like someone was choking her, after being cooped all day inside the one room where they had to cook and eat and sleep. But that was their own choice, made two years ago. They had given up the kitchen and decided to keep this room with its attached bathroom — the kitchen went with the other to the paying guests, in a natural division of the flat. She and Boman had agreed the bathroom was more important, what with little Adil's *soosoo* problem at nights, and the second baby they had been planning. A kitchen they could do without, by partitioning and using one side of their room for cooking and dining. The veranda was common because the only entrance to the flat was through it.

The arrangement was awkward. But Boman said that no wife of his would go out to work while there was breath in *his* lungs. The paying guests would be temporary, two years at best, till he got his raises and they could again afford the full rent. That was Boman's plan.

He laid it before Mr Karani one evening in the compound when they were both returning from work. Boman admired the chartered accountant on the third floor immensely. He always took his advice in all manner of things. Not that he lacked confidence in himself, he just enjoyed discussions with a man who was a CA; there was something about those two letters, especially since Boman's own studies had come to a halt after B.Com., when his father's fortunes had failed.

Mr Karani was full of dire forebodings. He warned that it was easier to get rid of a poisonous *kaankhajuro* which had crawled through your ear and nibbled its way to your brain than to evict a paying guest who had been allowed into your flat.

Boman was in a quandary. He had been looking for confirmation and support. Instead, he had run full tilt into contradiction and discouragement, and wished he had never spoken to Mr Karani. This was the problem in taking the CA's advice. If you disagreed with it, it sat inside you like a lump of incongenial food, noisily belligerent and causing indigestion.

For a few days, Mr Karani's warnings rumbled and growled and gnawed away at his plan, threatening it with disintegration, while Boman vacillated and went from extremes of confidence to extremes of uncertainty. Eventually, however, it turned out to be one of those rare instances when Boman ignored the CA's advice. He went ahead with his plan and told Kashmira he had inserted an ad in the *Jam-E-Jamshed*.

It was soon answered. An appointment was made, the flat was shown, and both parties were agreeable.

Then followed one and a half years of cordial coexistence with the paying guests. Boman began to feel that, for once, Mr Karani had been exaggerating. He was tempted to pull out the pedestal from under Mr Karani.

But the year and a half of cordial coexistence sped by and concluded abruptly when Ardesar and Khorshedbai received the notice to vacate. This notice to vacate would have far-reaching effects. It would bring new experiences into all their lives: courts and courtrooms, sleepless nights filled with paeans to the rising sun, a sadistic nose-digging lawyer for Boman, veranda-sweeping for Kashmira, signs and portents in dreams for Khorshedbai, pigeons (real and imagined) for Ardesar, thick and suffocating incense clouds for Boman and Kashmira, and finally, a taxi for Ardesar and an ambulance for Khorshedbai.

Its immediate result, however, was to make Khorshedbai emphatically declare to Ardesar that no one would peck her to pieces. For most of her life, Khorshedbai had carried at the back of her mind an image. It was a flock of crows pecking and tearing to shreds some dead creature lying in a gutter. At times the corpse was a kitten, at other times a puppy; sometimes it was even another crow. Whether she ever witnessed something of this sort or whether the image just grew out of various life experiences into a guiding metaphor, during times of adversity she would clench her teeth and repeat to herself that no one was going to peck her to pieces, she would fight back.

It was a year and a half ago that the paying guests had moved in with their meagre possessions: two trunks, one holdall, a hefty parrot cage (empty and still bearing the former occupant's name: Pestonji Poputt), a wind-up gramophone, and one record: *Sukhi Sooraj*, a song of praise for the morning sun, its brittle 78-rpm shellac protected between soft sari layers in one of the trunks.

In those days, the two rooms did not stay locked. Khorshedbai would peek inside, wave to little Adil, and inquire how he was getting along. Sometimes Kashmira looked in on the elderly couple to ask if they needed anything. She noticed that two second-hand chairs and a small folding table had been added. On the table stood the cage of the deceased or disappeared Pestonji. Once, she saw Khorshedbai before the empty cage, gazing at the little swing inside. She felt a pang of compassion for the dear grey-haired lady, and imagined the burden of memories weighing heavily upon Khorshedbai's old shoulders as she stood and remembered her beloved pet. Khorshedbai beckoned her in, viced her arm in bony fingers, and said; "So sweet, Pestonji's whistle was, and so true." He still appeared in her dreams when there was trouble, she said, and communicated the future in whistles she alone could interpret.

That night when Kashmira told Boman all about it, he said the old lady definitely had at least one loose screw somewhere in the upper storey.

Minor irritants between the two parties were easily taken care of. Khorshedbai requested sole use of the veranda for her morning prayers. And she did not want Kashmira to emerge during her monthly. Boman and Kashmira agreed amusedly. Khorshedbai rose at five A.M. each day and, after brushing her teeth, unmuzzled her gramophone for *Sukhi Sooraj*, the fervent tribute to sunrise. As part of the mutual consideration pact, Boman and Kashmira requested that it not be played till after seven o'clock.

Khorshedbai soon became a familiar sight in the building. To and from her way to the *agyaari* or the bazaar, and sometimes, hand in hand with Ardesar, off to feed the pigeons at Chaupatty beach. Gradually, stories reached Kashmira's ears about the elderly couple, and how they came to be homeless at their age. Najamai from C Block stopped by whenever she uncovered something new from her numerous sources. She was concerned that Boman and Kashmira had taken strangers into their flat. So what if they too were Parsis, these days you could trust no one. It was one lesson she had learned, she said, after the murder in the fire-temple, when the *dustoorji* had been stabbed to death by a *chasniwalla* employed there. Thus Najamai made it her bounden responsibility to make known the truth, but was not really successful.

In one version, it was the result of a family feud; many years ago Ardesar had sworn never to set foot in his father's house as long as a certain person lived there. Although soft-spoken Ardesar swearing to do or not do anything was highly improbable.

Another story went that something quite shameful had come to pass between Khorshedbai and one unnamed male occupant, a relative of Ardesar's, and they had had no choice but to pack up and leave after the affair. But here again it was impossible to imagine prim, *agyaari*-going Khorshedbai with sari-covered head in any kind of liaison.

Yet another tale, and the saddest of them all, had it that the couple, after a long and arduous life of working and scrimping and saving, had managed to educate and send their only son to Canada. Some years later he sponsored them. So they got rid of their flat and went, only to find he was not the son they once knew; after a period of misery and ill-treatment at his hands they returned to Bombay, homeless and heartbroken.

Kashmira did not pay much attention to these stories. But sometimes, when she picked up the mail dropped on the veranda by the postman, she would see a letter for Ardesar and Khorshedbai from Canada. The cruel son? The return address had the same last name. But if they were mistreated in Canada, returning to Bombay made no sense. Especially since there was no flat. Sons could be ungrateful, yes, but you could not run away from it. Better to remain where at least the food and air and water were good.

Kashmira would hand over the letter with a remark about the pretty foreign stamp, hoping to elicit a comment, perhaps a clue to the writer's identity. All Khorshedbai ever said was thanks, then she took her arm and led her in beside the cage, to tell more about the life of Pestonji.

When the doctor said yes, Kashmira was pregnant, Boman thought it was time to use the whole flat again. With two children they would need both rooms.

One day, soon after the glad tidings, he stopped Mr Karani in the compound. More out of habit than anything else, he wanted to discuss the best way of making the paying guests leave.

"Boman *dikra*, what shall I tell you?" said Mr Karani, shaking his head sorrowfully, "whatever advice can I give? If there was a *kaankhajuro* inside your skull, gnawing through your brain, I could say: hold a smelly chunk of mutton beside your ear, that will tempt it to come racing out on its one hundred legs. But what can I tell you about paying guests? To get rid of that problem there is no remedy except death."

Mr Karani went on in this way for a while, and when he felt that Boman had suffered enough, suggested he go to see the trustees of Firozsha Baag.

But there was to be no help from that quarter.

Boman sought out the one to whom he had slipped an expensive envelope one and a half years ago for the favour of turning the trustees' collective blind eye (a delicate organ, but nurtured to operate without hindrance of ruth or compassion) upon the arrival of paying guests in the ground floor of B Block. Impossible, the oily man said. He spoke without relinquishing the look of grave concern (practised for several years) that proclaimed: here I stand, a pillar of the community, ready to help the poor and the needy at any hour of the day or night. Impossible, he repeated, there could not be paying guests living in any flat of Firozsha Baag, it was against the policy, Boman had to be mistaken; either that, or Boman had broken the rules.

Boman left. He turned to his brother-in-law Rustomji in A Block. Rustomji was a lawyer, he would have something sensible to say for sure. Boman had always sized up Kashmira's brother as a tough, no-nonsense kind of person, and surely that was the individual to talk to in this tricky situation.

"*Saala ghéla!*" vociferated Rustomji. "Worst bloody thing you have done, taking paying guests. Where had your brain gone, committing such foolishness? You should have asked me before taking them in, now what is the use. First you are setting a fire, then running to dig the well." Boman waited meekly, murmuring: "That's true, that's true." The impassioned outburst had to be suffered patiently when you wanted tough, no-nonsense advice for free.

Then Boman told him about his meeting with the trustee. It gave Rustomji the appropriate opportunity for some harmless spleen-venting. "*Arré*, those rascals won't give a glass of water to a thirsty man. In their office, their chairs don't need cushions because they have piles of trust money squeezed under their arses." Rustomji thrust his hands behind and upwards, and Boman, laughing appreciatively, said: "That's too good, *yaar*, too good!"

Rustomji enjoyed compliments; he continued.

"Four years ago when my WC was leaking, *saala* thieves took five weeks to repair it. Every day my poor Mehroo would phone, and some bloody bugger would say, today or tomorrow, for sure. For five weeks I had to go next door to Hirabai Hansotia every morning. Finally I sent them such a stiff letter, it must have sizzled their arses. Repairing was done double-quick." Boman gave him one of his awe-and-admiration looks.

It paid off. Rustomji now came to what Boman was waiting for. "Legal channels are what you should follow, make the court work for you," said he. "It will not be easy, mark my words, tenancy laws are such. But if you are lucky it will not get that far. A lawyer's letter might be enough to scare them out. Sometimes a lawyer's letter gives the best laxative." He wrote down the name of one who specialized in tenancy law.

When Kashmira learned of the procedure they would follow, she did not like it at all. She wanted to invite the paying guests for tea, announce the good news, then discuss the room. The baby would not be here for another seven months. She could look in the *Jam-E-Jamshed* columns and help them find another place. As Boman himself had said, between the two they must have easily scored more than a century. It would be hard moving again at their age, they could use her assistance.

Once, Kashmira's devout ambition was to do some kind of social work. Rustomji had been able to indulge a similar desire years ago by joining the Social Service League at St Xavier's College, and had eventually worked it out of his system. In recent times he had laboured hard to build up his reputation for hard-heartedness and apathy which, he made no bones about expressing, were essential for survival. But when her time came, Kashmira was not allowed to join the SSL because boys and girls went on work-camps together, and all kinds of stories were told about what when on there be-tween the sexes. She had to repeatedly listen to her parents and her brother say things like: charity begins at home, or: self-help is the best help, which made no sense to her then or now.

Boman said inviting the paying guests to tea was out of the ques-tion. These days human nature was such that courtesy was usually misinterpreted as weakness. Better to do it firmly and officially, through proper channels, with a lawyer's letter telling them to vacate in two months.

When the paying guests received the notice, Khorshedbai im-mediately and emphatically declared that no one would peck her to pieces. Then she told Ardesar that it was no surprise, she knew it was coming: Pestonji had recently appeared in a dream, and his cage had been nowhere in sight. Frantically beating his clipped wings, he had flopped around the veranda from corner to corner, squawking pitifully, and it had taken a long time to comfort him.

Ardesar wanted to tell Boman there was no need for lawyers and notices. They just needed a little time. But Khorshedbai forbade him. She saw beaks getting ready to peck, and was going to give them a fight, that was all. Standing before the cage, she set the swing going with her finger. "Prayerful people like us have nothing to fear," she said, and swayed with the to-and-fro rocking of the swing.

Six months of futile and wearying procedures then began. The lawyer Rustomji had recommended was a sadistic little tub of a fellow who dug his nose insolently in the presence of his clients. It delighted him to see Boman writhe in anxiety as he told him about the laws regarding tenancy and sub-tenancy, and how difficult it was to prove extreme hardship and evict someone.

"There are laws to protect the poor," Boman said bitterly after he got home, "and laws to protect the rich. But middle-class people like us get the bamboo, all the way."

"Chhee! Don't talk like that!" said Kashmira, intolerant of dirty speech. Clothes and language were two things in which she insisted on cleanliness. In other matters she let Boman have his way. During happier times, she had allowed him to do things which would have horrified her had they been described in words. How Boman yearned for those nights again. When he would reach out his hand in the darkness after little Adil had fallen asleep, and she would turn her soft, warm body towards him, and know exactly what to do. Darkness was all she required, and silence: silence of words — other sounds, such as moans and whimpers, she did not mind, in fact they even excited her, of that he was certain.

Kashmira continued with bitterness: "If you had let me get a job instead, none of this would ever have happened." Boman, turning over those night-time moments of ecstasy within his memory, smiled wistfully, and she did not understand why.

The weeks during which Khorshedbai littered in the morning and Kashmira swept in the evening commenced following the day of the final courthouse appearance. That day saw Kashmira enter the eighth month of her pregnancy. It saw Pestonji flutter his way again into Khorshedbai's dreams. And it saw the end of Boman's futile and wearying procedures to secure the eviction.

Boman had not foreseen a complete defeat. At most, on grounds of compassion, a longer notice period. He had spent the last few weeks returning utmost courtesy for Khorshedbai's daily vituperation, displaying the grace and generosity only the victor can afford, and which, in his mind, he already was.

When the verdict came it crushed him. And to see Boman humbled emboldened Khorshedbai. A brave front might have kept her vengeance within reasonable limits of decency, but brave fronts were now beyond Boman.

That day, Khorshedbai and Ardesar went directly from the courthouse to the *agyaari*, and made an offering of a ten-rupee sandalwood log instead of the regular fifty-paise stick. She was ebullient by the time they reached home. She washed and wiped the photoframes containing the moustached and pugreed countenances of her forefathers on the Other Side, as well as the cage, and filled fresh water in the drinking pan. Then, all evening long she lit sticks of *agarbatti* before the photoframes and cage, wreathing her departed ones in a fog thicker than the one they must have encountered when crossing Chinvad Bridge to the Other Side.

The heavy incense began to spread. It strayed into the other room and nauseated Kashmira and Boman. It filled their pots and pans and destroyed their appetites; lingered over bedsheets and slunk inside pillowcases; slipped through the slats and squatted under their bed. The relentless and pungent scent insinuated itself into their eyes and noses, and swam boldly through their skulls, muddling their minds and curdling their senses, until Khorshedbai had taken possession of their flat and their beings. Little Adil complained about the smell too. They calmed him down and put him to bed early, then retired, nursing headaches and shame and disappointment.

But Khorshedbai denied them the balm of sleep. When silence had fallen beyond the wall, she wound up her gramophone. She pointed the horn towards the region where the beds would be on the other side, and played the only record that she possessed. The only record, as she told Ardesar whenever he wanted to augment the collection, that anyone need possess. The strains of *Sukhi Sooraj*, the stridulant paean to the rising sun, borne on the vocal cords of the shrill woman buried in the crackling, hissing grooves of the 78's shellac, journeyed beyond the wall and into the darkness where Boman and Kashmira had sought refuge. They clung together, helpless, soothing each other's pain through repeated playings.

Then the horn was folded away. The last sticks of *agarbatti* smouldered into diminutive tapers. And when Khorshedbai finally felt sleep overpowering her, she struggled against it, unwilling to let the day's blessed events cease their circuit of her mind. Such were her stars, though, that when sleep did triumph, it only brought more joy. Pestonji visited, and whistled, and fluttered through her sleeping hours.

In the morning she remembered the dream distinctly: Pestonji was sitting in his large rectangular custom-built cage which, for some reason, was out on the veranda. She brought him peanuts. Pestonji proceeded to crack them methodically and thoroughly, then tossed the shells and nuts out of the cage. He threw them all out. Very surprising, because Pestonji had always been a neat and tidy parrot, he even did his potty in one corner of the cage only, never let fly haphazardly like others. Maybe he was not in the mood for peanuts. So she gave him two peppers. Long green ones. He did the same thing again. Tore them into little pieces, threw them across the length and breadth of the veranda.

It was only then that she understood Pestonji's message.

And while she was preparing the first of her veranda parcels, guided by the divine afflatus from Pestonji, Boman awoke, his confidence renewed. He told Kashmira there was no need to worry, he would get rid of the paying guests one way or another. He whistled as he lingered over the selection of a tie. When the knot turned out perfect at the first attempt, his self-assurance was fully restored. He kissed Kashmira and left for work, urging her to continue with their locked-door policy. And in the evening he discovered Khorshedbai's revenge scattered over the veranda.

Boman and Kashmira decided to pretend that nothing was wrong. They went out with a broom and dustpan. She swept away the garbage. He whistled as insouciantly as he could. She hummed along. He maintained a protective stance in the doorway. His tie and jacket gleamed like talismans of civility amidst Khorshedbai's manufactured squalor. He always returned from work as crisp and neat as he left in the morning. Kashmira loved this about him, she used to say he made their room classy the minute he walked in; at night he would delay changing into pyjamas for as long as possible.

Khorshedbai watched with satisfaction through the crack in the door. The beaks lifted against her had been humbled and turned away without a single peck. She said to Ardesar, "Look at him standing *chingo-mingo* in his fancy dress, making his pregnant wife clean it." Ardesar barely heard her. The pigeons were cooing and feeding from his hands, the occasional flutter of their wings fanning his face.

Days went by, then weeks. The veranda littering entered its second month, and Kashmira approached her ninth. She said, "What is going to happen now, Bomsi, how much longer?" He reassured her that he was making a plan.

"Not like the plan you made that time, I hope. Talking big, that you would scare them with a lawyer."

"Don't worry, Kashoo darling," he soothed, "this one will be perfect." He blamed her bitter reproach on the pregnancy. But the truth smarted.

That night he lay in bed unable to sleep. The paying guests were on his mind. Nowadays, it was the only thing he thought about.

What was going to happen? He couldn't admit there wasn't a plan and upset her. He turned over on his right side and stretched out his legs. A few moments later he folded them up into his stomach. Still not comfortable. He straightened them again. It was no use. He turned over on his left side, rose on one elbow, and adjusted the pillow. Kashmira said to please lie quietly if he couldn't sleep, and at least let her, she was worn out with the housework and the extra sweeping every evening, and it wouldn't be long before five o'clock struck and Khorshedbai wound up her gramophone.

What Boman did not have a shred of before the case concluded, he now had in abundance: evidence to evict the paying guests. On grounds of extreme hardship, harassment, harmful influences, something like that — the odious lawyer had quoted sections and paragraphs, finger in nose. Now he needed some way to package it for presenting to the court. Witnesses, of course. Hardly anyone in Firozsha Baag was unaware of Khorshedbai's doings on the veranda. Those who had not seen had at least heard of them. Those who wanted to see could walk past B Block at eleven o'clock.

He spoke to Mr Karani first. Boman had expected more support from him during these difficult months. But each time they met, Mr Karani, clutching his brief case and leaning on his umbrella, stood in the compound and droned on about the black market or the latest government swindle. The closest he let himself get to Boman's domestic dilemma was when he politely inquired about Kashmira's health.

Now Boman confronted him with his proposal.

"There is one principle in my life, Boman *dikra*," said Mr Karani, "which I never transgress: the three-monkeys principle." He mimed, placing his hands over his eyes, ears, and mouth. "Besides," he said, "the Mrs would never let me be a witness. Ever since that *tamaasha* in the Baag about Jaakaylee and the ghost they saw, and the rubbish that people were talking about crazy ayah and crazy *bai*, she pinched her ears and swore, and made me do the same, to have nothing to do with these lowbreds and churls in Firozsha Baag." Realizing what he'd just said, he embarrassedly patted Boman's shoulder: "She didn't mean you, of course, but it is a principle, you understand." He winked and gave him the from-one-man-to-another look: "Always obey the Mrs. My motto is: be coward-ly and be happy, try to be brave and you're soon in the grave."

Boman was bitterly disappointed. What bloody nonsense about the three-monkeys principle. Where did the monkeys go when he did his income tax, or helped his clients with theirs? Henpecked hypocrite. And selfish. But still a smart man, that Boman could not deny.

Next he tried Rustomji, who gruffly dismissed the suggestion as impossible: "Sorry, but enough time I spend in courtrooms, as it is."

And Najamai said: "Me, a widow, living all alone, how can I go falling in the middle of a court *lufraa*? And at my age making un-necessary enemies. No *bawa*, please forgive me, you will have to find someone else." This refusal hurt the most. She had shown so much concern all along. And now this blunt answer.

It might have tempered Boman's bitterness had he known that it would not be long now before Najamai would, in fact, become their saviour; that Najamai, with a beckon of her arm, would deliver them from the paying guests, from the fate worse than a brain-devouring *kaankhajuro*.

But in the meantime he spent his days exhausting the list of possible witnesses in the Baag. When he began making petitions to those who were as good as strangers, he realized he was reaching the end of hope. The one man who would have helped him, as surely as there was earth beneath and sky above, who had been worth more than all of B Block put together, and who had more goodness in his dried scabs of psoriasis than in the hearts of all these others, was long dead: the kind and noble Dr Mody. And Mrs Mody now lived a cloistered life, spending her days in prayer and seclusion. He had gone to see her a few times, but on each occasion she came to the door with her prayer book in her hands and beckoned him away, making vague sounds from behind tightly shut lips: parting them for profane speech would have rendered everything prayed up to that point useless.

There was someone who would be willing to speak in court, Boman knew: the Muslim who lived in the next flat. But desperate as Boman was, he would not stoop to that, to ask him to testify against a fellow Parsi.

The time for Kashmira's confinement came. She checked into the Awabai Petit Lying-In Hospital. Khorshedbai continued with her eleven o'clock routine, dancing her dance of disorder to the tinkling of bangles. Now Boman would clean up each night after visiting Kashmira at the hospital, and to see him crouching with broom and dustpan made Khorshedbai wild with delight. She could not hold still at the crack of her door, and kept dragging Ardesar up to make him look, against his will, at how low the mighty had to bend despite tie and jacket.

Poor Ardesar cowered inside, ashamed, and worried for her soul. His happiest moments came when he fed the pigeons at Chaupatty beach. He spent a lot of time there these days, alone: now Khotty refused to go. They waddled around his feet as he moved into their midst. He stopped every now and then, standing perfectly still, to let them pick playfully at his shoelaces. It made him sigh contentedly to see the way their throats trembled when they made their soft cooing sounds. The pigeons were the best part of living in this flat near Chaupatty beach.

In the end, the neighbours were willing to testify against the paying guests. There were so many volunteers that Boman could have picked and chosen. Even Mrs Karani assured him that she would make Mr Karani be a witness, whether he wanted to or not, three monkeys or no three monkeys, so outraged was she about what had happened.

But as it turned out, there was no need. The paying guests went quietly: Khorshedbai first, by ambulance, everyone knew where; then Ardesar, no one knew where, by taxi.

It happened soon after Kashmira returned from her confinement, determined not to spend her days behind locked doors with the new baby. Parturition had endowed her with fresh courage and strength. So she strolled out on the veranda whenever her legs felt like stretching or her lungs longed for fresh air. Even at eleven o'clock she emerged undaunted.

Khorshedbai was not impressed by this new show of defiance. She continued to scatter and toss and sprinkle; the veranda, after all, was for common use as per the sub-tenancy agreement. But she was careful to skirt Kashmira's immediate vicinity.

One morning, after Boman had left for work, Kashmira heard the soft, single flap of envelopes alighting on the veranda. The postman. She went to pick up the letters and stood scanning them: the ones for the paying guests landed back on the floor.

Then Najamai passed by in the compound and beckoned her out.

It was this gesture of Najamai's, innocent and friendly, that was responsible for changing the tide of the neighbours' apathy. Hers was the credit for the events now to follow, which would make them all eager to bear witness, but for which there would be no need because that single beckon in itself would get rid of the paying guests.

The gesture, potent as it turned out to be, would have been useless if Kashmira had elected not to go outside. Or if she had gone outside but returned quickly. Or if she had gone outside with the baby. Fortunately, none of these things happened.

Was there any little item, Najamai asked, that she could get for her while she was out shopping? Kashmira said thanks, but Boman usually got all they needed on his way home from work in the evening. What a good husband, said Najamai, then inquired about the new baby, and if there was any change in the madwoman's behaviour because of the baby. None, said Kashmira, and she would rather die than let the lunatic's shadow even fall upon the little one.

They stood by the steps of B Block, talking thus for some minutes: the precise number of minutes, as it turned out, that were required for the events (triggered by the beckoning arm) to gather momentum.

When Kashmira returned inside, the first thing she saw was the baby's cot: empty. A vague fear of this sort of thing always used to lurk inside her. But she had managed to keep it bottled away under control in a remote part of her mind.

Now it escaped its bounds and pounded in her head, pumped through her veins and arteries, filled her lungs and the pit of her stomach. It felt ice-cold as it made its way. Call Boman, call the police, call for help, the fear screamed inside her, while the place where it used to be bottled up said stay calm, think clearly, take a deep breath. She rushed out to the veranda, willing to consider absurd possibilities: maybe the baby was precocious, already knew how to crawl, had crawled away, swaddling clothes and all, and was hiding somewhere.

While she dashed from room to veranda and veranda to room, a soft whimpering penetrated her panic. It came from Khorshedbai's quarters. The door was ajar, and she peered inside. Uncertain of what she was seeing, she opened the door to let in more light from the veranda, then screamed, just once: a loud piercing scream. Behind it was gathered the combined force of the ice-cold fear and the place where the fear used to be bottled up.

Unaware of what her beckoning arm had precipitated, Najamai was almost at the end of the compound. She heard the scream and retrieved her steps. By then, Kashmira was yelling for assistance to any kind soul who could hear to come and save her child. Najamai repeated the cry for help outside C Block as she hurried towards B.

And help arrived within seconds. Later, Najamai would go over the list with Kashmira; from this day forward, in Najamai's eyes the Baag had only two kinds of Parsis: the ones who had been shameless enough to ignore the call for help and the ones who had responded. Among the latter were retired Nariman Hansotia who was just stepping out to drive to the library, his wife Hirabai, Mrs Karani from upstairs with Jaakaylee in tow, Mrs Bulsara wearing her *mathoobanoo*, Mrs Boyce, the spinster Tehmina in slippers and duster-coat, the watchman from his post at the compound gate — Najamai would remember them all, what they said, how they behaved, what they were wearing.

The hastily marshalled column entered the veranda with Najamai at its head, and stopped at the paying guests' door. The screaming had emptied Kashmira of all words. She pointed within, propping herself up against the doorjamb.

Inside, Khorshedbai was leaning over the locked parrot cage. She seemed to have noticed no part of the commotion. The neighbours looked with curiosity that turned to horror as soon as their eyes adjusted to Khorshedbai's dim room. There was a lull in the noise and confusion, a stunned silence for moments, during which the bangles on Khorshedbai's wrists could be heard tinkling.

Ardesar sat on a chair with his face hidden in his hands. He was shaking visibly. The baby, liberated from the swaddling clothes, was inside the cage. Intermittent whistling came from Khorshedbai, mixed with soft kissing sounds or a series of rapid little clicks with tongue against palate. From her fingers she teasingly dangled two green peppers, long and thin, over the baby's face.

Squatter

Squatter

Whenever Nariman Hansotia returned in the evening from the Cawasji Framji Memorial Library in a good mood the signs were plainly evident.

First, he parked his 1932 Mercedes-Benz (he called it the apple of his eye) outside A Block, directly in front of his ground-floor veranda window, and beeped the horn three long times. It annoyed Rustomji who also had a ground-floor flat in A Block. Ever since he had defied Nariman in the matter of painting the exterior of the building, Rustomji was convinced that nothing the old coot did was untainted by the thought of vengeance and harassment, his retirement pastime.

But the beeping was merely Nariman's signal to let Hirabai inside know that though he was back he would not step indoors for a while. Then he raised the hood, whistling "Rose Marie," and leaned his tall frame over the engine. He checked the oil, wiped here and there with a rag, tightened the radiator cap, and lowered the hood. Finally, he polished the Mercedes star and let the whistling modulate into the march from *The Bridge On The River Kwai*. The boys playing in the compound knew that Nariman was ready now to tell a story. They started to gather round.

"*Sahibji*, Nariman Uncle," someone said tentatively and Nariman nodded, careful not to lose his whistle, his bulbous nose flaring slightly. The pursed lips had temporarily raised and reshaped his Clark Gable moustache. More boys walked up. One called out, "How about a story, Nariman Uncle?" at which point Nariman's eyes began to twinkle, and he imparted increased energy to the polishing. The cry was taken up by others, "Yes, yes, Nariman Uncle, a story!" He swung into a final verse of the march. Then the lips relinquished the whistle, the Clark Gable moustache descended. The rag was put away, and he began.

"You boys know the great cricketers: Contractor, Polly Umrigar, and recently, the young chap, Farokh Engineer. Cricket *aficionados*, that's what you all are." Nariman liked to use new words, especially big ones, in the stories he told, believing it was his duty to expose young minds to as shimmering and varied a vocabulary as possible; if they could not spend their days at the Cawasji Framji Memorial Library then he, at least, could carry bits of the library out to them.

The boys nodded; the names of the cricketers were familiar.

"But does any one know about Savukshaw, the greatest of them all?" They shook their heads in unison.

"This, then, is the story about Savukshaw, how he saved the Indian team from a humiliating defeat when they were touring in England." Nariman sat on the steps of A Block. The few diehards who had continued with their games could not resist any longer when they saw the gathering circle, and ran up to listen. They asked their neighbours in whispers what the story was about, and were told: Savukshaw the greatest cricketer. The whispering died down and Nariman began.

"The Indian team was to play the indomitable MCC as part of its tour of England. Contractor was our captain. Now the MCC being the strongest team they had to face, Contractor was almost certain of defeat. To add to Contractor's troubles, one of his star batsmen, Nadkarni, had caught influenza early in the tour, and would definitely not be well enough to play against the MCC. By the way, does anyone know what those letters stand for? You, Kersi, you wanted to be a cricketer once."

Kersi shook his head. None of the boys knew, even though they had heard the MCC mentioned in radio commentaries, because the full name was hardly ever used.

Then Jehangir Bulsara spoke up, or Bulsara Bookworm, as the boys called him. The name given by Pesi *paadmaroo* had stuck even though it was now more than four years since Pesi had been sent away to boarding-school, and over two years since the death of Dr Mody. Jehangir was still unliked by the boys in the Baag, though they had come to accept his aloofness and respect his knowledge and intellect. They were not surprised that he knew the answer to Nariman's question: "Marylebone Cricket Club."

"Absolutely correct," said Nariman, and continued with the story. "The MCC won the toss and elected to bat. They scored four hundred and ninety-seven runs in the first inning before our spinners could get them out. Early in the second day's play our team was dismissed for one hundred and nine runs, and the extra who had taken Nadkarni's place was injured by a vicious bumper that opened a gash on his forehead." Nariman indicated the spot and the length of the gash on his furrowed brow. "Contractor's worst fears were coming true. The MCC waived their own second inning and gave the Indian team a follow-on, wanting to inflict an inning's defeat. And this time he had to use the second extra. The second extra was a certain Savukshaw."

The younger boys listened attentively; some of them, like the two sons of the chartered accountant in B Block, had only recently been deemed old enough by their parents to come out and play in the compound, and had not received any exposure to Nariman's stories. But the others like Jehangir, Kersi, and Viraf were familiar with Nariman's technique.

Once, Jehangir had overheard them discussing Nariman's stories, and he could not help expressing his opinion: that unpredictability was the brush he used to paint his tales with, and ambiguity the palette he mixed his colours in. The others looked at him with admiration. Then Viraf asked what exactly he meant by that. Jehangir said that Nariman sometimes told a funny incident in a very serious way, or expressed a significant matter in a light and playful manner. And these were only two rough divisions, in between were lots of subtle gradations of tone and texture. Which, then, was the funny story and which the serious? Their opinions were divided, but ultimately, said Jehangir, it was up to the listener to decide.

"So," continued Nariman, "Contractor first sent out his two regular openers, convinced that it was all hopeless. But after five wickets were lost for just another thirty-eight runs, out came Savukshaw the extra. Nothing mattered any more."

The street lights outside the compound came on, illuminating the iron gate where the watchman stood. It was a load off the watchman's mind when Nariman told a story. It meant an early end to the hectic vigil during which he had to ensure that none of the children ran out on the main road, or tried to jump over the wall. For although keeping out riff-raff was his duty, keeping in the boys was as important if he wanted to retain the job.

"The first ball Savukshaw faced was wide outside the off stump. He just lifted his bat and ignored it. But with what style! What panache! As if to say, come on, you blighters, play some polished cricket. The next ball was also wide, but not as much as the first. It missed the off stump narrowly. Again Savukshaw lifted his bat, boredom written all over him. Everyone was now watching closely. The bowler was annoyed by Savukshaw's arrogance, and the third delivery was a vicious fast pitch, right down on the middle stump.

"Savukshaw was ready, quick as lightning. No one even saw the stroke of his bat, but the ball went like a bullet towards square leg.

"Fielding at square leg was a giant of a fellow, about six feet seven, weighing two hundred and fifty pounds, a veritable Brobdingnagian, with arms like branches and hands like a pair of huge *sapaat*, the kind that Dr Mody used to wear, you remember what big feet Dr Mody had." Jehangir was the only one who did; he nodded. "Just to see him standing there was scary. Not one ball had got past him, and he had taken some great catches. Savukshaw purposely aimed his shot right at him. But he was as quick as Savukshaw, and stuck out his huge *sapaat* of a hand to stop the ball. What do you think happened then, boys?"

The older boys knew what Nariman wanted to hear at this point. They asked, "What happened, Nariman Uncle, what happened?" Satisfied, Nariman continued.

"A howl is what happened. A howl from the giant fielder, a howl that rang through the entire stadium, that soared like the cry of a banshee right up to the cheapest seats in the furthest, highest corners, a howl that echoed from the scoreboard and into the pavilion, into the kitchen, startling the chap inside who was preparing tea and scones for after the match, who spilled boiling water all over himself and was severely hurt. But not nearly as bad as the giant fielder at square leg. Never at any English stadium was a howl heard like that one, not in the whole history of cricket. And why do you think he was howling, boys?"

The chorus asked, "Why, Nariman Uncle, why?"

"Because of Savukshaw's bullet-like shot, of course. The hand he had reached out to stop it, he now held up for all to see, and *dhur-dhur, dhur-dhur* the blood was gushing like a fountain in an Italian piazza, like a burst water-main from the Vihar-Powai reservoir, dripping onto his shirt and his white pants, and sprinkling the green grass, and only because he was such a giant of a fellow could he suffer so much blood loss and not faint. But even he could not last forever; eventually, he felt dizzy, and was helped off the field. And where do you think the ball was, boys, that Savukshaw had smacked so hard?"

And the chorus rang out again on the now dark steps of A Block: "Where, Nariman Uncle, where?"

"Past the boundary line, of course. Lying near the fence. Rent asunder. Into two perfect leather hemispheres. All the stitches had ripped, and some of the insides had spilled out. So the umpires sent for a new one, and the game resumed. Now none of the fielders dared to touch any ball that Savukshaw hit. Every shot went to the boundary, all the way for four runs. Single-handedly, Savukshaw wiped out the deficit, and had it not been for loss of time due to rain, he would have taken the Indian team to a thumping victory against the MCC. As it was, the match ended in a draw."

Nariman was pleased with the awed faces of the youngest ones around him. Kersi and Viraf were grinning away and whispering something. From one of the flats the smell of frying fish swam out to explore the night air, and tickled Nariman's nostrils. He sniffed appreciatively, aware that it was in his good wife Hirabai's pan that the frying was taking place. This morning, he had seen the pomfret she had purchased at the door, waiting to be cleaned, its mouth open and eyes wide, like the eyes of some of these youngsters. It was time to wind up the story.

"The MCC will not forget the number of new balls they had to produce that day because of Savukshaw's deadly strokes. Their annual ball budget was thrown badly out of balance. Any other bat would have cracked under the strain, but Savukshaw's was seasoned with a special combination of oils, a secret formula given to him by a *sadhu* who had seen him one day playing cricket when he was a small boy. But Savukshaw used to say his real secret was practice, lots of practice, that was the advice he gave to any young lad who wanted to play cricket."

The story was now clearly finished, but none of the boys showed any sign of dispersing. "Tell us about more matches that Savukshaw played in," they said.

"More nothing. This was his greatest match. Anyway, he did not play cricket for long because soon after the match against the MCC he became a champion bicyclist, the fastest human on two wheels. And later, a pole-vaulter — when he glided over on his pole, so graceful, it was like watching a bird in flight. But he gave that up, too, and became a hunter, the mightiest hunter ever known, absolutely fearless, and so skilful, with a gun he could have, from the third floor of A Block, shaved the whisker of a cat in the backyard of C Block."

"Tell us about that," they said, "about Savukshaw the hunter!"

The fat ayah, Jaakaylee, arrived to take the chartered accountant's two children home. But they refused to go without hearing about Savukshaw the hunter. When she scolded them and things became a little hysterical, some other boys tried to resurrect the ghost she had once seen: "Ayah *bhoot!* Ayah *bhoot!*" Nariman raised a finger in warning — that subject was still taboo in Firozsha Baag; none of the adults was in a hurry to relive the wild and rampageous days that Pesi *paadmaroo* had ushered in, once upon a time, with the *bhoot* games.

Jaakaylee sat down, unwilling to return without the children, and whispered to Nariman to make it short. The smell of frying fish which had tickled Nariman's nostrils ventured into and awakened his stomach. But the story of Savukshaw the hunter was one he had wanted to tell for a long time.

"Savukshaw always went hunting alone, he preferred it that way. There are many incidents in the life of Savukshaw the hunter, but the one I am telling you about involves a terrifying situation. Terrifying for us, of course; Savukshaw was never terrified of anything. What happened was, one night he set up camp, started a fire and warmed up his bowl of chicken-*dhansaak*."

The frying fish had precipitated famishment upon Nariman, and the subject of chicken-*dhansaak* suited him well. His own mouth watering, he elaborated: "Mrs Savukshaw was as famous for her *dhansaak* as Mr was for hunting. She used to put in tamarind and brinjal, coriander and cumin, cloves and cinnamon, and dozens of other spices no one knows about. Women used to come from miles around to stand outside her window while she cooked it, to enjoy the fragrance and try to penetrate her secret, hoping to identify the ingredients as the aroma floated out, layer by layer, growing more complex and delicious. But always, the delectable fragrance enveloped the women and they just surrendered to the ecstasy, forgetting what they had come for. Mrs Savukshaw's secret was safe."

Jaakaylee motioned to Nariman to hurry up, it was past the children's dinner-time. He continued: "The aroma of savoury spices soon filled the night air in the jungle, and when the *dhansaak* was piping hot he started to eat, his rifle beside him. But as soon as he lifted the first morsel to his lips, a tiger's eyes flashed in the bushes! Not twelve feet from him! He emerged licking his chops! What do you think happened then, boys?"

"What, what, Nariman Uncle?"

Before he could tell them, the door of his flat opened. Hirabai put her head out and said, "*Chaalo ni*, Nariman, it's time. Then if it gets cold you won't like it."

That decided the matter. To let Hirabai's fried fish, crisp on the outside, yet tender and juicy inside, marinated in turmeric and cayenne — to let that get cold would be something that *Khoedaiji* above would not easily forgive. "Sorry boys, have to go. Next time about Savukshaw and the tiger."

There were some groans of disappointment. They hoped Nariman's good spirits would extend into the morrow when he returned from the Memorial Library, or the story would get cold.

But a whole week elapsed before Nariman again parked the apple of his eye outside his ground-floor flat and beeped the horn three times. When he had raised the hood, checked the oil, polished the star and swung into the "Colonel Boogie March," the boys began drifting towards A Block.

Some of them recalled the incomplete story of Savukshaw and the tiger, but they knew better than to remind him. It was never wise to prompt Nariman until he had dropped the first hint himself, or things would turn out badly.

Nariman inspected the faces: the two who stood at the back, always looking superior and wise, were missing. So was the quiet Bulsara boy, the intelligent one. "Call Kersi, Viraf, and Jehangir," he said, "I want them to listen to today's story."

Jehangir was sitting alone on the stone steps of C Block. The others were chatting by the compound gate with the watchman. Someone went to fetch them.

"Sorry to disturb your conference, boys, and your meditation, Jehangir," Nariman said facetiously, "but I thought you would like to hear this story. Especially since some of you are planning to go abroad."

This was not strictly accurate, but Kersi and Viraf did talk a lot about America and Canada. Kersi had started writing to universities there since his final high-school year, and had also sent letters of inquiry to the Canadian High Commission in New Delhi and to the U.S. Consulate at Breach Candy. But so far he had not made any progress. He and Viraf replied with as much sarcasm as their unripe years allowed, "Oh yes, next week, just have to pack our bags."

"Riiiight," drawled Nariman. Although he spoke perfect English, this was the one word with which he allowed himself sometimes to take liberties, indulging in a broadness of vowel more American than anything else. "But before we go on with today's story, what did you learn about Savukshaw, from last week's story?"

"That he was a very talented man," said someone.

"What else?"

"He was also a very lucky man, to have so many talents," said Viraf.

"Yes, but what else?"

There was silence for a few moments. Then Jehangir said, timidly: "He was a man searching for happiness, by trying all kinds of different things."

"Exactly! And he never found it. He kept looking for new experiences, and though he was very successful at everything he attempted, it did not bring him happiness. Remember this, success alone does not bring happiness. Nor does failure have to bring unhappiness. Keep it in mind when you listen to today's story."

A chant started somewhere in the back: "We-want-a-story! We-want-a-story!"

"Riiiight," said Nariman. "Now, everyone remembers Vera and Dolly, daughters of Najamai from C Block." There were whistles and hoots; Viraf nudged Kersi with his elbow, who was smiling wistfully. Nariman held up his hand: "Now now, boys, behave yourselves. Those two girls went abroad for studies many years ago, and never came back. They settled there happily.

"And like them, a fellow called Sarosh also went abroad, to Toronto, but did not find happiness there. This story is about him. You probably don't know him, he does not live in Firozsha Baag, though he is related to someone who does."

"Who? Who?"

"Curiosity killed the cat," said Nariman, running a finger over each branch of his moustache, "and what's important is the tale. So let us continue. This Sarosh began calling himself Sid after living in Toronto for a few months, but in our story he will be Sarosh and nothing but Sarosh, for that is his proper Parsi name. Besides, that was his own stipulation when he entrusted me with the sad but instructive chronicle of his recent life." Nariman polished his glasses with his handkerchief, put them on again, and began.

"At the point where our story commences, Sarosh had been living in Toronto for ten years. We find him depressed and miserable, perched on top of the toilet, crouching on his haunches, feet planted firmly for balance upon the white plastic oval of the toilet seat.

"Daily for a decade had Sarosh suffered this position. Morning after morning, he had no choice but to climb up and simulate the squat of our Indian latrines. If he sat down, no amount of exertion could produce success.

"At first, this inability was no more than mildly incommodious. As time went by, however, the frustrated attempts caused him grave anxiety. And when the failure stretched unbroken over ten years, it began to torment and haunt all his waking hours."

Some of the boys struggled hard to keep straight faces. They suspected that Nariman was not telling just a funny story, because if he intended them to laugh there was always some unmistakable way to let them know. Only the thought of displeasing Nariman and prematurely terminating the story kept their paroxysms of mirth from bursting forth unchecked.

Nariman continued: "You see, ten years was the time Sarosh had set himself to achieve complete adaptation to the new country. But how could he claim adaptation with any honesty if the acceptable catharsis continually failed to favour him? Obtaining his new citizenship had not helped either. He remained dependent on the old way, and this unalterable fact, strengthened afresh every morning of his life in the new country, suffocated him.

"The ten-year time limit was more an accident than anything else. But it hung over him with the awesome presence and sharpness of a guillotine. Careless words, boys, careless words in a moment of lightheartedness, as is so often the case with us all, had led to it.

"Ten years before, Sarosh had returned triumphantly to Bombay after fulfilling the immigration requirements of the Canadian High Commission in New Delhi. News of his imminent departure spread amongst relatives and friends. A farewell party was organized. In fact, it was given by his relatives in Firozsha Baag. Most of you will be too young to remember it, but it was a very loud party, went on till late in the night. Very lengthy and heated arguments took place, which is not the thing to do at a party. It started like this: Sarosh was told by some what a smart decision he had made, that his whole life would change for the better; others said he was making a mistake, emigration was all wrong, but if he wanted to be unhappy that was his business, they wished him well.

"By and by, after substantial amounts of Scotch and soda and rum and Coke had disappeared, a fierce debate started between the two groups. To this day Sarosh does not know what made him raise his glass and announce: 'My dear family, my dear friends, if I do not become completely Canadian in exactly ten years from the time I land there, then I will come back. I promise. So please, no more arguments. Enjoy the party.' His words were greeted with cheers and shouts of hear! hear! They told him never to fear embarrassment; there was no shame if he decided to return to the country of his birth.

"But shortly, his poor worried mother pulled him aside. She led him to the back room and withdrew her worn and aged prayer book from her purse, saying, 'I want you to place your hand upon the *Avesta* and swear that you will keep that promise.'

"He told her not to be silly, that it was just a joke. But she insisted: '*Kassum khà* — on the *Avesta*. One last thing for your mother. Who knows when you will see me again?' and her voice grew tremulous as it always did when she turned deeply emotional. Sarosh complied, and the prayer book was returned to her purse.

"His mother continued: 'It is better to live in want among your family and your friends, who love you and care for you, than to be unhappy surrounded by vacuum cleaners and dishwashers and big shiny motor cars.' She hugged him. Then they joined the celebration in progress.

"And Sarosh's careless words spoken at the party gradually forged themselves into a commitment as much to himself as to his mother and the others. It stayed with him all his years in the new land, reminding him every morning of what must happen at the end of the tenth, as it reminded him now while he descended from his perch."

Jehangir wished the titters and chortles around him would settle down, he found them annoying. When Nariman structured his sentences so carefully and chose his words with extreme care as he was doing now, Jehangir found it most pleasurable to listen. Sometimes, he remembered certain words Nariman had used, or combinations of words, and repeated them to himself, enjoying again the beauty of their sounds when he went for his walks to the Hanging Gardens or was sitting alone on the stone steps of C Block. Mumbling to himself did nothing to mitigate the isolation which the other boys in the Baag had dropped around him like a heavy cloak, but he had grown used to all that by now.

Nariman continued: "In his own apartment Sarosh squatted

barefoot. Elsewhere, if he had to go with his shoes on, he would carefully cover the seat with toilet paper before climbing up. He learnt to do this after the first time, when his shoes had left telltale footprints on the seat. He had had to clean it with a wet paper towel. Luckily, no one had seen him.

"But there was not much he could keep secret about his ways. The world of washrooms is private and at the same time very public. The absence of feet below the stall door, the smell of faeces, the rustle of paper, glimpses caught through the narrow crack between stall door and jamb — all these added up to only one thing: a foreign presence in the stall, not doing things in the conventional way. And if the one outside could receive the fetor of Sarosh's business wafting through the door, poor unhappy Sarosh too could detect something malodorous in the air: the presence of xenophobia and hostility."

What a feast, thought Jehangir, what a feast of words! This would be the finest story Nariman had ever told, he just knew it.

"But Sarosh did not give up trying. Each morning he seated himself to push and grunt, grunt and push, squirming and writhing unavailingly on the white plastic oval. Exhausted, he then hopped up, expert at balancing now, and completed the movement quite effortlessly.

"The long morning hours in the washroom created new difficulties. He was late going to work on several occasions, and one such day, the supervisor called him in: 'Here's your timesheet for this month. You've been late eleven times. What's the problem?' "

Here, Nariman stopped because his neighbour Rustomji's door creaked open. Rustomji peered out, scowling, and muttered: "*Saala* loafers, sitting all evening outside people's houses, making a nuisance, and being encouraged by grownups at that."

He stood there a moment longer, fingering the greying chest hair that was easily accessible through his *sudra*, then went inside. The boys immediately took up a soft and low chant: "Rustomji-the-curmudgeon! Rustomji-the-curmudgeon!"

Nariman help up his hand disapprovingly. But secretly, he was pleased that the name was still popular, the name he had given Rustomji when the latter had refused to pay his share for painting the building. "Quiet, quiet!" said he. "Do you want me to continue or not?"

"Yes, yes!" The chanting died away, and Nariman resumed the story.

"So Sarosh was told by his supervisor that he was coming late to work too often. What could poor Sarosh say?"

"What, Nariman Uncle?" rose the refrain.

"Nothing, of course. The supervisor, noting his silence, continued: 'If it keeps up, the consequences could be serious as far as your career is concerned.'

"Sarosh decided to speak. He said embarrassedly, 'It's a different kind of problem. I…I don't know how to explain…it's an immigration-related problem.'

"Now this supervisor must have had experience with other immigrants, because right away he told Sarosh, 'No problem. Just contact your Immigrant Aid Society. They should be able to help you. Every ethnic group has one: Vietnamese, Chinese — I'm certain that one exists for Indians. If you need time off to go there, no problem. That can be arranged, no problem. As long as you do something about your lateness, there's no problem.' That's the way they talk over there, nothing is ever a problem.

"So Sarosh thanked him and went to his desk. For the umpteenth time he bitterly rued his oversight. Could fate have plotted it, concealing the western toilet behind that shroud of anxieties which had appeared out of nowhere to beset him just before he left India? After all, he had readied himself meticulously for the new life. Even for the great, merciless Canadian cold he had heard so much about. How could he have overlooked preparation for the western toilet with its matutinal demands unless fate had conspired? In Bombay, you know that offices of foreign businesses offer both options in their bathrooms. So do all hotels with three stars or more. By practising in familiar surroundings, Sarosh was convinced he could have mastered a seated evacuation before departure.

"But perhaps there was something in what the supervisor said. Sarosh found a telephone number for the Indian Immigrant Aid Society and made an appointment. That afternoon, he met Mrs Maha-Lepate at the Society's office."

Kersi and Viraf looked at each other and smiled. Nariman Uncle had a nerve, there was more *lepate* in his own stories than any-where else.

"Mrs Maha-Lepate was very understanding, and made Sarosh feel at ease despite the very personal nature of his problem. She said, 'Yes, we get many referrals. There was a man here last month who couldn't eat Wonder Bread — it made him throw up.'

"By the way, boys, Wonder Bread is a Canadian bread which all happy families eat to be happy in the same way; the unhappy families are unhappy in their own fashion by eating other brands." Jehangir was the only one who understood, and murmured: "Tolstoy," at Nariman's little joke. Nariman noticed it, pleased. He continued.

"Mrs Maha-Lepate told Sarosh about that case: 'Our immigrant specialist, Dr No-Ilaaz, recommended that the patient eat cake instead. He explained that Wonder Bread caused vomiting because the digestive system was used to Indian bread only, made with Indian flour in the village he came from. However, since his system was unfamiliar with cake, Canadian or otherwise, it did not react but was digested as a newfound food. In this way he got used to Canadian flour first in cake form. Just yesterday we received a report from Dr No-Ilaaz. The patient successfully ate his first slice of whole-wheat Wonder Bread with no ill effects. The ultimate goal is pure white Wonder Bread.'

"Like a polite Parsi boy, Sarosh said, 'That's very interesting.' The garrulous Mrs Maha-Lepate was about to continue, and he tried to interject: 'But I — ' but Mrs Maha-Lepate was too quick for him: 'Oh, there are so many interesting cases I could tell you about. Like the woman from Sri Lanka — referred to us because they don't have their own Society — who could not drink the water here. Dr No-Ilaaz said it was due to the different mineral content. So he started her on Coca-Cola and then began diluting it with water, bit by bit. Six weeks later she took her first sip of unadulterated Cana-dian water and managed to keep it down.'

"Sarosh could not halt Mrs Maha-Lepate as she launched from one case history into another: 'Right now, Dr No-Ilaaz is working on a very unusual case. Involves a whole Pakistani family. Ever since immigrating to Canada, none of them can swallow. They choke on their own saliva, and have to spit constantly. But we are confident that Dr No-Ilaaz will find a remedy. He has never been stumped by any immigrant problem. Besides, we have an information network with other third-world Immigrant Aid Societies. We all seem to share a history of similar maladies, and regularly compare notes. Some of us thought these problems were linked to retention of original citizenship. But this was a false lead.'

"Sarosh, out of his own experience, vigorously nodded agreement. By now he was truly fascinated by Mrs Maha-Lepate's wealth of information. Reluctantly, he interrupted: 'But will Dr No-Ilaaz be able to solve my problem?'

" 'I have every confidence that he will,' replied Mrs Maha-Lepate in great earnest. 'And if he has no remedy for you right away, he will be delighted to start working on one. He loves to take up new projects.' "

Nariman halted to blow his nose, and a clear shrill voice travelled the night air of the Firozsha Baag compound from C Block to where the boys had collected around Nariman in A Block: "Jehangoo! O Jehangoo! Eight o'clock! Upstairs now!"

Jehangir stared at his feet in embarrassment. Nariman looked at his watch and said, "Yes, it's eight." But Jehangir did not move, so he continued.

"Mrs Maha-Lepate was able to arrange an appointment while Sarosh waited, and he went directly to the doctor's office. What he had heard so far sounded quite promising. Then he cautioned himself not to get overly optimistic, that was the worst mistake he could make. But along the way to the doctor's, he could not help thinking what a lovely city Toronto was. It was the same way he had felt when he first saw it ten years ago, before all the joy had dissolved in the acid of his anxieties."

Once again that shrill voice travelled through the clear night: "*Arré* Jehangoo! *Muà*, do I have to come down and drag you upstairs!"

Jehangir's mortification was now complete. Nariman made it easy for him, though: "The first part of the story is over. Second part continues tomorrow. Same time, same place." The boys were surprised, Nariman did not make such commitments. But never before had he told such a long story. They began drifting back to their homes.

As Jehangir strode hurriedly to C Block, falsettos and piercing shrieks followed him in the darkness: "*Arré* Jehangoo! *Muà* Jehangoo! Bulsara Bookworm! Eight o'clock Jehangoo!" Shaking his head, Nariman went indoors to Hirabai.

Next evening, the story punctually resumed when Nariman took his place on the topmost step of A Block: "You remember that we left Sarosh on his way to see the Immigrant Aid Society's doctor. Well, Dr No-Ilaaz listened patiently to Sarosh's concerns, then said, 'As a matter of fact, there is a remedy which is so new even the IAS does not know about it. Not even that Mrs Maha-Lepate who knows it all,' he added drolly, twirling his stethoscope like a stunted lasso. He slipped it on around his neck before continuing: 'It involves a minor operation which was developed with financial assistance from the Multicultural Department. A small device, *Crappus Non Interruptus*, or CNI as we call it, is implanted in the bowel. The device is controlled by an external handheld transmitter similar to the ones used for automatic garage door-openers — you may have seen them in hardware stores.' "

Nariman noticed that most of the boys wore puzzled looks and realized he had to make some things clearer. "The Multicultural Department is a Canadian invention. It is supposed to ensure that ethnic cultures are able to flourish, so that Canadian society will consist of a mosaic of cultures — that's their favourite word, mosaic — instead of one uniform mix, like the American melting pot. If you ask me, mosaic and melting pot are both nonsense, and ethnic is a polite way of saying bloody foreigner. But anyway, you understand Multicultural Department? Good. So Sarosh nodded, and Dr No-Ilaaz went on: 'You can encode the handheld transmitter with a personal ten-digit code. Then all you do is position yourself on the toilet seat and activate your transmitter. Just like a garage door, your bowel will open without pushing or grunting.' "

There was some snickering in the audience, and Nariman raised his eyebrows, whereupon they covered up their mouths with their hands. "The doctor asked Sarosh if he had any questions. Sarosh thought for a moment, then asked if it required any maintenance.

"Dr No-Ilaaz replied: 'CNI is semi-permanent and operates on solar energy. Which means you would have to make it a point to get some sun periodically, or it would cease and lead to constipation.

However, you don't have to strip for a tan. Exposing ten percent of your skin surface once a week during summer will let the device store sufficient energy for year-round operation.'

"Sarosh's next question was: 'Is there any hope that someday the bowels can work on their own, without operating the device?' at which Dr No-Ilaaz grimly shook his head: 'I'm afraid not. You must think very, very carefully before making a decision. Once CNI is implanted, you can never pass a motion in the natural way — neither sitting nor squatting.'

"He stopped to allow Sarosh time to think it over, then continued: 'And you must understand what that means. You will never be able to live a normal life again. You will be permanently different from your family and friends because of this basic internal modification. In fact, in this country or that, it will set you apart from your fellow countrymen. So you must consider the whole thing most carefully.'

"Dr No-Ilaaz paused, toyed with his stethoscope, shuffled some papers on his desk, then resumed: 'There are other dangers you should know about. Just as a garage door can be accidentally opened by a neighbour's transmitter on the same frequency, CNI can also be activated by someone with similar apparatus.' To ease the tension he attempted a quick laugh and said, 'Very embarrassing, eh, if it happened at the wrong place and time. Mind you, the risk is not so great at present, because the chances of finding yourself within a fifty-foot radius of another transmitter on the same frequency are infinitesimal. But what about the future? What if CNI becomes very popular? Sufficient permutations may not be available for transmitter frequencies and you could be sharing the code with others. Then the risk of accidents becomes greater.' "

Something landed with a loud thud in the yard behind A Block, making Nariman startle. Immediately, a yowling and screeching and caterwauling went up from the stray cats there, and the *kuchrawalli*'s dog started barking. Some of the boys went around the side of A Block to peer over the fence into the backyard. But the commotion soon died down of its own accord. The boys returned and, once again, Nariman's voice was the only sound to be heard.

"By now, Sarosh was on the verge of deciding against the operation. Dr No-Ilaaz observed this and was pleased. He took pride in being able to dissuade his patients from following the very remedies which he first so painstakingly described. True to his name, Dr No-Ilaaz believed no remedy is the best remedy, rather than prescribing this-mycin and that-mycin for every little ailment. So he continued: 'And what about our sons and daughters? And the quality of their lives? We still don't know the long-term effects of CNI. Some researchers speculate that it could generate a genetic deficiency, that the offspring of a CNI parent would also require CNI. On the other hand, they could be perfectly healthy toilet seat-users, without any congenital defects. We just don't know at this stage.'

"Sarosh rose from his chair: 'Thank you very much for your time, Dr No-Ilaaz. But I don't think I want to take such a drastic step. As you suggest, I will think it over very carefully.'

" 'Good, good,' said Dr No-Ilaaz, 'I was hoping you would say that. There is one more thing. The operation is extremely expensive, and is not covered by the province's Health Insurance Plan. Many immigrant groups are lobbying to obtain coverage for special immigration-related health problems. If they succeed, then good for you.'

"Sarosh left Dr No-Ilaaz's office with his mind made up. Time was running out. There had been a time when it was perfectly natural to squat. Now it seemed a grotesquely aberrant thing to do. Wherever he went he was reminded of the ignominy of his way. If he could not be westernized in all respects, he was nothing but a failure in this land — a failure not just in the washrooms of the nation but everywhere. He knew what he must do if he was to be true to himself and to the decade-old commitment. So what do you think Sarosh did next?"

"What, Nariman Uncle?"

"He went to the travel agent specializing in tickets to India. He bought a fully refundable ticket to Bombay for the day when he would complete exactly ten immigrant years — if he succeeded even once before that day dawned, he would cancel the booking.

"The travel agent asked sympathetically, 'Trouble at home?' His name was Mr Rawaana, and he was from Bombay too.

" 'No,' said Sarosh, 'trouble in Toronto.'

" 'That's a shame,' said Mr Rawaana. 'I don't want to poke my nose into your business, but in my line of work I meet so many people who are going back to their homeland because of problems here. Sometimes I forget I'm a travel agent, that my interest is to convince them to travel. Instead, I tell them: don't give up, God is great, stay and try again. It's bad for my profits but gives me a different, a spiritual kind of satisfaction when I succeed. And I succeed about half the time. Which means,' he added with a wry laugh, 'I could double my profits if I minded my own business.'

"After the lengthy sessions with Mrs Maha-Lepate and Dr No-Ilaaz, Sarosh felt he had listened to enough advice and kind words. Much as he disliked doing it, he had to hurt Mr Rawaana's feelings and leave his predicament undiscussed: 'I'm sorry, but I'm in a hurry. Will you be able to look after the booking?'

" 'Well, okay,' said Mr Rawaana, a trifle crestfallen; he did not relish the travel business as much as he did counselling immigrants. 'Hope you solve your problem. I will be happy to refund your fare, believe me.'

"Sarosh hurried home. With only four weeks to departure, every spare minute, every possible method had to be concentrated on a final attempt at adaptation.

"He tried laxatives, crunching down the tablets with a prayer that these would assist the sitting position. Changing brands did not help, and neither did various types of suppositories. He spent long stretches on the toilet seat each morning. The supervisor continued to reprimand him for tardiness. To make matters worse, Sarosh left his desk every time he felt the slightest urge, hoping: maybe this time.

"The working hours expended in the washroom were noted with unflagging vigilance by the supervisor. More counselling sessions followed. Sarosh refused to extinguish his last hope, and the supervisor punctiliously recorded 'No Improvement' in his daily log. Finally, Sarosh was fired. It would soon have been time to resign in any case, and he could not care less.

"Now whole days went by seated on the toilet, and he stubbornly refused to relieve himself the other way. The doorbell would ring only to be ignored. The telephone went unanswered. Sometimes, he would awake suddenly in the dark hours before dawn and rush to the washroom like a madman."

Without warning, Rustomji flung open his door and stormed: "Ridiculous nonsense this is becoming! Two days in a row, whole Firozsha Baag gathers here! This is not Chaupatty beach, this is not a squatters' colony, this is a building, people want to live here in peace and quiet!" Then just as suddenly, he stamped inside and slammed the door. Right on cue, Nariman continued, before the boys could say anything.

"Time for meals was the only time Sarosh allowed himself off the seat. Even in his desperation he remembered that if he did not eat well, he was doomed — the downward pressure on his gut was essential if there was to be any chance of success.

"But the ineluctable day of departure dawned, with grey skies and the scent of rain, while success remained out of sight. At the airport Sarosh checked in and went to the dreary lounge. Out of sheer habit he started towards the washroom. Then he realized the hopelessness of it and returned to the cold, clammy plastic of the lounge seats. Airport seats are the same almost anywhere in the world.

"The boarding announcement was made, and Sarosh was the first to step onto the plane. The skies were darker now. Out of the window he saw a flash of lightning fork through the clouds. For some reason, everything he'd learned years ago in St Xavier's about sheet lightning and forked lightning went through his mind. He wished it would change to sheet, there was something sinister and unpropitious about forked lightning."

Kersi, absorbedly listening, began cracking his knuckles quite unconsciously. His childhood habit still persisted. Jehangir frowned at the disturbance, and Viraf nudged Kersi to stop it.

"Sarosh fastened his seat-belt and attempted to turn his thoughts towards the long journey home: to the questions he would be expected to answer, the sympathy and criticism that would be thrust upon him. But what remained uppermost in his mind was the present moment — him in the plane, dark skies lowering, lightning on the horizon — irrevocably spelling out: defeat.

"But wait. Something else was happening now. A tiny rumble. Inside him. Or was it his imagination? Was it really thunder out-side which, in his present disoriented state, he was internalizing? No, there it was again. He had to go.

"He reached the washroom, and almost immediately the sign flashed to 'Please return to seat and fasten seat-belts.' Sarosh debated whether to squat and finish the business quickly, abandoning the perfunctory seated attempt. But the plane started to move and that decided him; it would be difficult now to balance while squatting.

"He pushed. The plane continued to move. He pushed again, trembling with the effort. The seat-belt sign flashed quicker and brighter now. The plane moved faster and faster. And Sarosh pushed hard, harder than he had ever pushed before, harder than in all his ten years of trying in the new land. And the memories of Bombay, the immigration interview in New Delhi, the farewell party, his mother's tattered prayer book, all these, of their own accord, emerged from beyond the region of the ten years to push with him and give him newfound strength."

Nariman paused and cleared his throat. Dusk was falling, and the frequency of B.E.S.T. buses plying the main road outside Firozsha Baag had dropped. Bats began to fly madly from one end of the compound to the other, silent shadows engaged in endless laps over the buildings.

"With a thunderous clap the rain started to fall. Sarosh felt a splash under him. Could it really be? He glanced down to make certain. Yes, it was. He had succeeded!

"But was it already too late? The plane waited at its assigned position on the runway, jet engines at full thrust. Rain was falling in torrents and takeoff could be delayed. Perhaps even now they would allow him to cancel his flight, to disembark. He lurched out of the constricting cubicle.

"A stewardess hurried towards him: 'Excuse me, sir, but you must return to your seat immediately and fasten your belt.'

" 'You don't understand!' Sarosh shouted excitedly. 'I must get off the plane! Everything is all right, I don't have to go any more...'

" 'That's impossible, sir!' said the stewardess, aghast. 'No one can leave now. Takeoff procedures are in progress!' The wild look in his sleepless eyes, and the dark rings around them scared her. She beckoned for help.

"Sarosh continued to argue, and a steward and the chief stewardess hurried over: 'What seems to be the problem, sir? You *must* resume your seat. We are authorized, if necessary, to forcibly restrain you, sir.'

"The plane began to move again, and suddenly Sarosh felt all the urgency leaving him. His feverish mind, the product of nightmarish days and torturous nights, was filled again with the calm which had fled a decade ago, and he spoke softly now: 'That…that will not be necessary…it's okay, I understand.' He readily returned to his seat.

"As the aircraft sped down the runway, Sarosh's first reaction was one of joy. The process of adaptation was complete. But later, he could not help wondering if success came before or after the ten-year limit had expired. And since he had already passed through the customs and security check, was he really an immigrant in every sense of the word at the moment of achievement?

"But such questions were merely academic. Or were they? He could not decide. If he returned, what would it be like? Ten years ago, the immigration officer who had stamped his passport had said, 'Welcome to Canada.' It was one of Sarosh's dearest memories, and thinking of it, he fell asleep.

"The plane was flying above the rainclouds. Sunshine streamed into the cabin. A few raindrops were still clinging miraculously to the windows, reminders of what was happening below. They sparkled as the sunlight caught them."

Some of the boys made as if to leave, thinking the story was finally over. Clearly, they had not found this one as interesting as the others Nariman had told. What dolts, thought Jehangir, they cannot recognize a masterpiece when they hear one. Nariman motioned with his hand for silence.

"But our story does not end there. There was a welcome-home party for Sarosh a few days after he arrived in Bombay. It was not in Firozsha Baag this time because his relatives in the Baag had a serious sickness in the house. But I was invited to it anyway. Sarosh's family and friends were considerate enough to wait till the jet lag had worked its way out of his system. They wanted him to really enjoy this one.

"Drinks began to flow freely again in his honour: Scotch and soda, rum and Coke, brandy. Sarosh noticed that during his absence all the brand names had changed — the labels were different and unfamiliar. Even for the mixes. Instead of Coke there was Thums-Up, and he remembered reading in the papers about Coca-Cola being kicked out by the Indian Government for refusing to reveal their secret formula.

"People slapped him on the back and shook his hand vigorously, over and over, right through the evening. They said: 'Telling the truth, you made the right decision, look how happy your mother is to live to see this day;' or they asked: 'Well, bossy, what changed your mind?' Sarosh smiled and nodded his way through it all, passing around Canadian currency at the insistence of some of the curious ones who, egged on by his mother, also pestered him to display his Canadian passport and citizenship card. She had been badgering him since his arrival to tell her the real reason: '*Saachoo kahé*, what brought you back?' and was hoping that tonight, among his friends, he might raise his glass and reveal something. But she remained disappointed.

"Weeks went by and Sarosh found himself desperately searching for his old place in the pattern of life he had vacated ten years ago. Friends who had organized the welcome-home party gradually disappeared. He went walking in the evenings along Marine Drive, by the sea-wall, where the old crowd used to congregate. But the people who sat on the parapet while waves crashed behind their backs were strangers. The tetrapods were still there, staunchly protecting the reclaimed land from the fury of the sea. He had watched as a kid when cranes had lowered these cement and concrete hulks of respectable grey into the water. They were grimy black now, and from their angularities rose the distinct stench of human excrement. The old pattern was never found by Sarosh; he searched in vain. Patterns of life are selfish and unforgiving.

"Then one day, as I was driving past Marine Drive, I saw some-one sitting alone. He looked familiar, so I stopped. For a moment I did not recognize Sarosh, so forlorn and woebegone was his countenance. I parked the apple of my eye and went to him, saying, 'Hullo, Sid, what are you doing here on your lonesome?' And he said, 'No no! No more Sid, please, that name reminds me of all my troubles.' Then, on the parapet at Marine Drive, he told me his unhappy and wretched tale, with the waves battering away at the tetrapods, and around us the hawkers screaming about coconut-water and sugar-cane juice and *paan*.

"When he finished, he said that he had related to me the whole sad saga because he knew how I told stories to boys in the Baag, and he wanted me to tell this one, especially to those who were planning to go abroad. 'Tell them,' said Sarosh, 'that the world can be a bewildering place, and dreams and ambitions are often paths to the most pernicious of traps.' As he spoke, I could see that Sarosh was somewhere far away, perhaps in New Delhi at his immigration interview, seeing himself as he was then, with what he thought was a life of hope and promise stretching endlessly before him. Poor Sarosh. Then he was back beside me on the parapet.

" 'I pray you, in your stories,' said Sarosh, his old sense of humour returning as he deepened his voice for his favourite *Othello* lines" — and here, Nariman produced a basso profundo of his own — " 'When you shall these unlucky deeds relate, speak of me as I am; nothing extenuate, nor set down aught in malice: tell them that in Toronto once there lived a Parsi boy as best as he could. Set you down this; and say, besides, that for some it was good and for some it was bad, but for me life in the land of milk and honey was just a pain in the posterior.' "

And now, Nariman allowed his low-pitched rumbles to turn into chuckles. The boys broke into cheers and loud applause and cries of "Encore!" and "More!" Finally, Nariman had to silence them by pointing warningly at Rustomji-the-curmudgeon's door.

While Kersi and Viraf were joking and wondering what to make of it all, Jehangir edged forward and told Nariman this was the best story he had ever told. Nariman patted his shoulder and smiled. Jehangir left, wondering if Nariman would have been as popular if Dr Mody was still alive. Probably, since the two were liked for different reasons: Dr Mody used to be constantly jovial, whereas Nariman had his periodic story-telling urges.

Now the group of boys who had really enjoyed the Savukshaw story during the previous week spoke up. Capitalizing on Nariman's extraordinarily good mood, they began clamouring for more Savukshaw: "Nariman Uncle, tell the one about Savukshaw the hunter, the one you had started that day."

"What hunter? I don't know which one you mean." He refused to be reminded of it, and got up to leave. But there was loud protest, and the boys started chanting, "We-want-Savukshaw! We-want-Savukshaw!"

Nariman looked fearfully towards Rustomji's door and held up his hands placatingly: "All right, all right! Next time it will be Savukshaw again. Savukshaw the artist. The story of the Parsi Picasso."

Lend Me
Your Light

Lend Me
Your Light

…your lights are all lit — then where do you go with your lamp?
My house is all dark and lonesome, — lend me your light.

Rabindranath Tagore
Gitanjali

We both left Bombay the same year. Jamshed first, for New York, then I, for Toronto. As immigrants in North America, sharing this common experience should have salvaged something from our acquaintanceship. It went back such a long way, to our school days at St Xavier's.

To sustain an acquaintance does not take very much. A friendship, that's another thing. Strange, then, that it has ended so completely, that he has erased himself out of our lives, mine and Percy's; now I cannot imagine him even as a mere bit player who fills out the action or swells a procession.

Jamshed was my brother's friend. The three of us went to the same school. Jamshed and my brother, Percy, both four years older than I, were in the same class, and spent their time together. They had to part company during lunch, though, because Jamshed did not eat where Percy and I did, in the school's drillhall-cum-lunchroom.

The tiffin carriers would stagger into the school compound with their long, narrow rickety crates balanced on their heads, each with fifty tiffin boxes, delivering lunches from homes in all corners of the city. When the boxes were unpacked, the drillhall would be filled with a smell that is hard to forget, thick as swill, while the individual aromas of four hundred steaming lunches started to mingle. The smell must have soaked into the very walls and ceiling, there to age and rancidify. No matter what the hour of the day, that hot and dank grotto of a drillhall smelled stale and sickly, the way a vomit-splashed room does even after it is cleaned up.

Jamshed did not eat in this crammed and cavernous interior. Not for him the air redolent of nauseous odours. His food arrived precisely at one o'clock in the chauffeur-driven, air-conditioned family car, and was eaten in the leather-upholstered luxury of the back seat, amidst his collection of hyphenated lavishness.

In the snug dining-room where chauffeur doubled as waiter, Jamshed lunched through his school-days, safe from the vicissitudes of climate. The monsoon might drench the tiffin carriers to the bone and turn cold the boxes of four hundred waiting schoolboys, but it could not touch Jamshed or his lunch. The tiffin carriers might arrive glistening and stinking of sweat in the hot season, with scorching hot tiffin boxes, hotter than they'd left the kitchens of Bombay, but Jamshed's lunch remained unaffected.

During the years of high school, my brother, Percy, began spending many weekend afternoons at his friend's house at Malabar Hill. Formerly, these were the afternoons when we used to join Pesi *paadmaroo* and the others for our most riotous times in the compound, the afternoons that the adults of Firozsha Baag would await with dread, not knowing what new terrors Pesi had devised to unleash upon the innocent and the unsuspecting.

But Percy dropped all this for Jamshed's company. And when he returned from his visits, Mummy would commence the questioning: What did they eat? Was Jamshed's mother home? What did the two do all afternoon? Did they go out anywhere? And so on.

Percy did not confide in me very much in those days. Our lives intersected during the lunch routine only, which counted for very little. For a short while we had played cricket together with the boys of Firozsha Baag. Then he lost interest in that too. He refused to come when Daddy would take the whole gang to the Marine **Dri** *maidaan* on Sunday mornings. And soon, like all younger brothe ⌐, I was seen mainly as a nuisance.

But my curiosity about Percy and Jamshed was satisfied by Mummy's interrogations. I knew that the afternoons were usually spent making model airplanes and listening to music. The airplanes were simple gliders in the early years; the records, mostly Mantovani and from Broadway shows. Later came more complex models with gasoline engines and remote control, and classical music from Bach to Poulenc.

The model-airplane kits were gifts from Jamshed's itinerant aunties and uncles, purchased during business trips to England or the U.S. Everyone except my brother and I seemed to have uncles and aunties smitten by wanderlust, and Jamshed's supply line from the western world guaranteed for him a steady diet of foreign clothes, shoes, and records.

One Saturday, Percy reported during question period that Jamshed had received the original soundtrack of *My Fair Lady.* This was sensational news. The LP was not available in Bombay, and a few privately imported or "smuggled" copies, brought in by people like Jamshed's relatives, were selling in the black market for two hundred rupees. I had seen the records displayed side by side with foreign perfumes, chocolates, and cheeses at the pavement stalls of smugglers along Flora Fountain.

Sometimes, these stalls were smashed up during police raids. I liked to imagine that one day a raid would occur as I was passing, and in the mêlée and chaos of the clash, *My Fair Lady* would fly through the air and land at my feet, unnoticed by anyone. Of course, there wasn't much I could have done with it following the miracle, because our old gramophone played only 78 rpms.

After strenuous negotiations in which Mummy, Percy, and I exhausted ourselves, Percy agreed to ask his friend if I could listen to the album. Arrangements were made. And the following Saturday we set off for Jamshed's house. From Firozsha Baag, the direction of Malabar Hill was opposite to the one we took to go to school every morning, and I was not familiar with the roads the bus travelled. The building had a marble lobby, and the lift zoomed us up smoothly to the tenth floor before I had time to draw breath. I was about to tell Percy that we needed one like this in Firozsha Baag, but the door opened. Jamshed welcomed us graciously, then wasted no time in putting the record on the turntable. After all, that was what I had come for.

The afternoon dragged by after the sound-track finished. Bored, I watched them work on an airplane. The box said it was a Sopwith Camel. The name was familiar from the Biggles books Percy used to bring home. I picked up the lid and read dully that the aircraft had been designed by the British industrialist and aeronautical engineer, Thomas Octave Murdoch Sopwith, born 1888, and had been used during the First World War. Then followed a list of the parts.

Later, we had lunch, and they talked. I was merely the kid brother, and nobody expected me to do much else but listen. They talked of school and the school library, of all the books that the library badly needed; and of the *ghatis* who were flooding the school of late.

In the particular version of reality we inherited, *ghatis* were always flooding places, they never just went there. *Ghatis* were flooding the banks, desecrating the sanctity of institutions, and taking up all the coveted jobs. *Ghatis* were even flooding the colleges and universities, a thing unheard of. Wherever you turned, the bloody *ghatis* were flooding the place.

With much shame I remember this word *ghati*. A suppurating sore of a word, oozing the stench of bigotry. It consigned a whole race to the mute roles of coolies and menials, forever unredeemable.

During one of our rare vacations to Matheran, as a child, I watched with detachment while a straining coolie loaded the family's baggage on his person. The big metal trunk was placed flat on his head, with the leather suitcase over it. The enormous hold-all was slung on his left arm, which he raised to steady the load on his head, and the remaining suitcase went in the right hand. It was all accomplished with much the same approach and consideration used in loading a cart or barrow — the main thing was balance, to avoid tipping over. This skeletal man then tottered off towards the train that would transport us to the little hill station. There, similar skeletal beings would be waiting with rickshaws. Automobiles were prohibited in Matheran, to preserve the pastoral purity of the place and the livelihood of the rickshawallas.

Many years later I found myself at the same hill station, a member of my college hikers' club, labouring up its slopes with a knapsack. Automobiles were still not permitted in Matheran, and every time a rickshaw sped by in a flurry of legs and wheels, we'd yell at the occupant ensconced within: "Capitalist pig! You bastard! Stop riding on your brother's back!" The bewildered passenger would lean forward for a moment, not quite understanding, then fall back into the cushioned comfort of the rickshaw.

But this kind of smug socialism did not come till much later. First we had to reckon with school, school uniforms, brown paper covers for textbooks and exercise books, and the mad morning rush for the school bus. I remember how Percy used to rage and shout at our scrawny *ghaton* if the pathetic creature ever got in his way as she swept and mopped the floors. Mummy would proudly observe, "He has a temper just like Grandpa's." She would also discreetly admonish Percy, since this was in the days when it was becoming quite difficult to find a new *ghaton*, especially if the first one quit due to abuse from the scion of the family and established her reasons for quitting among her colleagues.

I was never sure why some people called them *ghatons* and others, *gungas*. I supposed the latter was intended to placate — the collective conferment of the name of India's sacred river balanced the occasions of harshness and ill-treatment. But the good old days, when you could scream at a *ghaton* that you would kick her and hurl her down the steps, and expect her to show up for work next morning, had definitely passed.

After high school, Percy and Jamshed went to different colleges. If they met at all, it would be at concerts of the Bombay Chamber Orchestra. Along with a college friend, Navjeet, and some others, my brother organized a charitable agency that collected and distributed funds to destitute farmers in a small Maharashtrian village. The idea was to get as many of these wretched souls as possible out of the clutches of the village money-lenders.

Jamshed showed a very superficial interest in what little he knew

about Percy's activities. Each time they met, he would start with
how he was trying his best to get out of the country. "Absolutely no
future in this stupid place," he said. "Bloody corruption everywhere. And you can't buy any of the things you want, don't even get
to see a decent English movie. First chance I get, I'm going abroad.
Preferably the U.S."

After a while, Percy stopped talking about his small village, and
they only discussed the concert program or the soloist's performance that evening. Then their meetings at concerts ceased
altogether because Percy now spent very little time in Bombay.

Jamshed did manage to leave. One day, he came to say goodbye.
But Percy was away working in the small village: his charitable
agency had taken on the task full time. Jamshed spoke to those of
us who were home, and we all agreed that he was doing the right
thing. There just weren't any prospects in this country; nothing
could stop its downhill race towards despair and ruin.

My parents announced that I, too, was trying to emigrate, but to
Canada, not the U.S. "We will miss him if he gets to go," they told
Jamshed, "but for the sake of his own future, he must. There is a lot
of opportunity in Toronto. We've seen advertisements in
newspapers from England, where Canadian Immigration is
encouraging people to go to Canada. Of course, they won't adver-
tise in a country like India — who would want these bloody *ghatis*
to come charging into their fine land? — but the office in New
Delhi is holding interviews and selecting highly qualified
applicants." In the clichés of our speech was reflected the cliché
which the idea of emigration had turned into for so many. According to my parents, I would have no difficulty being approved, what
with my education, and my westernized background, and my
fluency in the English language.

And they were right. A few months later things were ready for my
departure to Toronto.

Then the neighbours began to arrive. Over the course of the last
seven days, they came to confer their blessings and good wishes
upon me. First was Bulsara Bookworm's mother, her hair in a bun
as usual and covered with the *mathoobanoo*. She said, "I know you
and Jehangir were never very good friends, but that does not matter at a time like this. He says best of luck." She put her arm over my

shoulder in lieu of a hug and said, "Don't forget your parents and all they did for you, maintain your good name at all times."

And Tehmina, too, using the occasion to let bygones be bygones with Mummy and Daddy, arrived sucking cloves and shuffling in slippers and duster-coat. Her cataracts were still a problem, refusing to ripen, she said.

Then one morning Nariman Hansotia stopped me in the compound. He was on his way to the Cawasji Framji Memorial Library, and I to the airline office for a final confirmation of my seat.

"Well, well," he said, "so you were serious when you used to tell everyone that you would go abroad. Who would have thought of it! Who would have imagined that Silloo Boyce's little Kersi would one day go to Canada. Knee high I had seen you, running around in the compound with your brother, trying to do everything he did. Well, lead a good life, do nothing to bring shame to you or the Parsi community. And don't just land there and say, where are the girls? like this other chap had done. Did I ever tell you that story?"

And Nariman launched into an anecdote: "A sex-crazy young fellow was going to California. For weeks he used to tell his friends about how the women there went around on the beaches with hardly any clothes on, and how easy it was to find women who would go with you for a little bit of this and that, and what a wonderful time he was going to have as soon as he got there. Well, when he landed at Los Angeles, he tried to joke with the immigration officer and asked him, 'Where are the girls?' What do you think happened then?"

"What, Nariman Uncle?"

"He was deported on the very next plane, of course. Never did find out where the girls were."

Good old Nariman Uncle. He would never stop telling his tales. We finally parted, and as he pulled out of the compound in his old Mercedes-Benz, someone called my name from the ground floor of A Block. It was Rustomji-the-curmudgeon, skulking in the shadows and waiting for Nariman to leave. He shook my hand and gruffly wished me well.

But as I slept on my last night in Bombay a searing pain in my eyes woke me up. It was one o'clock. I bathed my eyes and tried to get back to sleep. Half-jokingly, I saw myself as someone out of a

Greek tragedy, guilty of the sin of hubris for seeking emigration out of the land of my birth, and paying the price in burnt-out eyes: I, Tiresias, blind and throbbing between two lives, the one in Bombay and the one to come in Toronto...

In the morning, Dr Sidhwa arrived and said it was conjunctivitis, nothing very serious. But I would need some drops every four hours and protective dark glasses till the infection was gone. No charge, he said, because he was going to drop by anyway to say goodbye and good luck.

Just before noon came Najamai. She must have been saving herself for an auspicious *chogeryoori*. She sympathized about my eyes before bringing forth her portable celebration kit: a small silver *thaali* holding a garland, and a tiny cup for the vermilion. They were miniatures of her regular apparatus which was too heavy to lug around. She put the garland round my neck, made a large, bright red *teelo* on my forehead and hugged me several times: "Lots and lots of years you must live, see lots of life, study lots, earn lots, make us all very proud of you."

Then Najamai succumbed to reminiscing: "Remember when you used to come upstairs with the meat? Such a good boy, always helping your mother. And remember how you used to kill rats, with your bat, even for me? I always used to think, how brave for such a small boy to kill rats with a bat. And one day you even ran after Francis with it! Oh, I'll never forget that!"

She left, and Daddy found me a pair of dark glasses. And thus was spent my last day in Bombay, the city of all my days till then. The last glimpses of my bed, my broken cricket bat, the cracks in the plaster, the chest of drawers I shared with Percy till he went away to the small village, came through dark glasses; the neighbourhood I grew up in, with the chemist's store ("Open Twenty-Four Hours"), the Irani restaurant, the sugar-cane juice vendor, the fruit-and-vegetable stall in Tar Gully, all of these I surveyed through dark glasses; the huddle of relatives at the airport, by the final barrier through which only ticket holders can pass, I waved to and saw one last time through dark glasses.

Tense with excitement I walked across the tarmac. The slight chill I felt was due to the gusting night winds, I convinced myself.

Then, eyes red with conjunctivitis, pocket bulging with the

ridiculously large bottle of eye-drops, and mind confused by a thousand half-formed thoughts and doubts, I boarded the aircraft sitting white and roaring upon the concrete. I tried to imagine Mummy and Daddy on the visitors' gallery, watching me being swallowed up into its belly, I imagined them consoling each other and fighting back the tears (as they had promised me they would) while I vanished into the night.

After almost a year in Toronto I received a letter from Jamshed. From New York — a very neat missive, with an elegant little label showing his name and address. He wrote that he'd been to Bombay the previous month because in every single letter his mother had been pestering him to visit: "While there, I went to Firozsha Baag and saw your folks. Glad to hear you left India. But what about Percy? Can't understand what keeps him in that dismal place. He refuses to accept reality. All his efforts to help the farmers will be in vain. Nothing ever improves, just too much corruption. It's all part of the *ghati* mentality. I offered to help him immigrate if he ever changes his mind. I've got a lot of contacts now, in New York. But it's up to him to make up his mind," and on and on.

Finally: "Bombay is horrible. Seems dirtier than ever, and the whole trip just made me sick. I had my fill of it in two weeks and was happy to leave." He ended with a cordial invitation to New York.

What I read was only the kind of stuff I would have expected in a letter from Jamshed. That was the way we all used to talk in Bombay. Still, it irritated me. It was puzzling that he could express so much disdain and discontentment even when he was no longer living under those conditions. Was it himself he was angry with, for not being able to come to terms with matters as Percy had? Was it because of the powerlessness that all of us experience who, mistaking weakness for strength, walk away from one thing or another?

I started a most punctilious reply to his letter. Very properly, I thanked him for visiting my parents and his concern for Percy. Equally properly, I reciprocated his invitation to New York with one to Toronto. But I did not want to leave it at that. It sounded as if I was agreeing with him about Percy and his work, and about India.

So instead, I described the segment of Toronto's Gerrard Street known as Little India. I promised that when he visited, we would go to all the little restaurants there and gorge ourselves with *bhelpuri*, *panipuri*, *batata-wada*, *kulfi*, as authentic as any in Bombay; then we could browse through the shops selling imported spices and Hindi records, and maybe even see a Hindi movie at the Naaz Cinema. I often went to Little India, I wrote; he would be certain to have a great time.

The truth is, I have been there just once. And on that occasion I fled the place in a very short time, feeling extremely ill at ease and ashamed, wondering why all this did not make me feel homesick or at least a little nostalgic. But Jamshed did not have to know any of it. My letter must have told him that whatever he suffered from, I did not share it. For a long time afterwards I did not hear from him.

My days were always full. I attended evening classes at the University of Toronto, desultorily gathering philosophy credits, and worked during the day. I became a member of the Zoroastrian Society of Ontario. Hoping to meet people from Bombay, I also went to the Parsi New Year celebrations and dinner.

The event was held at a community centre rented for the occasion. As the evening progressed it took on, at an alarming rate, the semblance of a wedding party at Bombay's Cama Garden, with its attendant sights and sounds and smells, as we Parsis talked at the top of our voices, embraced heartily, drank heartily, and ate heartily. It was Cama Garden refurbished and modernized, Cama Garden without the cluster of beggars waiting by the entrance gate for the feast to end so they could come in and claim the dustbins.

My membership in the Society led to dinner invitations at Parsi homes. Many of the guests at these gatherings were not the type who would be regulars at Little India, but who might go there with the air of tourists, equipped with a supply of ohs and aahs for ejaculation at suitable moments, pretending to discover what they had always lived with.

These were people who knew all about the different airlines that flew to Bombay. These were the virtuosi of transatlantic travel. If someone inquired of the most recent traveller, "How was your trip to India?" another would be ready with "What airline?" The evening would then become a convention of travel agents expounding on the salient features of their preferred carriers.

After a few such copiously educational evenings, I knew what the odds were of my luggage getting lost if I travelled airline A. The best food was served on airline B. Departures were always delayed with airline C (the company had a *ghati* sense of time and punctuality, they said). The washrooms were filthy and blocked up on airline D (no fault of airline D, they explained, it was the low class of public that travelled on it).

Of Bombay itself the conversation was restricted to the shopping they'd done. They brought back tales of villainous shopkeepers who tried to cheat them because they sensed that here was the affluence of foreign exchange: "Very cunning, they all are. God knows how, but they are able to smell your dollars before you even open your wallet. Then they try to fool you in the way they fool all the other tourists. I used to tell them" — this, in broken Hindi — " 'go, go, what you thinking, I someone new in Mumbai? I living here thirty years, yes thirty, before going phoren.' Then they would bargain sensibly."

Others told of the way they had made a shrewd deal with shopkeepers who did not know the true value of brass and copper artifacts and knick-knacks, what did bloody *ghatis* know about such things anyway. These collectors of bric-a-brac, self-appointed connoisseurs of art and antiques, must have acquired their fancies along with their immigration visas.

But their number was small. And though they were as earnest about their hobbies as the others were, they never quite succeeded in holding the gathering transfixed the way the airline clique managed to. Art was not as popular as airlines were at these evenings.

Six months after Jamshed's trip to Bombay, I received a letter from my brother Percy. Among other things, he wrote about his commitment in the small village:

> Our work with the farmers started successfully. They got interest-free loans in the form of seed and fertilizer, which we purchased wholesale, and for the first time in years they did not have to borrow from those bloodthirsty money-lenders.
> Ever since we got there the money-lenders hated us. They

tried to persuade us to leave, saying that what we were doing was wrong because it was upsetting the delicate balance of village life and destroying tradition. We in turn pointed out things like exploitation, usury, inhumanity, and other abominations whose time was now up. We may have sounded like bold knights-errant, but they turned to threats and said it would soon become so unhealthy for us that we would leave quickly enough.

One day when we were out visiting a loan applicant, a farmer brought news that a gang of thugs wielding sticks and cudgels was waiting at the hut — our office and residence. So we stayed the night with the loan applicant and, in the morning, escorted by a band of villagers who insisted on coming along, started for our hut. But all we found were smouldering embers. It had been razed to the ground during the night, and no one had dared interfere.

Now we're back in Bombay, and Navjeet and I are working on a plan for our return. We've spoken to several reporters, and the work is getting much publicity. We're also collecting fresh donations, so that when we go back we won't fail for lack of funds.

Having read this far, I put down the letter for a moment. There you were, my brother, waging battles against corruption and evil, while I was watching sitcoms on my rented Granada TV. Or attending dinner parties at Parsi homes to listen to chit-chat about airlines and trinkets. And it was no use wishing that we had talked more to each other about our hopes and visions and dreams. I thought of our school-days, trying to locate the point when the gulf had appeared between us. Did it grow bit by bit or suddenly happen one morning? I cannot remember, but it did throw everything into silence and secrecy.

The rest of the letter concerned Jamshed's visit to Bombay six months ago:

I wish he'd stayed away, if not from Bombay then at least from me. At best, the time I spent with him was a waste. I expected that we would look at things differently, but was not prepared for the crassly materialistic boor that he's turned into. To think he was my "best friend" in school.

No doubt he believes the highlight of his visit came when he took some of us to dinner at the Rendezvous — nothing but the most expensive, of course. It was a spectacle to surpass anything he'd done so far. He reminded us to eat and drink all we wanted without minding the prices and enjoy ourselves as much as we could, because we wouldn't get such a chance again, at least, not until his next visit.

When the soup came he scolded the waiter that it was cold and sent it back. The rest of us sat silent and embarrassed. He looked at us nonchalantly, explaining that this was the only way to handle incompetence; Indians were too meek and docile, and should learn to stand up for their rights the way people do in the States.

We were supposed to be impressed by his performance, for we were in an expensive restaurant where only foreign tourists eat on the strength of their U.S. dollars. And here was one of our own, not intimidated within the walls of the five-star Taj Mahal Hotel. In our school-days we could only stand outside and watch the foreigners come and go, wondering what opulent secrets lay inside, what comforts these fair-skinned superior beings enjoyed. Here was one of our own showing us how to handle it all without feeling a trace of inferiority, and now we were ashamed of him.

We spent the evening watching Jamshed in disbelief, in silence, which he probably thought was due to the awesome splendour of our surroundings.

I was determined not to see him again, not even when he came to say goodbye on the day of his departure, and I don't intend to meet him when he visits Bombay the next time…

As I finished reading, I felt that my brother had been as irritated by Jamshed's presence as I had been by Jamshed's letter six months ago. But I did not write this to Percy. After all, I was planning to be in Bombay in four or five months. We could talk then. In just four months I would complete two years in Canada — long enough a separation, I supposed with a naive pomposity, to have developed a lucidity of thought which I would carry back with me and bring to bear on all of India's problems.

Soon it was time to go shopping for gifts. I packed chocolates, cheeses, jams, jellies, puddings, cake mixes, panty hose, stainless steel razor blades — all the items I used to see displayed in the stalls of the smugglers along Flora Fountain, always priced out of reach. I felt like one of those soldiers who, in wartime, accumulates strange things to use as currency for barter. What was I hoping to barter them for? Attention? Gratitude? Balm to soothe guilt or some other malady of the conscience? I wonder now. And I wonder more that I did not wonder then about it.

The suitcase I had come with proved insufficient. And although I bought a new one, an extra leather strap around each seemed wise, for they were both swelled to threatening dimensions.

Then, arms still sore from the typhoid and cholera inoculations, luggage bursting at the seams with a portable grocery store, and mind suffused with groundless optimism, I boarded the plane.

The aircraft was losing height in preparation for landing. The hard afternoon sun revealed the city I was coming back to after two years. When the plane had taken off two years ago, it had been in the dark of night, and all I saw from the sky through shaded and infected eyes were the airport lights of Santa Cruz. But now it was daytime, and I was not wearing dark glasses. I could see the parched land: brown, weary, and unhappy.

A few hours earlier the aircraft had made its scheduled landing in London, and the view from the air had been lush, everywhere green and hopeful. It enraged me as I contrasted it with what I was now seeing. Gone was the clearness with which I'd promised myself I would look at things. All that was left was a childish and helpless reaction. "It's not fair!" I wanted to stamp my foot and shout, "it's just not fair!"

Construction work was under way at the airport. The van transporting passengers from the aircraft to the terminal building passed improvised dwellings of corrugated metal, cardboard, packing crates, plastic sheets, even newspaper.

The van was reduced to a crawl in the construction zone. A few naked children emerged from the corrugated metal and cardboard and ran to keep up with us, screaming for money. When they came dangerously close to the van, the driver screamed back. On board was a group of four businessmen, and three of them tossed some change out the window. They sounded Australian. The fourth was the seasoned traveller, and the others hung on every word he said. He warned them, "If you try that when you're on the street, you'll create something like a bloody feeding frenzy of sharks." The children fell far behind when the construction zone ended and the van picked up speed.

Bombay seemed dirtier than ever. I remembered what Jamshed had written in his letter, and how it had annoyed me, but now I couldn't help thinking he was right. Hostility and tension seemed to be perpetually present in buses, shops, trains. It was disconcerting to discover I'd become unused to it. Now I knew what soldiers must experience in the trenches after a respite far behind the lines.

As if enacting a scene for my benefit with all the subtlety of a sixteenth-century morality play, a crowd clawed its way into a local train. All the players were there: Fate and Reality, and the latter's offspring, the New Reality, and also Poverty and Hunger, Virtue and Vice, Apathy and Corruption.

The drama began when the train, Reality, rolled into the station. It was overcrowded because everyone wanted to get on it: Virtue, Vice, Apathy, Corruption, all of them. Someone, probably Poverty, dropped his plastic lunch bag amidst the stampede, nudged on by Fate. Then Reality rolled out of the station with a gnashing and clanking of its metal, leaving in its wake the New Reality. And someone else, probably Hunger, matter-of-factly picked up Poverty's mangled lunch, dusted off a *chapati* which had slipped out of the trampled bag, and went his way. In all of this, was there a lesson for me? To trim my expectations and reactions to things, trim them down to the proper proportions?

I wasn't sure, but when I missed my bus an old instinctive impulse returned: to dash after it, to leap and join the crowd already hanging from the door rail. In the old days I would have been off and running. I used to pride my agility at this manoeuvre. After all, during rush hour it was the only way to catch a bus, or you'd be left at the bus-stop with the old and the feeble.

But while the first flush of confidence flowed through me, the bus had moved well into the stream of traffic. My momentary hesitation gave the game away. With the old and feeble was my place, as long as I was a tourist here, and not committed to life in the combat zone.

In Firozsha Baag things were still roughly the same, but Mrs Mody had died, and no one knew what Pesi was doing now. In fact, ever since he had been sent away to boarding-school some years ago, Pesi's doing were not spoken of at all. My friend Viraf of A Block, whom I had been unable to say goodbye to two years ago because he was away in Kharagpur studying at the Indian Institute of Technology, was absent for my hello as well. He did not return to Bombay because he had found a job in nearby Calcutta.

Tehmina had at last rid herself of the cataracts. She was suddenly very spry, very sure of herself in all she did. Along with her cataracts she had also jettisoned her old slippers and duster-coat. Her new ensemble consisted of a long, flowing floral-patterned kaftan and a smart pair of *chappals* with little heels that rang out her presence on the stairs and in the hallway.

But Najamai had aged considerably. She kept asking me why I had not yet been to see her daughters even though she had given me their addresses: Vera was somewhere in Alberta, and Dolly in British Columbia.

My brother, Percy, wrote from the small village that he wanted to meet me, but: "I cannot come to Bombay right now because I've received a letter from Jamshed. He's flying in from New York, and has written about reunions and great times for all the old crowd. That's out of the question as far as I'm concerned. I'm not going to see him again."

I wrote back saying I understood.

Our parents were disappointed. They had been so happy that the whole family would be together again for a while. And now this. They could not understand why Percy did not like Jamshed any more, and I'm sure at the back of their minds they thought their son envied his friend because of the fine success he'd made of himself in America. But who was I to explain things, and would they understand even if I tried? They truly believed that Jamshed was the smart young fellow, and Percy the idealist who forgot that charity begins at home.

This trip was not turning out to be anything I'd hoped it would. Jamshed was coming and Percy wasn't, our parents were disappointed with Percy, I was disappointed with them, and in a week I would be flying out of Bombay, confused and miserable. I could feel it already.

Without any destination in mind I left the house and took the first empty bus to come along. It went to Flora Fountain. The offices were now closing for the day. The dirty, yellow-grey buildings would soon spill out typists and clerks and peons into a swelling stream surging towards bus-stops and train stations.

Roadside stalls were open for business. This would be their busy hour. They were lined up along the edge of the pavement, displaying their merchandise. Here a profusion of towels and napkins from shocking pink to peacock green; there, the clatter and gleam of pots and pans; further down, a refreshment stall selling sizzling *samosas* and ice-cold sherbet.

The pavement across the road was the domain of the smugglers with their stalls of foreign goods. But they did not interest me, I stayed where I was. One man was peddling an assortment of toys. He demonstrated them all in turn, calling out, "Baba play and baby play! Daddy play and Mummy play!" Another, with fiendish vigour, was throwing glass bowls to the ground, yelling: "Un-ber-rakable! Un-ber-rakable!"

Sunlight began to fade as I listened to the hawkers singing their tunes. Kerosene lamps were lit in some of the stalls, punctuating at random the rows on both sides of the street.

Serenely I stood and watched. The disappointment which had overcome me earlier began to ebb. All was fine and warm within this moment after sunset when the lanterns were lit, and I began to feel a part of the crowds which were now flowing down Flora Fountain. I walked with them.

Suddenly, a hand on my shoulder made me turn around. It was Jamshed. "Bet you weren't expecting to see me in Bombay."

"Actually, I was. Percy wrote you were coming." Then I wished I hadn't volunteered this bit of information.

But there was no need to worry about awkward questions regarding Percy. For Jamshed, in fine fettle, had other thoughts he was anxious to share.

"So what are you doing here? Come shopping?" he asked jokingly, indicating the little stalls with a disdainful sweep of his hand. "Terrible, isn't it, the way these buggers think they own the streets — don't even leave you enough room to walk. The police should drive them off, break up their bloody stalls, really."

He paused. I wondered if I should say something. Something that Percy would love to hear me say. Like: these people were only trying to earn a meagre living by exercising, amidst a paucity of options, this one; at least they were not begging or stealing. But I didn't have a chance.

"God, what a racket! Impossible to take even a quiet little walk in this place. I tell you, I'll be happy when it's time to catch my plane back to New York."

It was hopeless. It was his letter all over again, the one he'd written the year before from New York. He had then temporarily disturbed the order I was trying to bring into my new life in Toronto, and I'd struck back with a letter of my own. But this time I just wanted to get away from him as quickly as possible. Before he made the peace of mind I was reaching out for dissipate, become forever unattainable.

Suddenly, I understood why Percy did not want to meet him again — he, too, sensed and feared Jamshed's soul-sapping presence.

Around us, all the pavement stalls were immersed in a rich dusk. Each one was now lit by a flickering kerosene lantern. What could I say to Jamshed? What would it take, I wondered, to light the lantern in his soul?

He was waiting for me to speak. I asked, perfunctorily, how much longer he would be in Bombay.

"Another week. Seven whole days, and they'll go so slowly. But I'll be dropping in at Firozsha Baag in a couple of days, tell Percy." We walked to my bus-stop. A beggar tugged at his sleeve and he mechanically reached in his pocket for change. Then we said good-night.

On the bus I thought about what to say if he asked me, two days later, why I hadn't mentioned that Percy was not coming.

As it turned out, I did not have to say anything.

Late next evening, Percy came home unexpectedly. I rushed to greet him, but his face revealed that he was not returning in this manner to give us a pleasant surprise. Something was dreadfully wrong. His colour was ashen. He was frightened and shaken, and struggled to retain his composure. He tried to smile as he shook my hand limply, but could not muster the effort to return my hug.

"What's the matter?" said Mother. "You don't look well."

Silently, Percy sat down and began to remove his shoes and socks. After a while he looked up and said, "They killed Navjeet."

No one spoke for the next few minutes. Percy sat with his socks dangling from his hands, looking sad, tired, defeated.

Then Mummy rose and said she would make tea. Over tea, he told us what had happened. Slowly, reluctantly at first, then faster, in a rush, to get the remembering and telling over with as soon as possible. "The money-lenders were ready to make trouble for us again. We didn't think they'd do anything as serious as the last time. The press was following our progress and had reported the arson in many newspapers. Yesterday we were out at the wholesaler's. Ordering seed for next year. But Navjeet had stayed behind. He was working on the accounts. When we returned he was lying unconscious. On the floor. His face and head were bleeding badly. We carried him to the makeshift clinic in the village — there is no hospital. The doctor said there was severe internal damage — massive head injuries — a few hours later he was dead."

There was silence again. Perhaps when we were together later, sharing our old room again, Percy would talk to me. But he lay on his bed in the darkness, wide awake, staring silently at the ceiling, tracing its old familiar cracks as I was, by the hints of streetlights straying through the worn curtains. Was there nothing to say? There had to be something I could do to help.

Strangely enough, it was Jamshed who provided this something the next day.

When he arrived in the evening, he presented Mummy with a box of chocolates and some cheese triangles. She asked him how he'd been enjoying his trip so far. He replied, true to form, "Oh Auntie, I'm tired of this place, really. The dust and heat and crowds — I've had enough of it." And Mummy nodded sympathetically.

Soon, the moment Percy had been dreading was at hand. Mummy asked him to narrate, for Jamshed's benefit, the events which had brought him home so suddenly. But Percy just shook his head, so she told the story herself.

When she finished, we shifted uneasily. What was next? But Jamshed could not contain himself. He heaved the sigh of the worldly-wise: "I told you from the beginning, all this was a waste of time and nothing would come of it, remember? Every time we met we would talk about it, and you used to make fun of me wanting to go abroad. But I still think the best thing for you is to move to the States. There is so much you could achieve there. There, if you are good at something, you are appreciated, and you get ahead. Not like here, where everything is controlled by uncle-auntie, and…."

When Jamshed concluded his harangue, Percy calmly turned to Mummy and said in his quiet voice, "Could we have dinner right away? I have to meet my friends at eight o'clock. To decide our next move in the village."

Five days later I was back in Toronto. I unpacked my suitcases, which were quite flat on the return trip and had not required the extra leather straps. I put my things away and displayed in the apartment the little knick-knacks bought in handicraft places and the Cottage Industries store.

Gradually, I discovered I'd brought back with me my entire burden of riddles and puzzles, unsolved. The whole sorry package was there, not lightened at all. The epiphany would have to wait for another time, another trip.

I mused, I gave way to whimsy: I Tiresias, throbbing between two lives, humbled by the ambiguities and dichotomies confront-ing me…

I thought of Jamshed and his adamant refusal to enjoy his trips to India, his way of seeing the worst in everything. Was he, too, waiting for some epiphany and growing impatient because, without it, life in America was bewildering? Perhaps the con-tempt and disdain which he shed was only his way of lightening his own load.

That Christmas, I received a card from Jamshed. The Christmas seal, postage stamp, address label were all neatly and correctly in place upon the envelope, like everything else about his surface existence. I put it down without opening it, wondering if this innocuous outer shell concealed more of his confusion, disdain, arrogance.

Later, I walked out of the apartment and down the hallway, and dropped the envelope down the chute of the garbage incinerator.

Exercisers

Exercisers

"If you don't want to take our word for it," said Jehangir Bulsara's parents to him, "that's fine. Ask Bhagwan Baba. Let *him* decide, with his holy wisdom, that the girl is unsuitable for you."

That was last week. Now the day of the journey was here; Mr and Mrs Bulsara, with Jehangir, were bound for Bhagwan Baba's dwelling place in the suburbs. From outside the gates of Firozsha Baag they took the bus to Bombay Central Station, and boarded the Sunday morning local.

Such guidance-seeking train journeys were customary for the parents, but this one was solely for Jehangir's benefit. "Your entire life's happiness is at stake," they had insisted. "When Bhagwan Baba speaks your eyes will open, all will become clear."

At first, Jehangir had refused to go. But: "You had double pneumonia when you were eight," Father had reminded him, "and even the doctor was despairing. I came to Bhagwan Baba and your health returned."

And Mother added, "After Father lost his job, who do you think helped, his friends, our relatives, who? Bhagwan Baba, and we have enough to eat and wear, thanks to him."

Thus it went, although the examples were dredged with difficulty

out of the past. Due to the passage of time they had relinquished
the greater part of their preternatural lustre, and appeared in a
disappointingly mundane light. But when Jehangir was younger,
he used to think it wonderful that there was a Baba who aided his
mother and father with blessings and advice and kind words. Life
was hard, always full of want and worry, and assistance from any
quarter was welcome. The little boy who used to sit on the steps of
C Block to watch the others at play, and who used to spend Sunday
mornings with Dr Mody and his stamps, would ask God every night
to help his father and mother.

The boy was now nineteen and in his third year at university,
but he still carried the distinct memories of poverty and anxiety,
memories of envelopes labelled Rent, School Fees, Ration,
Kerosene, Light, and Water, envelopes which were forever
examined and shuffled and re-examined because there was never
enough money in them (and never would be), and were worn
ragged and tattered along the edges due to such constant han-
dling and scrutinizing, as if the shuffling and sorting and re-
examining would lead to some discovery that would make the
money last longer.

So in the end Jehangir agreed to consult the holy man of the
suburbs and let him exercise his tenuous infallibility. He looked
out of the train window. What he had not realized, till the moment
of boarding, was the full baseness of it all. It struck suddenly, in the
pit of his stomach, like nausea. Cringing inwardly, he wondered
what *she* would say if she knew about the act of betrayal he was
shortly to perpetrate. Probably despise him forever, and he would
deserve it.

The suburban local was at the outskirts of Bombay; they would
arrive at their destination in forty-five minutes. The "17 Standees
Allowed" by the scratched and peeling sign had already been ex-
ceeded by the crush of Sunday morning commuters, but not to the
extent of a weekday train: as yet, there were no roof-riders or
window-clingers. In the sky the sun was higher than when the train
left Bombay Central. The heat began to strengthen rapidly now,
seeming to feed on itself, growing more oppressive with every
breath. From metal straps hung the standees, listless, upraised
arms revealing identical damp patches under sleeves of shirts and

blouses. Overhead, the fans turned ineffectively, whirring and rattling, their blades labouring with feeble rotations, trying to chop the air thick with heat and odour, scattering it around uselessly in the compartment.

In fitful sleep his parents leaned against each other. They swayed as one with the train's motion, on the wooden bench that constituted third-class seats. The bench, and the compartment in general, was randomly adorned with red stains of *paan*: the oral effluences of past passengers, relics of journeys done and gone. Time and dust had done their work, too, aging and dulling the tobacco-betel-nut juices to varying degrees of redness.

Mother held a brown paper bag in her lap. It contained three oranges and three bananas for Bhagwan Baba. Offerings were not compulsory but people brought gifts out of gratitude, she had explained to Jehangir: "And Bhagwan Baba usually gives back half after blessing it. Very rich people bring expensive gifts, boxes of almonds and pistachios, large cartons of *mithai*, whole baskets of prime *alphonso* mango, sometimes even jewellery. But the beautiful thing is, he does no more for them than he does for the poorest. It is one of the signs of his saintliness."

All in the compartment were now asleep or trying to attain that envious state. Even the ones hanging from the straps like drowsy trapeze artists, lost in a swaying, somnolent exercise. Occasionally a new set of people entered when the train stopped. They were noisy and fidgety at first. But the contagion of lethargy quickly subdued them. They fell silent under the spell of the whirring fans which swivelled jerkily from side to side. With a nervous tic, twitching like victims of a heat-induced malady.

Sleep was one way to escape the discomfort; Jehangir shut his eyes to see if he could. He ceased bracing himself against the movement of the train, allowed the head and shoulders to droop forward to sway, and let his whole body sway with the train, unresisting. Like his parents' opposite him, his movement became one with the movement of the compartment. Rolling to and fro, swaying side to side, as the train decreed. Surrendering to the torridity of the air and the hypnotic drone of the fans, the close click-click of the standees' metal straps and the seemingly remote clackety-clack of the rails, he was ready to cross over from the edge of torpor into slumber, succumbing slowly to the swaying, swaying slowly.

The train stopped, and Jehangir straightened with a start. Did I really fall asleep? He anxiously scanned the platform for the station's name. No, this was not the one. The compartment lurched into motion. The train resumed its journey, and the possibility of sleep was now crowded out by thoughts of Bhagwan Baba, his parents, and her; but mainly of her.

She was the first girl he had ever gone out with.

Jehangir's school years had been devoid of girls. His parents could not afford the exhorbitant fees which, for some peculiar reason, were common to all coeducational high schools, and from whence issued rumours, periodically, about students being "dismissed for attempting sexual intercourse on school property." The rumours, vicariously relished and savoured when they reached the boys' schools, fuelled and stoked high the envy and frustration rife within those walls. Their occupants had a heavy study load. Besides the regular subjects, they learned to forgo things taken for granted by their wealthy counterparts in coeducational schools — things such as music lessons, camping trips, and guided tours to Jammu and Kashmir. But they discovered ways to make up for it. They learned how to use their eyes to undress their female teacher and gaze longingly at the outline of her bra, drop erasers or pencils and linger at floor level to retrieve them while she sat at her desk on an elevated platform (the days when she wore a sari were barren, black days), and carry home unforgettable images of flowery panties.

These pursuits went a long way in honing imaginations and developing agility and suppleness in tight places. Unfortunately, the supply of female teachers dwindled drastically in the higher grades, when their need was greatest. But the students believed that within the egalitarianism of university life all wrongs would be righted, and continued to believe until they arrived, bright-eyed and optimistic despite their awkwardness, to discover their faith had been groundless.

Jehangir had been trapped in St Xavier's Boys School; its effects lingered, and even in college his first two years had been fallow. He lacked the sophistication of the chaps from coeducational schools, in their Levis and other imported clothes, who took pleasure in flaunting the ease with which they mingled and joked in the college canteen before the gawky ones from boys' schools or the "vernacs" from non-English medium schools (at the bottom of the sophistication hierarchy) who continued shamefacedly to clothe themselves in old school uniforms at their parents' insistence to get the full wear out of them.

Jehangir suffered the superciliousness of the boys from coeducational schools with a silent rage. Sometimes he was consumed by bouts of inferiority which he palliated by trying to accept with calm resignation that the gulf between them and him was no wider than the one between him and the dolts in Firozsha Baag. But such fatalism did not make things less embittering. He despised their sardonic comments to the innocent ones who kept using 'periods' instead of 'lectures': "Periods, my friend, occur for menstruating females and schoolboys. In college we attend lectures." He envied their long and loud laughter laden with confidence, their clearly forceful and distinct speech during class discussions, which he could not help but compare to the diffident mumbles of the others.

He observed them, tried to learn from them and be like them, but remained inevitably mired in his reticence when it came to girls.

She started talking to him one day while they waited for choir practice to begin. It had taken a lot of courage, two years' worth of it, to join the college choir. As he correctly guessed, it was comprised mainly of members of that hateful species from coeducational schools who, in addition to their sartorial advantage, came equipped with prior experience from school choirs and corresponding portions of arrogance. All he had was a love of music and a good but untrained ear. After the first meeting he decided never to go again. He had felt like a gatecrasher at an exclusive party.

But a week went by during which he re-collected his courage, and the day for choir practice arrived. She was a soprano, he sang bass. She started the conversation, and Jehangir was relieved to find he had no trouble keeping it going. She had a lot to say, especially about Claude, the conductor: "The pompous jackass thinks all the girls in the choir are his personal property. The next time he puts his arm around me, I'm going to take his baton and poke it in his froggy eyes." Jehangir laughed, surprised at how naturally it came.

They had talked often after that. His fear of blushing when spoken to, or stumbling over his words if he thought they were being overheard gradually diminished. They discovered a common interest in reading, and she invited him to her house. He borrowed books, met her parents, and went back often for more. She sometimes mentioned movies she had seen or wanted to see, and how it would be fun to go together, but they always stopped short of making definite plans.

Jehangir had never been much of a cinema-goer. Amidst the bunch of envelopes marked Rent, Water, Light, and others, the last was labelled Pocket Money. But this one always stayed empty. And if sometimes he had enough money for a cinema ticket, there was no one at school or in Firozsha Baag he really cared to go with. The low opinion he had of the boys in the Baag, formed during the days of Pesi *paadmaroo* and the misery his life had been then, persisted. He preferred to sit on the steps of C Block and read, or watch the activity in the compound. Sometimes, he heard them heroically recounting their feats in the cinema: chucking paper balls of empty potato-chip bags at strangers, or hooting and whistling in the dark to provoke shushing sounds from the audience. He felt nothing but contempt for their puerile antics. A delight in Nariman Hansotia's yarns on the steps of A Block was the only thing he shared with them.

When Mrs Bulsara decided he was old enough to go out alone provided he always returned by eight o'clock, Jehangir varied the routine of his evenings. He began going for walks to the Hanging Gardens. His favourite place there was the children's playground after the children left at dusk. Then, it was occupied by men who transformed it into a gym every night. They came regularly, and improvised by using the various combinations of bars and railings of the slide or swing for pull-ups and push-ups, and the plank of the see-saw for sit-ups. They must have had an arrangement with the night-watchman, because the playground was strictly for children. Jehangir, hidden behind a bush or tree, watched the exercisers. They fascinated him. Their rippling, sweating muscles were magnified versions of the bodies of the boys in the school gym.

Watching their powerful torsos and limbs had a strange effect on his own skinny body, it sometimes triggered a longing for brawn and sinew in his slender arms and legs.

Later, in college, Jehangir stopped going to the Hanging Gardens. He was suddenly very conscious of his aloneness, and felt silly wandering around amidst ayahs with children or couples looking for solitude. Hiding and watching the exercisers did not seem right, either.

The cinema became his new haunt. In the dark movie theatres it did not matter that he was alone. If he sat next to a girl, he would fantasize that she had come with him and was throbbing just like him. He let his elbow touch her arm as if by accident on the arm-rest they shared. When she edged past him during intermission or after the movie, he gently grazed the back of her thighs with his knees, almost like a light caress. He would maneouvre to make a show of allowing her maximum room, but made sure to get the most feel. Those were moments of pure ecstasy, moments which he re-lived in bed at night. Sometimes, if there was a particularly active couple next to him, he spent more time watching them than the screen, employing the contortions of a head trained in school under desks and benches. But a stiff neck and an ache at his centre were his only companions when he emerged from the theatre.

Several choir practices later, she went with him to the cinema, and Jehangir found it hard to believe that he had not come alone again to the darkened hall of possibilities. After the intermission she was gently massaging her right wrist, having sprained it the day before. He asked if it was hurting terribly, and later remembered the moment with pride, that he had had the courage and presence of mind to stroke the wrist without a word when she held it out for him over his lap. The stirring which began at his centre swelled with each stroke; after a while their fingers entwined, clumsily, until the index, middle, and ring found their proper places, and interlocked in a tight clasp. He was tremendously aroused but did not dare do anything else. Much too soon the flag appeared on the screen and the audience rose for *Jana Gana Mana*. His tremendous arousal was quickly doused. All that remained was a nasty ache, the unpleasant residue of lust unreleased, as though he had been kneed in the groin.

It was a while since the train had stopped at a station. Jehangir crossed his legs. He was disgusted with himself. Getting excited again at the mere memory of holding hands. He had read in various magazines and books that boys of fifteen in America enjoyed regular sex, and had the privacy to do it, while he at nineteen was still a virgin, worked up just at the thought of holding her hand, and it was all very unfair and frustrating.

The train was passing by farmland. The fields were sere, brown and bare, and the little vegetation persisting tenaciously was parched yellow. The monsoons were late again, and here, outside the city, the delay was writ harsh across the landscape.

In the city, too, there were hardships. The quota of tap water had been curtailed, and Jehangir had been waking up at five A.M. for the past month to help Mother fill up storage drums for bathing and cleaning and cooking, before the supply was cut off at six A.M.

Scrawny cattle foraged amidst the stubble in the fields. Telegraph poles whizzed by, menacingly close. Poles which periodically cracked open the skulls of commuters who travelled hanging from doors and windows, and provided fodder for the death toll faithfully recorded by city newspapers. A death toll sharing the inconspicuity of inside pages. Side by side with assaults on scheduled castes in one village and murders of *harijans* by brahmins in another.

When he had brought her home the first time, it had been for a very short visit. He had warned his parents beforehand, praying that Mother would take the hint and remove the *mathoobanoo* from her head; the white mulmul square made her look like a backward village Parsi from Navsari, he had recently decided. But he was not spared what he thought was a moment of shame and embarrassment. There were quick introductions and several awkward silences, then they left for choir practice.

Later, when Jehangir returned, Mother said during dinner that he should not be seeing so much of the girl. "This is not the time for going out with girls anyway. The proper time will come after finishing college, when you are earning your own living and can afford it." In the meantime, if he did go out occasionally after asking for permission, he would have to continue to be home by eight o'clock. It would not do to stay out later than that and let things get too serious.

Jehangir said that he would be home by eight if she did not wear that *mathoobanoo*.

"I am not going to tolerate your ifs-bifs," said Mrs Bulsara, covering her hurt with brusqueness, "what I am saying is for your own good." It was obvious, she said, that the girl came from a family better off than they were, her life-style would make him uncomfortable. "Trust a mother's instinct. It is only your happiness I think of. Besides, she is the first girl you have gone out with, you might meet someone you like more. Then what?"

"Then I'll stop going out with her."

"But what of her feelings? You might be giving her serious hopes."

"No one has any serious hopes. It's so silly, all these objections."

"It is always a serious matter where a girl is involved. You will not understand that at your age."

Dinner finished without any real unpleasantry. But not for many nights after that. The dinner-table talk grew sharper as days passed. At first, words were chosen carefully in an effort to preserve a semblance of democratic discussion. Soon, however, the tensions outgrew all such efforts, and a nightly routine of debilitating sarcasm established itself. Every dinner saw the same denunciations brought forth, sometimes with a new barb twisted through them.

"There's something about the way she talks. Without proper respect."

"Saw what she was wearing? Such a short skirt. And too much makeup."

"Because you are going out with her you think electricity is free of charge? Ironing shirt and pant from morning till evening." The ancient dented serving-spoon, descended through hands of foremothers, struck the pot of brinjal with a plangency denoting more to come.

"Why must a girl wear so much makeup unless she is hiding something underneath."

"Shines his shoes till I can see my unhappy face. More shoe polish has been used after meeting her than in all the years before."

"If she does not respect your parents, how will she respect you? Your whole life will be unhappy."

Father said only one thing: "Trust your mother's instincts. I always do, they are never wrong."

Things rapidly became worse. Not a day passed without quarrelling. They said things to each other which they would not have dreamt of saying at one time; bitter, vindictive things. Every few days there was a reconciliation at Father's insistence, with sincere hugs and tears of remorse which sprang from the depths of their beings, so fervent was the desire to let peace and understanding reign again. But this would last for a short time only. The strange new emotions and forces which had taken hold, indecipherable and inscrutable, would soon be manifest again; then the quarrels and hurtful words would resume.

After the first few visits Jehangir did not bring her home any more. Besides, she always refused to come under some pretext — she had felt the antagonism that silently burgeoned on her arrival. There was no outward sign of it, on the surface all was decorum and grace, welcome and kindness. But to sense what lay underneath did not take much. She also picked up the unintentional hints he dropped during those evenings when they met after an excessively trying time at home. Then she would try to help him, and before they parted he would agree to stand up to his parents, become independent, and many more promises.

But the promises were always smothered by a fresh wave of reproaches awaiting him at home. If he managed to speak in the spirit of autonomy that she had inspired in him earlier in the evening, it still turned out unfavourably.

"See?" Mother would say with mournful satisfaction, "see how it proves my point that she is a bad influence? He goes to her and returns with such cruel words in his mouth. And who put them there, that is all I am asking. Because such words were not there before. Now I must start all over again to remove her effect on him. Then he will be more like the son I once knew. But how long can I go on like this, how long?" she would conclude dolefully, whereupon Jehangir abandoned the balance of his painstakingly prepared words.

He looked at his parents now, supporting each other as they slept through heat and dust. The photograph was in his wallet. They had told him to bring it along. He had taken it with her camera during the college picnic at Elephanta Caves. She later gave him a copy. It was a black-and-white, and as he gazed at it he could feel the soft brown of her eyes drawing him in, ready to do her will. The will of my enchantress, he liked to imagine.

Mother had taken to going through his trousers and wallet. He was aware of these secret searches but had said nothing, not wanting to add to her sorrow and to the bitterness that filled the house.

The day after he received the photograph, she triumphantly found it: "What is this, why must you carry her photo with you?"

"What right did you have to look in my wallet?"

"What right? What right, he says! To his own mother he says what right! A mother does not need any rights. A mother exercises her judgement out of love. A mother does whatever she knows is right for her son."

The photograph was brought up constantly for days after, and with each passing day the rhetoric grew increasingly forceful and wildly inventive.

"It is not enough to see her makeup-covered face in the evening. He must also keep her photograph."

"People have been made to go crazy by a photo with a magic spell on it. Maybe her parents are involved in this, trying to snare my son for their daughter."

"She knows you will go to study in America one day and settle there. By thrusting her photo on you she is making sure you will sponsor her. Oh yes, it begins with a photograph."

"Be careful you don't forget your own mother's face, you don't have much time to see it these days."

And always, the eight o'clock ultimatum: "Remember, the door will never open for you after eight o'clock."

In the end Mother was glad to have the photograph. "One good thing she did by giving it to you. Now we have something to show Bhagwan Baba."

The train braked in preparation for the approaching station. A *kayrawalli* climbed aboard to flop upon the floor with her basket of plantains. She mopped her brow with one corner of her sari, rubbed her eyes, and sat with drawn-up knees after administering a good scratching in some region under the sari-folds. Any minute now she'll start badgering the passengers to buy her plantains, thought Jehangir. But she sat where she was, enervated, with no inclination to acquire business. Perhaps she did not dare to wake the slumbering people. In school they used to say that for a quarter rupee a *kayrawalli* would lift her sari and flash for you. For a rupee she would even perform with a plantain. He wondered if it was true.

The glass bangles on her wrists tinkled as the train swayed along, and she fell asleep. The plantains in her basket looked bruised and battered, beginning to show black patches because of the heat. They would have to be thrown away if they remained unsold. Granny had a saying about eating them: a plantain in the morning turns to gold in the stomach and a plantain at noon is silver; a plantain in the evening turns to brass in the belly, but a plantain at night is iron in the gut.

He wondered why the *kayrawalli* was travelling away from the city and towards the suburbs. People like her brought fruit to the city. Maybe she was on the wrong train.

Just like Father and Mother and me. To think that I put the thought in their heads.

Once, in the midst of a bitter outburst, he had said, "Why don't you ask your famous Bhagwan Baba if he also handles matchmaking? Maybe he'll be in my favour." He spoke with what he thought was biting sarcasm. Everything now had a habit of degenerating into a sarcasm contest.

But they liked the idea very much. "It was only a joke," Jehangir pleaded, sarcasm retreating in alarm.

Mother and Father thought it was the best way to decide his future. They tried to convince him to make the visit. Mother was harshly dictatorial at first, then lachrymose and pleading. "What we want," she tearfully entreated, "is for you to come and talk to Bhagwan Baba about the girl, to find out if she is right for you. Agree that Bhagwan Baba is never wrong, believe again as you believed once when you were younger."

And Jehangir stopped objecting when reminded of the many miracles wrought within the world of his childhood. Miracles were no doubt easier to believe in that long ago world. But the memories began to prey on his notions of loyalty to the past, his nostalgia for a home happy and loving despite its material meagreness, and guilt for considering (however briefly) repudiation of Bhagwan Baba. Besides, he reasoned, he had nothing to lose, it could not get worse. If he was lucky, a favourable pronouncement would make things much easier.

And with the agreement to take Bhagwan Baba's advice, a measure of calm returned to their lives. Hostilities were suspended and the harsh words temporarily silenced.

The *kayrawalli* awoke and balanced the basket of plantains on her head. She got off at the next station, which was also the one Jehangir and his parents were waiting for.

The medium-sized house had a spacious veranda at the front. A wooden bench sat on the veranda, and around the house a lush vegetable garden with several pumpkin vines and tomato plants. Tucked away in one corner was a large bench-swing, hanging still. Still, too, was the greenery in the garden. Not a breath of breeze.

A large crowd was waiting for Bhagwan Baba. People stood in a line leading up to the veranda, in silence or soft conversation, reverent hands clutching packets with offerings for Bhagwan Baba. There was none of the hysterical activity usually associated with holy men, no burning of incense, no chanting, no peddling of holy pictures or religious artifacts.

Jehangir's parents explained that when Bhagwan Baba was ready he came out to the wooden bench. The visitors then went up to the veranda and sat with him, one by one or in a group if it was a group consultation.

A man just ahead of them in line overheard, and spoke up as though waiting for the cue: "There is *no*thing to worry about. Bhagwan Baba is *won*derful. What*ever* he will say or do, it is only for your own benefit." Bhagwan Baba started granting audiences at eleven A.M. It was now eleven-thirty. With the air of one privy to special information the man said, "Bhagwan Baba knows best. If he is late it is for a good reason." His hands performed practised gestures to embellish the earnestly devout speech: fingers bunched together to describe a vertical line in the air; right index finger wisely held aloft and lowered through an arc into the left hand; palms together in a clasp; and so on. "We are only simple human beings, so *how* to understand *eve*rything Bhagwan Baba will say or do, how to know *why* his spirituality is manifesting in one way and not in another?" He paused, then added unctuously, "For us, it is only to stand and wait till Baba is ready to mingle with poor souls like you and me."

Jehangir found the man's effusive devotional talk embarrassing. He wished his parents would stop encouraging him by nodding pious looks of agreement. Bhagwan Baba appeared now, supported by two men. Something like a collective suspiration was audible in the garden. Then the scattered whispering fell silent. He was dressed in a white *kurta-pyjama*, and looked quite frail, with bare feet. His head was bald but he had a white beard. A short stubbly beard. And he wore dark glasses.

"Sometimes he takes off the glasses," the man whispered, "then at once puts them back on. *Eve*ryone waits for that, to see his eyes. *Exactly* what it means I don't understand. But it is absolutely significant, *most* definitely."

Two little boys and their older sister climbed onto the bench-swing in the corner of the vegetable garden. Their clambering set it into a gentle, squeaky oscillation. The sister sustained the motion of the swing with a pushing-kicking movement of her legs. During the forward swing her skirt billowed, then fell with the retreat; forward and back, billowed and fell.

Out of a long-formed habit Jehangir, craning, positioned himself to obtain the best view. When he had newly started going to college he discovered a pastime to which the Law of Diminishing Returns did not apply. The excitement of descending the stairs sometimes kept him from paying proper attention during class. There were two flights to each floor, and as he rounded the splendidly carved newel at the end of the first flight, his eyes lifted upwards. Above him flowed a stream of panties, a cascade of crotches out of the heavens, while he descended slowly, hand upon the balustrade to keep his balance, for it was heady stuff.

The thrills of this sport suffered greatly after that day at choir practice when she spoke to him. He realized that she could be amidst the descending crowd while his head was thrown back at a right angle to his trunk. It would be mortifying if she spotted him in this stance, she who believed him shy and, doubtless, pure of mind. Like Mother who, until recently, would say with pride, "My Jehangir, such a quiet good boy, *aitlo dahyo*, won't make *choon* or *chaan*. Does everything I tell him." What a revelation if she could enter his prurient mind. Ironic that two women so different could share the same misconception, both beguiled in identical ways.

The bench-swing reminded him of the exercisers in the children's playground. He now gave that place a wide berth when he visited the Hanging Gardens, preferring to think that the playground and the exercisers belonged to a part of his life which had concluded for good. He wondered if the exercisers still went there every night, if their muscles had developed further since he last saw them more than two years ago.

The children lost interest in the swing. It slowed down, steadying into its former stillness, with the squeaks coming further and further apart, then dying away completely. Jehangir turned away from it, feeling victorious after his sighting. Not only had he succeeded, he had done so in Bhagwan Baba's garden amidst devotees thinking pious thoughts, and the touch of blasphemy was particularly satisfying. The sanctimonious fellow in front had been quiet for a while, not sharing any more of his insider's information. His turn was next. He smiled at Jehangir and his parents, and stepped up to the veranda. The sun had progressed in its descent, and the pumpkin vines and tomatoes would soon need watering. A slight breeze was evident in the faint rustle of leaves.

Now they were first in line. Jehangir's apprehension and uncertainty returned. He began digging frantically in his trousers for the photograph before remembering that on the train, while his parents slept, he had transferred it from his wallet to his shirt pocket. "How do we start this?" he asked. "Do I show the photo first?"

Mother said she would take care of that. All he should do was listen carefully when Bhagwan Baba spoke.

From Bhagwan Baba's house to the railway station was a short walk along a dirt road. Jehangir and his parents hurried along silently in the face of a rising wind. A somber, rainless cloud cover dominated the sky.

The dirt road was deserted. The sun's midday sharpness had been replaced by a heavy, stifling air mass moving over the land. Clouds of dust rose at the least provocation and Mother held a handkerchief over her nose and mouth. A few simple shacks and shanties on either side of the road were the only structures on the barren plain. Their sunken-cheeked occupants watched with empty eyes as the three figures made their way to the station.

The shelter of the waiting-room was a relief. It was deserted except for the man attending to the cold-drink stand. They purchased three bottles of Limca and settled on a bench to await their train. The bottles were closer to tepid than the ice-cold promised by the sign, but the drink was refreshing.

Bathrooms were located next to the cold-drink stand. From behind one of the doors emerged the song of a broken tap, the copious drip splashing in complex, agitated rhythms upon the stone floor.

"Shortage of water everywhere. But listen, listen to the shameful waste," said Father. He sipped Limca through the straw, anticipating the final empty gurgle to signal the end. "It was a little disappointing. He removed his dark glasses to see the photo, but did not say much. And three hours in line."

Mother said, "That is normal. Bhagwan Baba never speaks unless you ask him specific things. Jehangir did not open his mouth *sidhō-padhrō*, to speak clearly. Not one word. What do you expect Bhagwan Baba to do?"

"But you said you would explain…"

"I said I would begin for you. That does not mean you show no interest in what is your problem."

"I don't have a problem. You do because you don't like her." The entire day had passed without argument. Now it seemed the heat and dust would take their toll.

"I never said I do not like *her*. But no sense talking to you, you don't want to understand. We decided to come, you should have shown more concern. Now we still don't know what is the best thing for you."

Jehangir returned the empty Limca bottles to the cold-drink counter. A ceiling fan hung motionless in the waiting-room, and he pointed to it when the cold-drink man caught his eye. "Power shortage," the cold-drink man replied. "No lights even. At night I sell by lantern light. And kerosene is not cheap. So price of cold-drinks had to go up."

Jehangir nodded indifferently and returned to the bench. Father said, "Bhagwan Baba did not say much. But it seems to me he did give an answer. He said life is a trap, full of webs. Ask yourself, what does the sensible person do if a trap is facing him? Avoid, get away from it. So I think Bhagwan Baba was saying that Jehangir should stay away from that girl." He was pleased with his interpretation.

"But if that was what Bhagwan Baba meant, why not say it plainly?" said Mother. "Every other time he has given us plain answers, simple language."

"I don't know. There is always a reason for what Bhagwan Baba does. That much I know. To me his words sounded like a warning for Jehangir."

"But Jehangir is not saying anything. Again you are staying quiet, like you did with Bhagwan Baba. Tell us whatever is on your mind."

And he was tempted to tell: of the sight which had shocked and embarrassed him one night when he had come home, changed his clothes, and left them on the pile for the *gunga* to wash next morning. A few minutes later he had returned, having forgotten his pen in one of the pockets. But Mother was there, sniffing, scrutinizing the gusset under the light. To find smells of illicit sex? Stains to corroborate her suspicions of the girl's sluttishness? Evidence that her boy had been ravished by a flesh-and-blood succubus? She had started counting garments for next day's washing quota when she saw him.

Trying to conceal the rough edge of resentment that crept into his voice now, he was only partly successful. "You keep saying the girl, the girl, the girl. You know her name is Behroze, why don't you use it? Do you think if you pronounce her name she will become more real than she is?"

His parents shifted uncomfortably. "You never talk to us these days," said Mother. "You were not like that in school. How you used to come home and tell me everything. The little butter we

could afford I would always save for you, make your tea, help
with homework. And how you used to go running to Dr Mody
every Sunday at ten o'clock, do you remember, with your
stamps." Those happy years brought a wistful smile to her face.
She reached out as if to stroke his cheek. But the memories also
exacerbated the imperfection of the present, and she left the
gesture unfinished.

"We never treated you like other parents when you misbehaved.
That old Karani woman in B Block, she used to make her boy stand
naked out on the steps for punishment, to shame him. A brilliant
CA he is now, but to this day the poor man has not completely
recovered from that cruelty. And Dr Mody, rest his soul, would slap
his son Pesi left-right on the face. Outside in the compound for all
Firozsha Baag to see." Mother paused, remembered the point she
was trying to make, and continued.

"Maybe it is because you have changed so much that we fret. You
used to care about our problems, worry just like Daddy and me.
More and more selfish you seem to be now, so what am I to think?
That your new life in college, and your new friends, and that girl —
Behroze — have changed you."

"Again we are starting to argue. No use talking of it now," said
Father, "when we are all so tired."

"But I want to tell you what I think," said Jehangir. "Bhagwan
Baba talked about a trap. He also said no one can do anything
about it. No one means not you or I or Bhagwan Baba himself. So
what is the point of a warning no one can act upon?"

"You see what I mean?" asked Mother, turning in despair to
Father. "What I mean when I say he has changed? He takes all these
logic and philosophy courses in college and gives us smart answers.
We begged and borrowed to pay his college fees, and this is the
result. Not afraid even to twist the words of Bhagwan Baba. Don't
forget, all your smartness and your ambition to go to America will
come to nothing. This girl will change you and keep you here.
Then you will finish your days like your father and me, in poverty
and filth."

The suburban local to Bombay Central was announced over
the loudspeaker. As the train swept in, Mother realized that
the brown paper bag of oranges blessed by Bhagwan Baba was

missing. Jehangir raced into the waiting-room and back to the compartment where they had found seats.

"You can eat one every day for the next three days," Mother said. "It will help you think clearly about your problem."

Jehangir did not tell Behroze about Bhagwan Baba. She would dismiss him as a fake, lumping him in the same category as the quacks and charlatans of whom there was no dearth in Bombay, who sold their charms and potions and had a thriving trade among the educated and the uneducated alike. It would lead to an argument, and he did not want to have to defend Bhagwan Baba.

That week, he missed choir practice and went to the Hanging Gardens. He walked, taking the short cut up the hill as he had done so many times with her. He mulled over the words of Bhagwan Baba. Not that it matters one way or the other what he meant, he kept assuring himself. A trap, he had said. Did he mean Behroze trapped me? That was absurd. Why would she want to? If anything, he had trapped Behroze, luring her with his melancholy looks and the sad and gentle air which so became him and his shyness. Or had Bhagwan Baba meant trap in a larger — sort of cosmic — sense, so that he and his parents and Behroze were all trapped, and must work out their lives within its confines? This interpretation at least had some metaphysical appeal to it.

The sun was on the verge of setting when he arrived at the Gardens. There was yet another possibility: that he could not break with Behroze even if he wanted because these things were out of man's control. Ludicrous, the thought that he was seeing her impelled by some higher force.

On weekdays the Gardens were empty except for ayahs with their charges and the elderly out for a constitutional. They left when it got dark. Then couples arrived to seek privacy behind bushes and trees. But shortly after dusk a gang of men roamed through the Gardens, flushing out twosomes in their sanctuaries. They would stand around and snicker, or yell out obscene encouragement punctuated by lewd flourishes of hands and fingers, till the couples took flight in frustration and embarrassment.

Jehangir walked till the sun went down. The ayahs and the little children departed with their prams and toys, and across the greying skies a flock of sparrows ushered them to the exits, chirping urgently. He could go on seeing Behroze as if nothing had changed. But then the squabbles, the scenes verging on hysteria, the bitter taunting would continue to fester. In one way Bhagwan Baba's words made sense; life is a trap — I cannot solve both problems. How long could such terrible discord persist without rupturing something vital? He never understood that so much unhappiness could come upon the happy, loving family they used to be. A horrible end would come of it, some awful mess, if things continued in their clamorous, disturbed manner.

He emerged from the Gardens through the gate opposite the one he had entered by. Where the *shik-kababwalla* sat. Fanning his coals, and the skewers ready in his basket, loaded with bits of beef and liver. Nodding at Jehangir in recognition. Then across the road and into Kamala Nehru Park, with its hedges sculpted into the shapes of animals and birds. In bright sunlight, when freshly trimmed, the figures were delightful to look at. But now the hour was passing through the final moments of dusk, and the shapes were indefinable. Looming in a strange, unearthly manner. Possessing neither the randomness of nature nor the manicured discipline imposed by man.

He left quickly. Something eerie about the place. Back into the Hanging Gardens, to retrace his steps homeward, down the hill.

And then a slight detour occurred to him, through the children's playground. His heart raced a little as he approached, wondering if the exercisers would be there.

He heard their panting before he saw them, and hurried to turn the bend in the hedge and position himself at his old place. Unnoticed, he watched their sweating bodies perform. The old fascination returned at the sight of their rippling, bulging muscles. In their rhythm and symmetry, in the sureness of their pulse, in the obedient responses of their limbs he rediscovered what he had always found strangely enticing, and remembered the days in the gym at St Xavier's: the smell of sweat, the camaraderie that flowed, the slapping of flesh, the search for the hairiest chest, bushiest armpit, longest pubic hair, the grabbing and jostling, all the fun which he was never a part of, always ignored by the boys, always isolated.

And now, regarding these fellows building bodies by night, a wild urge came over him. To step out of his concealed spot and touch their muscles, feel the hardness, make his body join theirs in the exercises. To engage in good-hearted physical competition, to see who could do the most push-ups, to arm-wrestle, to grunt and heave together.

But it was only momentary. I was never good at such things, I'll look foolish. He laughed at himself and left, feeling better now. As if the straining, exerting muscles of these men at exercise had kneaded away the disquietude and anxiety he had been feeling about Behroze, about Bhagwan Baba, about his parents. Nothing is a trap, I exercise control over my own destiny.

To discover where he had been, Mother began some skilful questioning. She stalked around, observing his face for suspicious-looking marks or blemishes, his shirt and collar for questionable discolouration. Instead of ignoring this customary examination he said, "You won't see anything. Behroze never puts on makeup when we got out for *kissie-koatie*."

She clutched at her throat with both hands. "When a son speaks so shamelessly to his mother it is the end." And Father scolded in his mild way: "It is a disgrace when you talk like that."

Next evening he was drawn again to the Hanging Gardens. Lack of rain was obvious in the fading lushness of the lawns, but what green remained was still soothing. All the fountains were dry, their coloured lights switched off, and the little waterfall was a slope of grey sun-dried rock. After a few minutes of aimless strolling he went down to the overhang. It was the most secluded spot in the Gardens, at the edge overlooking the sea. Thick with bushes and trees on all three sides, and two wooden benches affording a spectacular view of Chaupatty Beach, from the Queen's Necklace along Marine Drive to the modern skyscrapers mushrooming at Nariman Point.

Behroze and he had come here once when both benches were unoccupied, on a slightly cool December evening. There was a gentle breeze. They sat down, his arm around her, watching the sky till the first star appeared. The gang of voyeurs was nowhere in sight, and Jehangir had a plan: to turn her head and kiss her when it was darker. A few moments later she reached her hands up to his face — she must have had a plan, too. But there were footsteps. He froze, then tore away from her hands.

The newcomers, a man and woman, occupied the other bench and began kissing desperately. The man's hands seemed to be everywhere, down her blouse, up her skirt. Jehangir and Behroze did not need to look; they could feel the heat of the feverish activity.

When Jehangir finally snatched a glance, the man was supine on the bench, his fly undone. The woman's face buried in his lap. Moans of pleasure. And a vague memory was transported from a great distance, pitting his intense desire to watch against an urgent need to leave, to cover up his eyes, to blot it all out: it was an evening on the veranda of their flat; the little boy stood with Mother at the window, taking the evening air and looking out beyond the compound wall. A boisterous group of men approached from the direction of Tar Gully, and down the main road three young women. As they closed the distance between them, one of the men suddenly cupped his hands around his crotch and said something the little boy could not hear, something about suck and mouth and money. There was giggling among the girls. The little boy tried hard to see what happened next. But Mother dragged him away, saying he shouldn't be looking at the filthy behaviour of wicked *mawaalis* and evil women; he should forget what he saw and heard or God would punish him and their whole house.

The evening had been spoilt. As they got up to leave, the night-watchman who patrolled the Gardens appeared. The fellating couple remained oblivious to the banging of his nightstick and other diversionary tactics. Finally, without going closer, in stentorian *Pathani* tones he called out, "*Arré bhaisahib*, lying on the benches is prohibited, please sit up straight," and the couple broke apart.

The night-watchman left; Jehangir and Behroze followed. Jehangir cast one backward glance: the couple was down again upon the bench, her mouth upon his lap. And fleeing the overhang, he recalled the panicked tearing of his own face from Behroze's hands. "I'm sorry," he said, "I just couldn't help it." He bundled up his frustrated desires into a tight, aching package and descended the hill in silence. Images of the couple on the bench abandoning themselves to their wild and desperate lust had danced unendingly before his eyes.

Jehangir sat on the grass now, under a lamp just outside the overhang. The overhang and its benches. Benches everywhere.

Paan-stained ones in the train were third-class seats. Bhagwan Baba's veranda bench — sit on it and he told you a riddle. The one in the waiting-room was for drinking lukewarm Limca. And the overhang bench — reserved for sucking lessons, and wet dreams that trickled down your thighs to make embarrassing starched pyjama legs, which the *gunga* probably examined with interest when she washed the clothes.

A shower of gravel descended upon him, striking his head and neck and back. He jumped up. Saw three boys sprinting away. Started to give chase, then stopped. What will I do even if I manage to catch the urchins?

He was trembling and could not sit down again. Breathing hard. Quick short breaths. Hands shaking. Armpits damp. He decided to walk. To the children's playground. The gym-by-night. Where children's game equipment became the parallel bars of the poor; where the stone-broke used the see-saw to bench-press, with flagstones for weights. Yes, they would build their muscles, one way or another.

As the twilight faded the exercisers arrived, and stripped down to *lungoatee* and vest. A little adjustment of the pouch with a swift downward movement. Tucking in and fine-tuning of the formation within. Then tightening expertly the knots of the waistband.

Their bodies moved through the various exercises, and once again Jehangir felt the urge to join them, join them in their sweating, rippling activity. He imagined meeting them every evening, taking off his clothes with them, down to his shorts and *sudra*; they would sweat and pant together, a community of men, and when the exercises were done they would all go arm in arm, laughing and joking, for a hot and spicy *shik-kabab* and sugar-cane juice. He could even learn to smoke a *bidi* with them.

He seriously considered taking up exercising. He was tired of being a skinny-armed, stoop-shouldered weakling. He would start in private, at home, and after his body strengthened he could join them in the open air. Surely they would welcome him. It would be a fraternity sufficient and complete.

He would go to Behroze's house on Saturday and say he had to speak to her about a serious matter. Make a clean break.

He prepared a mental list. He decided to conclude by saying that their relationship was making everyone unhappy: first, his parents were; she was, too, because they did not like her; besides, she could not tolerate their influence on him. Now she could resume her life as it was before he trespassed into it. Yes, trespassed, that was a good word, he'd use it.

The Kamala Nehru Park beckoned from across the road, through the dusk. The *maali* must have been at work, cuttings and twigs and leaves lay in heaps around the hedges. The sculptures looked magnificent, the birds on the verge of flight, the camel and elephant and giraffe about to lumber off into the darkness. But all of them ultimately frozen. Trapped, like Bhagwan Baba said. The words of Bhagwan Baba. Should be labelled A Philosophy For The Faint Of Heart And Weak Of Spirit. Or better still, The Way Of The Sculpted Hedges.

Behroze was alone when Jehangir arrived on Saturday evening. Her parents were out, so was the servant.

"You missed choir practice on Thursday," she said accusingly, crossing her legs. Her skirt slipped above the knee, exposing part of her thigh, and she did not pull it down.

Jehangir sensed nervously that somewhere in this was a challenge to him. The trace of hostility in the air narrowed the distance between them and made the room more intimate. Outside in the compound a game of volleyball was in progress, and the dull thud as the ball met flesh and bone could be heard inside the flat.

"I'm sorry. I had something very important to do. It concerns us. I would like to talk to you about it." The note of formality in his short, complete sentences sounded reassuringly in his ears. "This is the first time you've been alone at home," he ventured with an echo of her accusing tone.

"You didn't come since last weekend. Maybe my parents think we've broken up, and they didn't need to stick around to guard my virginity."

Jehangir turned away to look outside the window. He felt very uncomfortable when she talked like this. The flat was on the ground floor at an elevation that raised it above the compound, and he could see the volleyball in its flight over the net but not the boys who smacked it. A few minutes of daylight remained. When the room began edging towards darkness she reached out to switch on the table-lamp. Her movement caused the skirt to rise a little more.

"They've gone to a wedding at Albless Baag. Won't be back till eleven o'clock," she said.

"And Shanti?"

"Gone to visit her family. Has the weekend off."

"I could not come last Sunday, I went with my parents to Bhagwan Baba — "

"Your string is showing again," she interrupted. He reached behind, thinking his *kusti* had slipped out over the waistband of his trousers.

She laughed scornfully. "Not your *kusti*, I meant your mother's extra-long apron string. Anyway, tell me about your Baba. This should be good."

"If you're going to mock me even before I…"

"I'm sorry, go on."

Jehangir described the visit to Bhagwan Baba and the pronouncement. He paused before announcing his own decision about them. She adjusted her skirt properly over the knee and said, "But does that make any difference? Surely you don't believe all that mumbo-jumbo."

"But that's not the reason — "

"Your parents will try anything, you know they hate me."

"They don't hate you," he started, and stopped. His well-tempered sentences wrought for the occasion now seemed silly — he realized he had known it all along, even as he rehearsed the words in the Hanging Gardens. He looked outside. The volleyball no longer flew over the net, and the boys had either gone home or down to the *bhelpuriwalla* for a snack. The sudden gloom was due to the sky's fierce clouding, which had overtaken the gradual change from dusk to night. In the window the curtains flapped, violently at times.

The decision made in the Hanging Gardens was no comfort. No comfort at all. Refused to buoy him up. Instead, it suddenly started to dissolve. Where was the peace and serenity he experienced that night in the Hanging Gardens? How could it come and go so quickly? To recapture his elusive confidence he imagined himself in the Gardens amidst the community of exercising men, sculpted hedges, chirping sparrows. But they swam pointlessly through his mind now. It was all meaningless.

Drawn by his anguished face, she came and sat beside him on the sofa. She slipped her hand in his; the scorn had gone out of her eyes, leaving them soft and brown. She moved closer, and he put his arm around her. His confusion and anxiety started to evaporate. He remembered the other time on the overhang bench: what would have been their first kiss had been interrupted by the unrestrained, coarse, unabashed passion of the other couple. To-day there would be no interruptions. She switched off the lamp. Outside, there was the first rumbling of thunder, very distant, and the first drops of rain. The fresh, wholesome smell of earth was soon in the air.

It was still raining when Jehangir was racing homeward. People waited, huddled under awnings of shops or overhangs of buildings, under whatever shelter was afforded till the shower passed. There was gladness on all faces at the rain which had at long last arrived.

Outside a *jhopadpatti*, where even at the best of times a hundred and twenty residents depended on one water tap or the fortuity of a malfunctioning fire-hydrant, the joy of celebration was the most intense. Children and grownups soaped their bodies, tattered clothes and all, and stood gratefully under the cleansing waters from heaven. Mothers washed naked babies to the accompaniment of gleeful squeals. Some women were scouring their grimy, greasy pots and pans. Little rivulets of soapy water were soon running down the pavements leading from the *jhopadpatti* into the main street.

Jehangir was soaked to the skin. But he did not notice it, as he noticed nothing else around him. He was oblivious to the celebration of rain, to its freshness and abundance, to the delicious coolness and comfort that graced the air which barely an hour ago had been vile and full of threat.

With long desperate strides he splashed through the puddles. Some of them were ankle-deep, and his shoes were soon water-logged, but he hurried along. The rubbled pavement abandoned in mid-construction was impossible, so he took to the road.

A car fixed his soaking figure in its headlights, honking in annoyance. Sweat mingled with the rain-water coursing down his face. Waiting for a bus back to Firozsha Baag in this weather was pointless, it would take too long. He was panting hard, gasping for breath, but did not slow down. And his wretched, anguished mind would not be rid of her seated figure on the sofa, her hair over her soft brown eyes in which there were traces of moisture.

And to think that just a few minutes before he'd been sitting beside her on the same sofa, they were holding each other so close. Things could not be more perfect, it had seemed to him at that moment.

"Isn't this like a Hindi movie?" she had said smiling, adding wickedly to make him blush, "only thing is, I should be wearing a sari made transparent by rain. Even the thunder and lightning sound-track is perfect for lovers." Lovers? Was that a hint? She had stroked his hair. "Tell your parents and your Baba they did not succeed."

Jehangir had rested his cheek against hers, at peace with life and all its tangled complexities. His eyes wandered around in the dark, passed over the clock (a flash of lightning showed eight-fifteen), the outline of the bookcase, the piano and the frowning bust of Beethoven.

Eight-fifteen. Was that the right time? He had to find out. The radium-painted numbers of his watch dial would glow in the dark and show the correct time. He shifted, uneasy, and tried to move his hand. But she'd noticed immediately.

"If you want to look at your watch don't be so sneaky about it." She shook off his hand.

"I'm supposed to be home by eight." He looked at his watch.

"I know. You remind me every time you see me."

"In my watch it's almost eight. It's set with the clock at home. We eat dinner by it," he added apologetically, as if that would set things right. Short, complete sentences again, for reassurance. He got up.

"Going home on time for your mother is more important than — ?" and she broke off. Her eyes rested for a moment on the cushions which lay about the sofa, comfortably rumpled, still holding the heat of their bodies, then returned to his face. He did not reply, just glanced at his watch again. Tidying up in great haste, he tucked in his shirt, put the crease back in pants, smoothed down the tousled hair: raced with the clock of Mother.

Behroze watched in stark disbelief at this exhibition of terror, the transformation from man to cowering child. "Calm down, will you? Your mother's world won't end if you are late. Haven't you learned yet? All these are just her tactics to — "

"I've told you before I know they are tactics," he snapped back, "and I'm doing it all because I want to, because her life has been troubled enough, because I don't want to add more misery to it. Because, because, because! Do you want me to repeat everything again?"

Then he had stooped to pull up his socks. As he was leaving he turned around, and that was when he saw what he'd least expected — two tiny tears moistening her lower lashes.

And side by side with this image that refused to go away was the sickening thought which had struck in the pit of his stomach, like nausea — the one interpretation of Bhagwan Baba's words which he had never considered during all his rumination in the Hanging Gardens: that the trap was the one laid by Bhagwan Baba himself. To trick him into ending it this way.

He rushed through the streets like a madman, shivering, tormented and confused, glancing at his watch again and again. His breath was coming hard, he thought he would collapse. Finally, he turned into the compound and stumbled up the three steps of the C Block entrance and into the lift.

He rang the doorbell. Just one short burst. His finger slid off, the arm fell limply to his side. There was no energy to complete the prearranged signal of rings that the family members used: two short and one long.

Mother opened the door narrowly, leaving on the chain. "Trying to fool me or what, with just one ring?"

Jehangir shook his head. He clung feebly to the door, wanting to speak, but the words could not form through the panting.

"You know what time it is?"

He nodded, holding up his watch. Eight-thirty.

"This time you crossed the limit. Your father says be patient, he is just a boy. Just a boy, yes, but the boy has climbed to the roof." She shook off his hand and slammed the door shut.

Still leaning against the door, he reached for the bell and rang it. Desperately, again and again, two short bursts and one long burst, two short and one long, over and over, as if that familiar signal would magically open the door. It remained shut. From inside the flat, silence. His arm fell. He slid to the floor and settled down to wait.

His breathing returned to normal but the wet clothes clung to him, he was very cold. During his school years, Mother used to accompany him on rainy mornings with a towel, a change of socks and shoes; at school she would dry his feet, help him into fresh socks, exchange his gumboots for the dry shoes.

He pulled his handkerchief and wiped his face, then pushed back the wet hair. The door was exposed to a gusting wind from the balcony. It made him shiver, and he shuffled into the narrow corridor sheltered by the staircase. He looked at his watch. Still eight-thirty. Must have stopped, clogged with rain water. It was a gift from Mother and Father for getting first class with distinction in his SSC exams. He hoped the neighbours would not open their doors: the news would spread through all three blocks of Firozsha Baag. Then the boys would find new names for him. He fell into a light sleep, leaning against the wall, till the soft clanking of the chain being removed from the door woke him up.

Swimming Lessons

Swimming Lessons

The old man's wheelchair is audible today as he creaks by in the hallway: on some days it's just a smooth whirr. Maybe the way he slumps in it, or the way his weight rests has something to do with it. Down to the lobby he goes, and sits there most of the time, talking to people on their way out or in. That's where he first spoke to me a few days ago. I was waiting for the elevator, back from Eaton's with my new pair of swimming-trunks.

"Hullo," he said. I nodded, smiled.

"Beautiful summer day we've got."

"Yes," I said, "it's lovely outside."

He shifted the wheelchair to face me squarely. "How old do you think I am?"

I looked at him blankly, and he said, "Go on, take a guess."

I understood the game; he seemed about seventy-five although the hair was still black, so I said, "Sixty-five?" He made a sound between a chuckle and a wheeze: "I'll be seventy-seven next month." Close enough.

I've heard him ask that question several times since, and everyone plays by the rules. Their faked guesses range from sixty to seventy. They pick a lower number when he's more depressed than usual. He reminds me of Grandpa as he sits on the sofa in the lobby, staring out vacantly at the parking lot. Only difference is, he sits with the stillness of stroke victims, while Grandpa's Parkinson's disease would bounce his thighs and legs and arms all over the place. When he could no longer hold the *Bombay Samachar* steady enough to read, Grandpa took to sitting on the veranda and staring emptily at the traffic passing outside Firozsha Baag. Or waving to anyone who went by in the compound: Rustomji, Nariman Hansotia in his 1932 Mercedes-Benz, the fat ayah Jaakaylee with her shopping-bag, the *kuchrawalli* with her basket and long bamboo broom.

The Portuguese woman across the hall has told me a little about the old man. She is the communicator for the apartment building. To gather and disseminate information, she takes the liberty of unabashedly throwing open her door when newsworthy events transpire. Not for Portuguese Woman the furtive peerings from thin cracks or spyholes. She reminds me of a character in a movie, *Barefoot In The Park* I think it was, who left empty beer cans by the landing for anyone passing to stumble and give her the signal. But PW does not need beer cans. The gutang-khutang of the elevator opening and closing is enough.

The old man's daughter looks after him. He was living alone till his stroke, which coincided with his youngest daughter's divorce in Vancouver. She returned to him and they moved into this low-rise in Don Mills. PW says the daughter talks to no one in the building but takes good care of her father.

Mummy used to take good care of Grandpa, too, till things became complicated and he was moved to the Parsi General Hospital. Parkinsonism and osteoporosis laid him low. The doctor explained that Grandpa's hip did not break because he fell, but he fell because the hip, gradually growing brittle, snapped on that fatal day. That's what osteoporosis does, hollows out the bones and turns effect into cause. It has an unusually high incidence in the Parsi community, he said, but did not say why. Just one of those mysterious things. We are the chosen people where osteoporosis is concerned. And divorce. The Parsi community has the highest divorce rate in India. It also claims to be the most westernized community in India. Which is the result of the other? Confusion again, of cause and effect.

The hip was put in traction. Single-handed, Mummy struggled valiantly with bedpans and dressings for bedsores which soon appeared like grim spectres on his back. *Mamaiji*, bent double with her weak back, could give no assistance. My help would be enlisted to roll him over on his side while Mummy changed the dressing. But after three months, the doctor pronounced a patch upon Grandpa's lungs, and the male ward of Parsi General swallowed him up. There was no money for a private nursing home. I went to see him once, at Mummy's insistence. She used to say that the blessings of an old person were the most valuable and potent of all, they would last my whole life long. The ward had rows and rows of beds; the din was enormous, the smells nauseating, and it was just as well that Grandpa passed most of his time in a less than conscious state.

But I should have gone to see him more often. Whenever Grandpa went out, while he still could in the days before parkinsonism, he would bring back pink and white sugar-coated almonds for Percy and me. Every time I remember Grandpa, I remember that; and then I think: I should have gone to see him more often. That's what I also thought when our telephone-owning neighbour, esteemed by all for that reason, sent his son to tell us the hospital had phoned that Grandpa died an hour ago.

The postman rang the doorbell the way he always did, long and continuous; Mother went to open it, wanting to give him a piece of her mind but thought better of it, she did not want to risk the vengeance of postmen, it was so easy for them to destroy letters; workers nowadays thought no end of themselves, strutting around like peacocks, ever since all this Shiv Sena agitation about Maharashtra for Maharashtrians, threatening strikes and Bombay bundh *all the time, with no respect for the public; bus drivers and conductors were the worst, behaving as if they owned the buses and were doing favours to commuters, pulling the bell before you were in the bus, the driver purposely braking and moving with big jerks to make the standees lose their balance, the conductor so rude if you did not have the right change.*

But when she saw the airmail envelope with a Canadian stamp her face lit up, she said wait to the postman, and went in for a fifty paisa piece, a little baksheesh *for you, she told him, then shut the door and kissed the envelope, went in running, saying my son has written, my son has sent a letter, and Father looked up from the newspaper and said, don't get too excited, first read it, you know what kind of letters he writes, a few lines of empty words, I'm fine, hope you are all right, your loving son — that kind of writing I don't call letter-writing.*

Then Mother opened the envelope and took out one small page and began to read silently, and the joy brought to her face by the letter's arrival began to ebb; Father saw it happening and knew he was right, he said read aloud, let me also hear what our son is writing this time, so Mother read: My dear Mummy and Daddy, Last winter was terrible, we had record-breaking low temperatures all through February and March, and the first official day of spring was colder than the first official day of winter had been, but it's getting warmer now. Looks like it will be a nice warm summer. You asked about my new apartment. It's small, but not bad at all. This is just a quick note to let you know I'm fine, so you won't worry about me. Hope everything is okay at home.

After Mother put it back in the envelope, Father said everything about his life is locked in silence and secrecy, I still don't understand why he bothered to visit us last year if he had nothing to say; every letter of his has been a quick note so we won't worry — what does he think we worry about, his health, in that country everyone eats well whether they work or not, he should be worrying about us with all the black market and rationing, has he forgotten already how he used to go to the ration-shop and wait in line every week; and what kind of apartment description is that, not bad at all; and if it is a Canadian weather report I need from him, I can go with Nariman Hansotia from A Block to the Cawasji Framji Memorial Library and read all about it, there they get newspapers from all over the world.

The sun is hot today. Two women are sunbathing on the stretch of patchy lawn at the periphery of the parking lot. I can see them clearly from my kitchen. They're wearing bikinis and I'd love to take a closer look. But I have no binoculars. Nor do I have a car to saunter out to and pretend to look under the hood. They're both luscious and gleaming. From time to time they smear lotion over their skin, on the bellies, on the inside of the thighs, on the shoulders. Then one of them gets the other to undo the string of her top and spread some there. She lies on her stomach with the straps undone. I wait. I pray that the heat and haze make her forget, when it's time to turn over, that the straps are undone.

But the sun is not hot enough to work this magic for me. When it's time to come in, she flips over, deftly holding up the cups, and reties the top. They arise, pick up towels, lotions and magazines, and return to the building.

This is my chance to see them closer. I race down the stairs to the lobby. The old man says hullo. "Down again?"

"My mailbox," I mumble.

"It's Saturday," he chortles. For some reason he finds it extremely funny. My eye is on the door leading in from the parking lot.

Through the glass panel I see them approaching. I hurry to the elevator and wait. In the dimly lit lobby I can see their eyes are having trouble adjusting after the bright sun. They don't seem as attractive as they did from the kitchen window. The elevator arrives and I hold it open, inviting them in with what I think is a gallant flourish. Under the fluorescent glare in the elevator I see their wrinkled skin, aging hands, sagging bottoms, varicose veins. The lustrous trick of sun and lotion and distance has ended.

I step out and they continue to the third floor. I have Monday night to look forward to, my first swimming lesson. The high school behind the apartment building is offering, among its usual assortment of macramé and ceramics and pottery classes, a class for non-swimming adults.

The woman at the registration desk is quite friendly. She even gives me the opening to satisfy the compulsion I have about explaining my non-swimming status.

"Are you from India?" she asks. I nod. "I hope you don't mind my asking, but I was curious because an Indian couple, husband and wife, also registered a few minutes ago. Is swimming not encouraged in India?"

"On the contrary," I say. "Most Indians swim like fish. I'm an exception to the rule. My house was five minutes walking distance from Chaupatty beach in Bombay. It's one of the most beautiful beaches in Bombay, or was, before the filth took over. Anyway, even though we lived so close to it, I never learned to swim. It's just one of those things."

"Well," says the woman, "that happens sometimes. Take me, for instance. I never learned to ride a bicycle. It was the mounting that used to scare me, I was afraid of falling." People have lined up behind me. "It's been very nice talking to you," she says, "hope you enjoy the course."

The art of swimming had been trapped between the devil and the deep blue sea. The devil was money, always scarce, and kept the private swimming clubs out of reach; the deep blue sea of Chaupatty beach was grey and murky with garbage, too filthy to swim in. Every so often we would muster our courage and Mummy would take me there to try and teach me. But a few minutes of paddling was all we could endure. Sooner or later something would float up against our legs or thighs or waists, depending on how deep we'd gone in, and we'd be revulsed and stride out to the sand.

Water imagery in my life is recurring. Chaupatty beach, now the high-school swimming pool. The universal symbol of life and regeneration did nothing but frustrate me. Perhaps the swimming pool will overturn that failure.

When images and symbols abound in this manner, sprawling or rolling across the page without guile or artifice, one is prone to say, how obvious, how skilless; symbols, after all, should be still and gentle as dewdrops, tiny, yet shining with a world of meaning. But what happens when, on the page of life itself, one encounters the ever-moving, all-engirdling sprawl of the filthy sea? Dewdrops and oceans both have their rightful places; Nariman Hansotia certainly knew that when he told his stories to the boys of Firozsha Baag.

The sea of Chaupatty was fated to endure the finales of life's everyday functions. It seemed that the dirtier it became, the more crowds it attracted: street urchins and beggars and beachcombers, looking through the junk that washed up. (Or was it the crowds that made it dirtier? — another instance of cause and effect blurring and evading identification.)

Too many religious festivals also used the sea as repository for their finales. Its use should have been rationed, like rice and kerosene. On Ganesh Chaturthi, clay idols of the god Ganesh, adorned with garlands and all manner of finery, were carried in processions to the accompaniment of drums and a variety of wind instruments. The music got more frenzied the closer the procession got to Chaupatty and to the moment of immersion.

Then there was Coconut Day, which was never as popular as Ganesh Chaturthi. From a bystander's viewpoint, coconuts chucked into the sea do not provide as much of a spectacle. We used the sea, too, to deposit the leftovers from Parsi religious ceremonies, things such as flowers, or the ashes of the sacred sandalwood fire, which just could not be dumped with the regular garbage but had to be entrusted to the care of Avan Yazad, the guardian of the sea. And things which were of no use but which no one had the heart to destroy were also given to Avan Yazad. Such as old photographs.

After Grandpa died, some of his things were flung out to sea. It was high tide; we always checked the newspaper when going to perform these disposals; an ebb would mean a long walk in squelchy sand before finding water. Most of the things were probably washed up on shore. But we tried to throw them as far out as possible, then waited a few minutes; if they did not float back right away we would pretend they were in the permanent safekeeping of Avan Yazad, which was a comforting thought. I can't remember everything we sent out to sea, but his brush and comb were in the parcel, his *kusti*, and some Kemadrin pills, which he used to take to keep the parkinsonism under control.

Our paddling sessions stopped for lack of enthusiasm on my part. Mummy wasn't too keen either, because of the filth. But my main concern was the little guttersnipes, like naked fish with little buoyant penises, taunting me with their skills, swimming underwater and emerging unexpectedly all around me, or pretending to masturbate — I think they were too young to achieve ejaculation. It was embarrassing. When I look back, I'm surprised that Mummy and I kept going as long as we did.

I examine the swimming-trunks I bought last week. Surf King, says the label, Made in Canada-Fabriqué Au Canada. I've been learning bits and pieces of French from bilingual labels at the supermarket too. These trunks are extremely sleek and streamlined hipsters, the distance from waistband to pouch tip the barest minimum. I wonder how everything will stay in place, not that I'm boastful about my endowments. I try them on, and feel that the tip of my member lingers perilously close to the exit. Too close, in fact, to conceal the exigencies of my swimming lesson fantasy: a gorgeous woman in the class for non-swimmers, at whose sight I will be instantly aroused, and she, spying the shape of my desire, will look me straight in the eye with her intentions; she will come home with me, to taste the pleasures of my delectable Asian brown body whose strangeness has intrigued her and unleashed uncontrollable surges of passion inside her throughout the duration of the swimming lesson.

I drop the Eaton's bag and wrapper in the garbage can. The swimming-trunks cost fifteen dollars, same as the fee for the ten weekly lessons. The garbage bag is almost full. I tie it up and take it outside. There is a medicinal smell in the hallway; the old man must have just returned to his apartment.

PW opens her door and says, "Two ladies from the third floor were lying in the sun this morning. In bikinis."

"That's nice," I say, and walk to the incinerator chute. She reminds me of Najamai in Firozsha Baag, except that Najamai employed a bit more subtlety while going about her life's chosen work.

PW withdraws and shuts her door.

Mother had to reply because Father said he did not want to write to his son till his son had something sensible to write to him, his questions had been ignored long enough, and if he wanted to keep his life a secret, fine, he would get no letters from his father.

But after Mother started the letter he went and looked over her shoulder, telling her what to ask him, because if they kept on writing the same questions, maybe he would understand how interested they were in knowing about things over there; Father said go on, ask him what his work is at the insurance company, tell him to take some courses at night school, that's how everyone moves ahead over there, tell him not to be discouraged if his job is just clerical right now, hard work will get him ahead, remind him he is a Zoroastrian: manashni, gavashni, kunashni, *better write the translation also: good thoughts, good words, good deeds — he must have forgotten what it means, and tell him to say prayers and do* kusti *at least twice a day.*

Writing it all down sadly, Mother did not believe he wore his sudra *and* kusti *anymore, she would be very surprised if he remembered any of the prayers; when she had asked him if he needed new* sudras *he said not to take any trouble because the Zoroastrian Society of Ontario imported them from Bombay for their members, and this sounded like a story he was making up, but she was leaving it in the hands of God, ten thousand miles away there was nothing she could do but write a letter and hope for the best.*

Then she sealed it, and Father wrote the address on it as usual because his writing was much neater than hers, handwriting was important in the address and she did not want the postman in Canada to make any mistake; she took it to the post office herself, it was impossible to trust anyone to mail it ever since the postage rates went up because people just tore off the stamps for their own use and threw away the letter, the only safe way was to hand it over the counter and make the clerk cancel the stamps before your own eyes.

Berthe, the building superintendent, is yelling at her son in the parking lot. He tinkers away with his van. This happens every fine-weathered Sunday. It must be the van that Berthe dislikes because I've seen mother and son together in other quite amicable situations.

Berthe is a big Yugoslavian with high cheekbones. Her nationality was disclosed to me by PW. Berthe speaks a very rough-hewn English, I've overheard her in the lobby scolding tenants for late rents and leaving dirty lint screens in the dryers. It's exciting to listen to her, her words fall like rocks and boulders, and one can never tell where or how the next few will drop. But her Slavic yells at her son are a different matter, the words fly swift and true, well-aimed missiles that never miss. Finally, the son slams down the hood in disgust, wipes his hands on a rag, accompanies mother Berthe inside.

Berthe's husband has a job in a factory. But he loses several days of work every month when he succumbs to the booze, a word Berthe uses often in her Slavic tirades on those days, the only one I can understand, as it clunks down heavily out of the tight-flying formation of Yugoslavian sentences. He lolls around in the lobby, submitting passively to his wife's tongue-lashings. The bags under his bloodshot eyes, his stringy moustache, stubbled chin, dirty hair are so vulnerable to the poison-laden barbs (poison works the same way in any language) emanating from deep within the powerful watermelon bosom. No one's presence can embarrass or dignify her into silence.

No one except the old man who arrives now. "Good morning," he says, and Berthe turns, stops yelling, and smiles. Her husband rises, positions the wheelchair at the favourite angle. The lobby will be peaceful as long as the old man is there.

It was hopeless. My first swimming lesson. The water terrified me. When did that happen, I wonder, I used to love splashing at Chaupatty, carried about by the waves. And this was only a swimming pool. Where did all that terror come from? I'm trying to remember.

Armed with my Surf King I enter the high school and go to the pool area. A sheet with instructions for the new class is pinned to the bulletin board. All students must shower and then assemble at eight by the shallow end. As I enter the showers three young boys, probably from a previous class, emerge. One of them holds his nose. The second begins to hum, under his breath: Paki Paki, smell like curry. The third says to the first two: pretty soon all the water's going to taste of curry. They leave.

It's a mixed class, but the gorgeous woman of my fantasy is missing. I have to settle for another, in a pink one-piece suit, with brown hair and a bit of a stomach. She must be about thirty-five. Plain-looking.

The instructor is called Ron. He gives us a pep talk, sensing some nervousness in the group. We're finally all in the water, in the shallow end. He demonstrates floating on the back, then asks for a volunteer. The pink one-piece suit wades forward. He supports her, tells her to lean back and let her head drop in the water.

She does very well. And as we all regard her floating body, I see what was not visible outside the pool: her bush, curly bits of it, straying out at the pink Spandex V. Tongues of water lapping against her delta, as if caressing it teasingly, make the brown hair come alive in a most tantalizing manner. The crests and troughs of little waves, set off by the movement of our bodies in a circle around her, dutifully irrigate her; the curls alternately wave free inside the crest, then adhere to her wet thighs, beached by the inevitable trough. I could watch this forever, and I wish the floating demonstration would never end.

Next we are shown how to grasp the rail and paddle, face down in the water. Between practising floating and paddling, the hour is almost gone. I have been trying to observe the pink one-piece suit, getting glimpses of her straying pubic hair from various angles. Finally, Ron wants a volunteer for the last demonstration, and I go forward. To my horror he leads the class to the deep end. Fifteen feet of water. It is so blue, and I can see the bottom. He picks up a metal hoop attached to a long wooden stick. He wants me to grasp the hoop, jump in the water, and paddle, while he guides me by the stick. Perfectly safe, he tells me. A demonstration of how paddling propels the body.

It's too late to back out; besides, I'm so terrified I couldn't find the words to do so even if I wanted to. Everything he says I do as if in a trance. I don't remember the moment of jumping. The next thing I know is, I'm swallowing water and floundering, hanging on to the hoop for dear life. Ron draws me to the rails and helps me out. The class applauds.

We disperse and one thought is on my mind: what if I'd lost my grip? Fifteen feet of water under me. I shudder and take deep breaths. This is it. I'm not coming next week. This instructor is an irresponsible person. Or he does not value the lives of non-white immigrants. I remember the three teenagers. Maybe the swimming pool is the hangout of some racist group, bent on eliminating all non-white swimmers, to keep their waters pure and their white sisters unogled.

The elevator takes me upstairs. Then gutang-khutang. PW opens her door as I turn the corridor of medicinal smells. "Berthe was screaming loudly at her husband tonight," she tells me.

"Good for her," I say, and she frowns indignantly at me.

The old man is in the lobby. He's wearing thick wool gloves. He wants to know how the swimming was, must have seen me leaving with my towel yesterday. Not bad, I say.

"I used to swim a lot. Very good for the circulation." He wheezes. "My feet are cold all the time. Cold as ice. Hands too."

Summer is winding down, so I say stupidly, "Yes, it's not so warm any more."

The thought of the next swimming lesson sickens me. But as I comb through the memories of that terrifying Monday, I come upon the straying curls of brown pubic hair. Inexorably drawn by them, I decide to go.

It's a mistake, of course. This time I'm scared even to venture in the shallow end. When everyone has entered the water and I'm the only one outside, I feel a little foolish and slide in.

Instructor Ron says we should start by reviewing the floating technique. I'm in no hurry. I watch the pink one-piece pull the swim-suit down around her cheeks and flip back to achieve perfect flotation. And then reap disappointment. The pink Spandex triangle is perfectly streamlined today, nothing strays, not a trace of fuzz, not one filament, not even a sign of post-depilation irritation. Like the airbrushed parts of glamour magazine models. The barrenness of her impeccably packaged apex is a betrayal. Now she is shorn like the other women in the class. Why did she have to do it?

The weight of this disappointment makes the water less manageable, more lung-penetrating. With trepidation, I float and paddle my way through the remainder of the hour, jerking my head out every two seconds and breathing deeply, to continually shore up a supply of precious, precious air without, at the same time, seeming too anxious and losing my dignity.

I don't attend the remaining classes. After I've missed three, Ron the instructor telephones. I tell him I've had the flu and am still feeling poorly, but I'll try to be there the following week.

He does not call again. My Surf King is relegated to an unused drawer. Total losses: one fantasy plus thirty dollars. And no watery rebirth. The swimming pool, like Chaupatty beach, has produced a stillbirth. But there is a difference. Water means regeneration only if it is pure and cleansing. Chaupatty was filthy, the pool was not. Failure to swim through filth must mean something other than failure of rebirth — failure of symbolic death? Does that equal success of symbolic life? death of a symbolic failure? death of a symbol? What is the equation?

The postman did not bring a letter but a parcel, he was smiling because he knew that every time something came from Canada his baksheesh was guaranteed, and this time because it was a parcel Mother gave him a whole rupee, she was quite excited, there were so many stickers on it besides the stamps, one for Small Parcel, another Printed Papers, a red sticker saying Insured; she showed it to Father, and opened it, then put both hands on her cheeks, not able to speak because the surprise and happiness was so great, tears came to her eyes and she could not stop smiling, till Father became impatient to know and finally got up and came to the table.

When he saw it he was surprised and happy too, he began to grin, then hugged Mother saying our son is a writer, and we didn't even know it, he never told us a thing, here we are thinking he is still clerking away at the insurance company, and he has written a book of stories, all these years in school and college he kept his talent hidden, making us think he was just like one of the boys in the Baag, shouting and playing the fool in the compound, and now what a surprise; then Father opened the book and began reading it, heading back to the easy chair, and Mother so excited, still holding his arm, walked with him, saying it was not fair him reading it first, she wanted to read it too, and they agreed that he would read the first story, then give it to her so she could also read it, and they would take turns in that manner.

Mother removed the staples from the padded envelope in which he had mailed the book, and threw them away, then straightened the folded edges of the envelope and put it away safely with the other envelopes and letters she had collected since he left.

The leaves are beginning to fall. The only ones I can identify are maple. The days are dwindling like the leaves. I've started a habit of taking long walks every evening. The old man is in the lobby when I leave, he waves as I go by. By the time I'm back, the lobby is usually empty.

Today I was woken up by a grating sound outside that made my flesh crawl. I went to the window and saw Berthe raking the leaves in the parking lot. Not in the expanse of patchy lawn on the periphery, but in the parking lot proper. She was raking the black tarred surface. I went back to bed and dragged a pillow over my head, not releasing it till noon.

When I return from my walk in the evening, PW, summoned by the elevator's gutang-khutang, says, "Berthe filled six big black garbage bags with leaves today."

"Six bags!" I say. "Wow!"

Since the weather turned cold, Berthe's son does not tinker with his van on Sundays under my window. I'm able to sleep late.

Around eleven, there's a commotion outside. I reach out and switch on the clock radio. It's a sunny day, the window curtains are bright. I get up, curious, and see a black Olds Ninety-Eight in the parking lot, by the entrance to the building. The old man is in his wheelchair, bundled up, with a scarf wound several times round his neck as though to immobilize it, like a surgical collar. His daughter and another man, the car-owner, are helping him from the wheelchair into the front seat, encouraging him with words like: that's it, easy does it, attaboy. From the open door of the lobby, Berthe is shouting encouragement too, but hers is confined to one word: yah, repeated at different levels of pitch and volume, with variations on vowel-length. The stranger could be the old man's son, he has the same jet black hair and piercing eyes.

Maybe the old man is not well, it's an emergency. But I quickly scrap that thought — this isn't Bombay, an ambulance would have arrived. They're probably taking him out for a ride. If he is his son, where has he been all this time, I wonder.

The old man finally settles in the front seat, the wheelchair goes in the trunk, and they're off. The one I think is the son looks up and catches me at the window before I can move away, so I wave, and he waves back.

In the afternoon I take down a load of clothes to the laundry room. Both machines have completed their cycles, the clothes inside are waiting to be transferred to dryers. Should I remove them and place them on top of a dryer, or wait? I decide to wait. After a few minutes, two women arrive, they are in bathrobes, and smoking. It takes me a while to realize that these are the two disappointments who were sunbathing in bikinis last summer.

"You didn't have to wait, you could have removed the clothes and carried on, dear," says one. She has a Scottish accent. It's one of the few I've learned to identify. Like maple leaves.

"Well," I say, "some people might not like strangers touching their clothes."

"You're not a stranger, dear," she says, "you live in this building, we've seen you before."

"Besides, your hands are clean," the other one pipes in. "You can touch my things any time you like."

Horny old cow. I wonder what they've got on under their bathrobes. Not much, I find, as they bend over to place their clothes in the dryers.

"See you soon," they say, and exit, leaving me behind in an erotic wake of smoke and perfume and deep images of cleavages. I start the washers and depart, and when I come back later, the dryers are empty.

PW tells me, "The old man's son took him out for a drive today. He has a big beautiful black car."

I see my chance, and shoot back: "Olds Ninety-Eight."

"What?"

"The car," I explain, "it's an Oldsmobile Ninety-Eight."

She does not like this at all, my giving her information. She is visibly nettled, and retreats with a sour face.

Mother and Father read the first five stories, and she was very sad after reading some of them, she said he must be so unhappy there, all his stories are about Bombay, he remembers every little thing about his childhood, he is thinking about it all the time even though he is ten thousand miles away, my poor son, I think he misses his home and us and everything he left behind, because if he likes it over there why would he not write stories about that, there must be so many new ideas that his new life could give him.

But Father did not agree with this, he said it did not mean that he was unhappy, all writers worked in the same way, they used their memories and experiences and made stories out of them, changing some things, adding some, imagining some, all writers were very good at remembering details of their lives.

Mother said, how can you be sure that he is remembering because he is a writer, or whether he started to write because he is unhappy and thinks of his past, and wants to save it all by making stories of it; and Father said that is not a sensible question, anyway, it is now my turn to read the next story.

The first snow has fallen, and the air is crisp. It's not very deep, about two inches, just right to go for a walk in. I've been told that immigrants from hot countries always enjoy the snow the first year, maybe for a couple of years more, then inevitably the dread sets in, and the approach of winter gets them fretting and moping. On the other hand, if it hadn't been for my conversation with the woman at the swimming registration desk, they might now be saying that India is a nation of non-swimmers.

Berthe is outside, shovelling the snow off the walkway in the parking lot. She has a heavy, wide pusher which she wields expertly.

The old radiators in the apartment alarm me incessantly. They continue to broadcast a series of variations on death throes, and go from hot to cold and cold to hot at will, there's no controlling their temperature. I speak to Berthe about it in the lobby. The old man is there too, his chin seems to have sunk deeper into his chest, and his face is a yellowish grey.

"Nothing, not to worry about anything," says Berthe, dropping rough-hewn chunks of language around me. "Radiator no work, you tell me. You feel cold, you come to me, I keep you warm," and she opens her arms wide, laughing. I step back, and she advances, her breasts preceding her like the gallant prows of two ice-breakers. She looks at the old man to see if he is appreciating the act: "You no feel scared, I keep you safe and warm."

But the old man is staring outside, at the flakes of falling snow. What thoughts is he thinking as he watches them? Of childhood days, perhaps, and snowmen with hats and pipes, and snowball fights, and white Christmases, and Christmas trees? What will I think of, old in this country, when I sit and watch the snow come down? For me, it is already too late for snowmen and snowball fights, and all I will have is thoughts about childhood thoughts and dreams, built around snowscapes and winter-wonderlands on the Christmas cards so popular in Bombay; my snowmen and snowball fights and Christmas trees are in the pages of Enid Blyton's books, dispersed amidst the adventures of the Famous Five, and the Five Find-Outers, and the Secret Seven. My snowflakes are even less forgettable than the old man's, for they never melt.

It finally happened. The heat went. Not the usual intermittent coming and going, but out completely. Stone cold. The radiators are like ice. And so is everything else. There's no hot water. Naturally. It's the hot water that goes through the rads and heats them. Or is it the other way around? Is there no hot water because the rads have stopped circulating it? I don't care, I'm too cold to sort out the cause and effect relationship. Maybe there is no connection at all.

I dress quickly, put on my winter jacket, and go down to the lobby. The elevator is not working because the power is out, so I take the stairs. Several people are gathered, and Berthe has announced that she has telephoned the office, they are sending a man. I go back up the stairs. It's only one floor, the elevator is just a bad habit. Back in Firozsha Baag they were broken most of the time. The stairway enters the corridor outside the old man's apartment, and I think of his cold feet and hands. Poor man, it must be horrible for him without heat.

As I walk down the long hallway, I feel there's something different but can't pin it down. I look at the carpet, the ceiling, the wallpaper: it all seems the same. Maybe it's the freezing cold that imparts a feeling of difference.

PW opens her door: "The old man had another stroke yesterday. They took him to the hospital."

The medicinal smell. That's it. It's not in the hallway any more.

In the stories that he'd read so far Father said that all the Parsi families were poor or middle-class, but that was okay; nor did he mind that the seeds for the stories were picked from the sufferings of their own lives; but there should also have been something positive about Parsis, there was so much to be proud of: the great Tatas and their contribution to the steel industry, or Sir Dinshaw Petit in the textile industry who made Bombay the Manchester of the East, or Dadabhai Naoroji in the freedom movement, where he was the first to use the word swaraj, *and the first to be elected to the British Parliament where he carried on his campaign; he should have found some way to bring some of these wonderful facts into his stories, what would people reading these stories think, those who did not know about Parsis — that the whole community was full of cranky, bigoted people; and in reality it was the richest, most advanced and philanthropic community in India, and he did not need to tell his own son that Parsis had a reputation for being generous and family-oriented. And he could have written something also about the historic background, how Parsis came to India from Persia because of Islamic persecution in the seventh century, and were the descendants of Cyrus the Great and the magnificent Persian Empire. He could have made a story of all this, couldn't he?*

Mother said what she liked best was his remembering everything so well, how beautifully he wrote about it all, even the sad things, and though he changed some of it, and used his imagination, there was truth in it.

My hope is, Father said, that there will be some story based on his Canadian experience, that way we will know something about our son's life there, if not through his letters then in his stories; so far they are all about Parsis and Bombay, and the one with a little bit about Toronto, where a man perches on top of the toilet, is shameful and disgusting, although it is funny at times and did make me laugh, I have to admit, but where does he get such an imagination from, what is the point of such a fantasy; and Mother said that she would also enjoy some stories about Toronto and the people there; it puzzles me, she said, why he writes nothing about it, especially since you say that writers use their own experience to make stories out of.

Then Father said this is true, but he is probably not using his Toronto experience because it is too early; what do you mean, too early, asked Mother and Father explained it takes a writer about ten years time after an experience before he is able to use it in his writing, it takes that long to be absorbed internally and understood, thought out and thought about, over and over again, he haunts it and it haunts him if it is valuable enough, till the writer is comfortable with it to be able to use it as he wants; but this is only one theory I read somewhere, it may or may not be true.

That means, said Mother, that his childhood in Bombay and our home here is the most valuable thing in his life just now, because he is able to remember it all to write about it, and you were so bitterly saying he is forgetting where he came from; and that may be true, said Father, but that is not what the theory means, according to the theory he is writing of these things because they are far enough in the past for him to deal with objectively, he is able to achieve what critics call artistic distance, without emotions interfering; and what do you mean emotions, said Mother, you are saying he does not feel anything for his characters, how can he write so beautifully about so many sad things without any feelings in his heart?

But before Father could explain more, about beauty and emotion and inspiration and imagination, Mother took the book and said it was her turn now and too much theory she did not want to listen to, it was confusing and did not make as much sense as reading the stories, she would read them her way and Father could read them his.

My books on the windowsill have been damaged. Ice has been forming on the inside ledge, which I did not notice, and melting when the sun shines in. I spread them in a corner of the living-room to dry out.

The winter drags on. Berthe wields her snow pusher as expertly as ever, but there are signs of weariness in her performance. Neither husband nor son is ever seen outside with a shovel. Or anywhere else, for that matter. It occurs to me that the son's van is missing, too.

The medicinal smell is in the hall again, I sniff happily and look forward to seeing the old man in the lobby. I go downstairs and peer into the mailbox, see the blue and magenta of an Indian aerogramme with Don Mills, Ontario, Canada in Father's flawless hand through the slot.

I pocket the letter and enter the main lobby. The old man is there, but not in his usual place. He is not looking out through the glass door. His wheelchair is facing a bare wall where the wallpaper is torn in places. As though he is not interested in the outside world any more, having finished with all that, and now it's time to see inside. What does he see inside, I wonder? I go up to him and say hullo. He says hullo without raising his sunken chin. After a few seconds his grey countenance faces me. "How old do you think I am?" His eyes are dull and glazed; he is looking even further inside than I first presumed.

"Well, let's see, you're probably close to sixty-four."

"I'll be seventy-eight next August." But he does not chuckle or wheeze. Instead, he continues softly, "I wish my feet did not feel so cold all the time. And my hands." He lets his chin fall again.

In the elevator I start opening the aerogramme, a tricky business because a crooked tear means lost words. Absorbed in this while emerging, I don't notice PW occupying the centre of the hallway, arms folded across her chest: "They had a big fight. Both of them have left."

I don't immediately understand her agitation. "What…who?"

"Berthe. Husband and son both left her. Now she is all alone."

Her tone and stance suggest that we should not be standing here talking but do something to bring Berthe's family back. "That's very sad," I say, and go in. I picture father and son in the van, driving away, driving across the snow-covered country, in the dead of winter, away from wife and mother; away to where? how far will they go? Not son's van nor father's booze can take them far enough. And the further they go, the more they'll remember, they can take it from me.

All the stories were read by Father and Mother, and they were sorry when the book was finished, they felt they had come to know their son better now, yet there was much more to know, they wished there were many more stories;

*and this is what they mean, said Father, when they say that the whole story
can never be told, the whole truth can never be known; what do you mean,
they say, asked Mother, who they, and Father said writers, poets,
philosophers. I don't care what they say, said Mother, my son will write as
much or as little as he wants to, and if I can read it I will be happy.*

*The last story they liked the best of all because it had the most in it about
Canada, and now they felt they knew at least a little bit, even if it was a very
little bit, about his day-to-day life in his apartment; and Father said if he
continues to write about such things he will become popular because I am
sure they are interested there in reading about life through the eyes of an immigrant, it provides a different viewpoint; the only danger is if he changes
and becomes so much like them that he will write like one of them and lose
the important difference.*

The bathroom needs cleaning. I open a new can of Ajax and scour
the tub. Sloshing with mug from bucket was standard bathing procedure in the bathrooms of Firozsha Baag, so my preference now
is always for a shower. I've never used the tub as yet; besides, it
would be too much like Chaupatty or the swimming pool, wallow-
ing in my own dirt. Still, it must be cleaned.

When I've finished, I prepare for a shower. But the clean gleaming tub and the nearness of the vernal equinox give me the urge to
do something different today. I find the drain plug in the
bathroom cabinet, and run the bath.

I've spoken so often to the old man, but I don't know his name. I
should have asked him the last time I saw him, when his wheelchair
was facing the bare wall because he had seen all there was to see
outside and it was time to see what was inside. Well, tomorrow. Or
better yet, I can look it up in the directory in the lobby. Why didn't
I think of that before? It will only have an initial and a last name,
but then I can surprise him with: hullo Mr Wilson, or whatever it is.

The bath is full. Water imagery is recurring in my life: Chaupatty
beach, swimming pool, bathtub. I step in and immerse myself up to
the neck. It feels good. The hot water loses its opacity when the
chlorine, or whatever it is, has cleared. My hair is still dry. I close my
eyes, hold my breath, and dunk my head. Fighting the panic, I stay
under and count to thirty. I come out, clear my lungs and breathe
deeply.

I do it again. This time I open my eyes under water, and stare blindly without seeing, it takes all my will to keep the lids from closing. Then I am slowly able to discern the underwater objects. The drain plug looks different, slightly distorted; there is a hair trapped between the hole and the plug, it waves and dances with the movement of the water. I come up, refresh my lungs, examine quickly the overwater world of the washroom, and go in again. I do it several times, over and over. The world outside the water I have seen a lot of, it is now time to see what is inside.

The spring session for adult non-swimmers will begin in a few days at the high school. I must not forget the registration date.

The dwindled days of winter are now all but forgotten; they have grown and attained a respectable span. I resume my evening walks, it's spring, and a vigorous thaw is on. The snowbanks are melting, the sound of water on its gushing, gurgling journey to the drains is beautiful. I plan to buy a book of trees, so I can identify more than the maple as they begin to bloom.

When I return to the building, I wipe my feet energetically on the mat because some people are entering behind me, and I want to set a good example. Then I go to the board with its little plastic letters and numbers. The old man's apartment is the one on the corner by the stairway, that makes it number 201. I run down the list, come to 201, but there are no little white plastic letters beside it. Just the empty black rectangle with holes where the letters would be squeezed in. That's strange. Well, I can introduce myself to him, then ask his name.

However, the lobby is empty. I take the elevator, exit at the second floor, wait for the gutang-khutang. It does not come: the door closes noiselessly, smoothly. Berthe has been at work, or has made sure someone else has. PW's cue has been lubricated out of existence.

But she must have the ears of a cockroach. She is waiting for me. I whistle my way down the corridor. She fixes me with an accusing look. She waits till I stop whistling, then says: "You know the old man died last night."

I cease groping for my key. She turns to go and I take a step towards her, my hand still in my trouser pocket. "Did you know his name?" I ask, but she leaves without answering.

Then Mother said, the part I like best in the last story is about Grandpa, where he wonders if Grandpa's spirit is really watching him and blessing him, because you know I really told him that, I told him helping an old suffering person who is near death is the most blessed thing to do, because that person will ever after watch over you from heaven, I told him this when he was disgusted with Grandpa's urine-bottle and would not touch it, would not hand it to him even when I was not at home.

Are you sure, said Father, that you really told him this, or you believe you told him because you like the sound of it, you said yourself the other day that he changes and adds and alters things in the stories but he writes it all so beautifully that it seems true, so how can you be sure; this sounds like another theory, said Mother, but I don't care, he says I told him and I believe now I told him, so even if I did not tell him then it does not matter now.

Don't you see, said Father, that you are confusing fiction with facts, fiction does not create facts, fiction can come from facts, it can grow out of facts by compounding, transposing, augmenting, diminishing, or altering them in any way; but you must not confuse cause and effect, you must not confuse what really happened with what the story says happened, you must not loose your grasp on reality, that way madness lies.

Then Mother stopped listening because, as she told Father so often, she was not very fond of theories, and she took out her writing pad and started a letter to her son; Father looked over her shoulder, telling her to say how proud they were of him and were waiting for his next book, he also said, leave a little space for me at the end, I want to write a few lines when I put the address on the envelope.